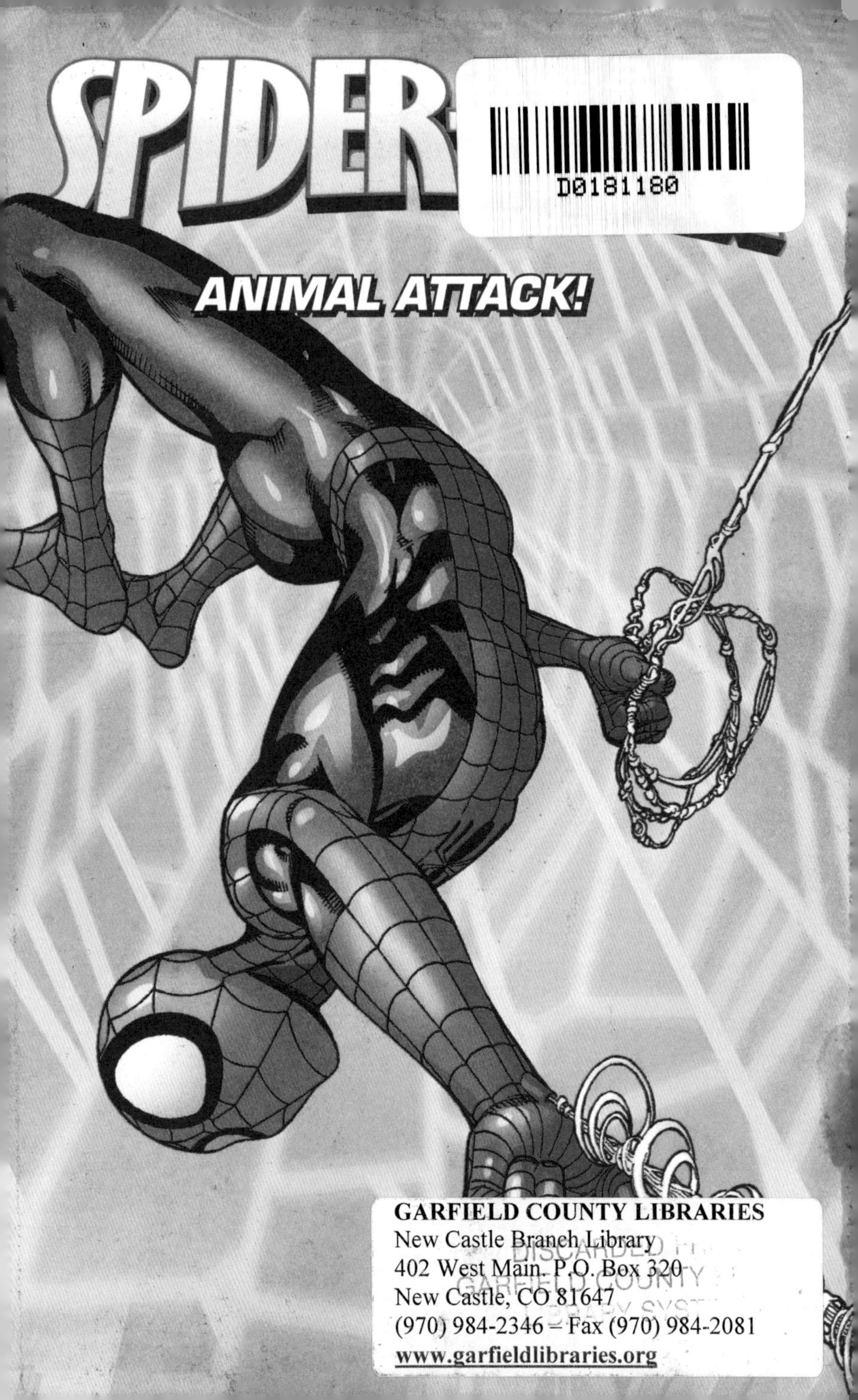

SPIDER-

ANIMAL ATTACK!

D0181180

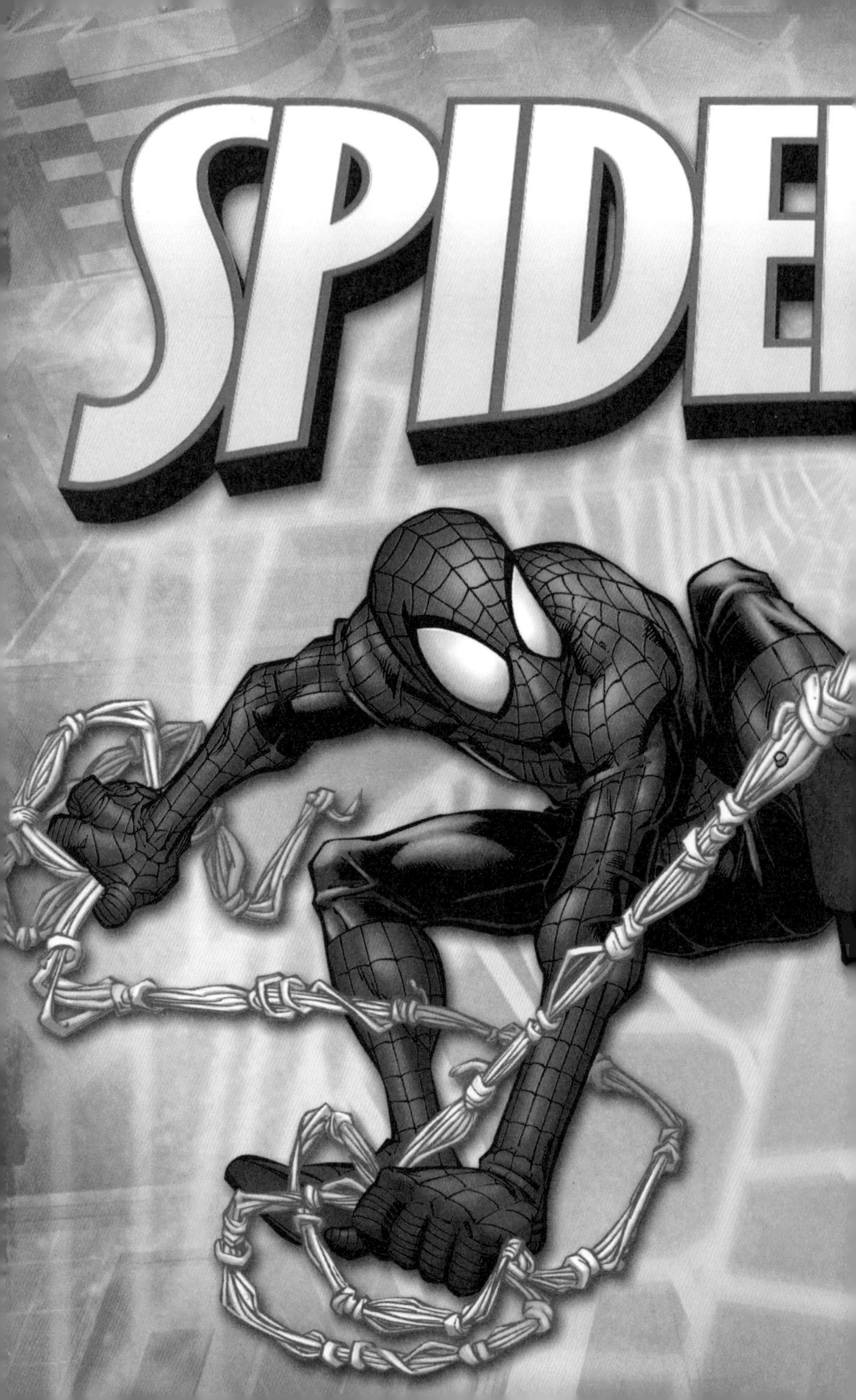
SPIDE

R-MAN

ANIMAL ATTACK!

Writers: **Marc Sumerak, Roger Langridge & Paul Benjamin**

Pencilers: **Sanford Greene, Sonny Liew & Juan Santacruz**

Inkers: **Nathan Massengill, Sonny Liew & Juan Santacruz**

Colors: **Sotocolor's A. Street & Sonny Liew**

Letters: **Dave Sharpe**

Cover Artists: **Francis Tsai, Patrick Scherberger, Carlos Ferreira & Graham Nolan**

Assistant Editor: **Jordan D. White**

Consulting Editors: **Mark Paniccia & Ralph Macchio**

Editor: **Nathan Cosby**

Collection Editor: **Cory Levine**

Assistant Editors: **Alex Starbuck & John Denning**

Editors, Special Projects: **Jennifer Grünwald & Mark D. Beazley**

Senior Editor, Special Projects: **Jeff Youngquist**

Senior Vice President of Sales: **David Gabriel**

Vice President of Creative: **Tom Marvelli**

Editor in Chief: **Joe Quesada**

Publisher: **Dan Buckley**

Executive Producer: **Alan Fine**

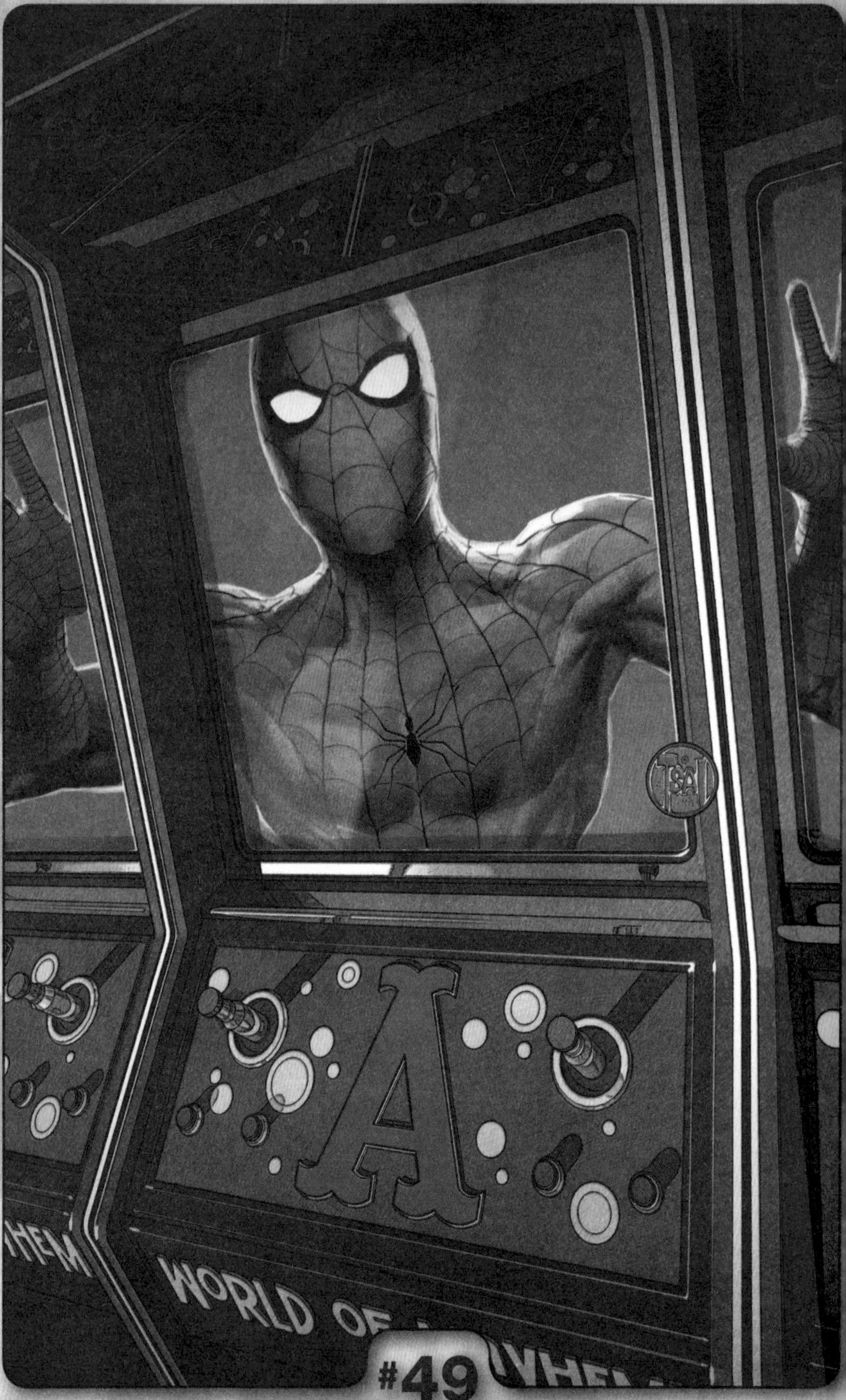
WORLD OF
#49

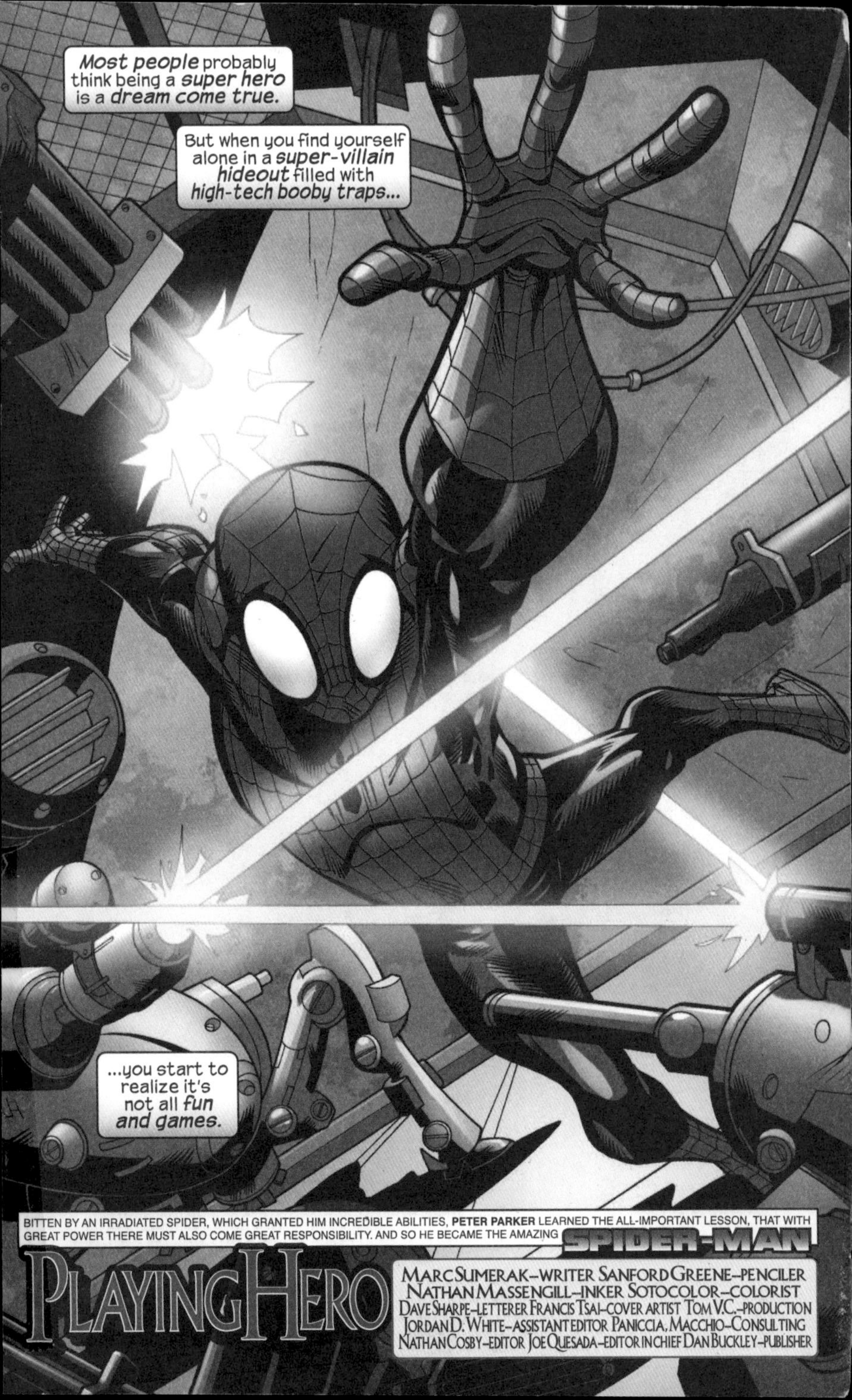

Most people probably think being a super hero is a dream come true.
But when you find yourself alone in a super-villain hideout filled with high-tech booby traps...
...you start to realize it's not all fun and games.
BITTEN BY AN IRRADIATED SPIDER, WHICH GRANTED HIM INCREDIBLE ABILITIES, PETER PARKER LEARNED THE ALL-IMPORTANT LESSON, THAT WITH GREAT POWER THERE MUST ALSO COME GREAT RESPONSIBILITY. AND SO HE BECAME THE AMAZING SPIDER-MAN
PLAYING HERO
MARC SUMERAK–WRITER SANFORD GREENE–PENCILER
NATHAN MASSENGILL–INKER SOTOCOLOR–COLORIST
DAVE SHARPE–LETTERER FRANCIS TSAI–COVER ARTIST TOM V.C.–PRODUCTION
JORDAN D. WHITE–ASSISTANT EDITOR PANICCIA, MACCHIO–CONSULTING
NATHAN COSBY–EDITOR JOE QUESADA–EDITOR IN CHIEF DAN BUCKLEY–PUBLISHER

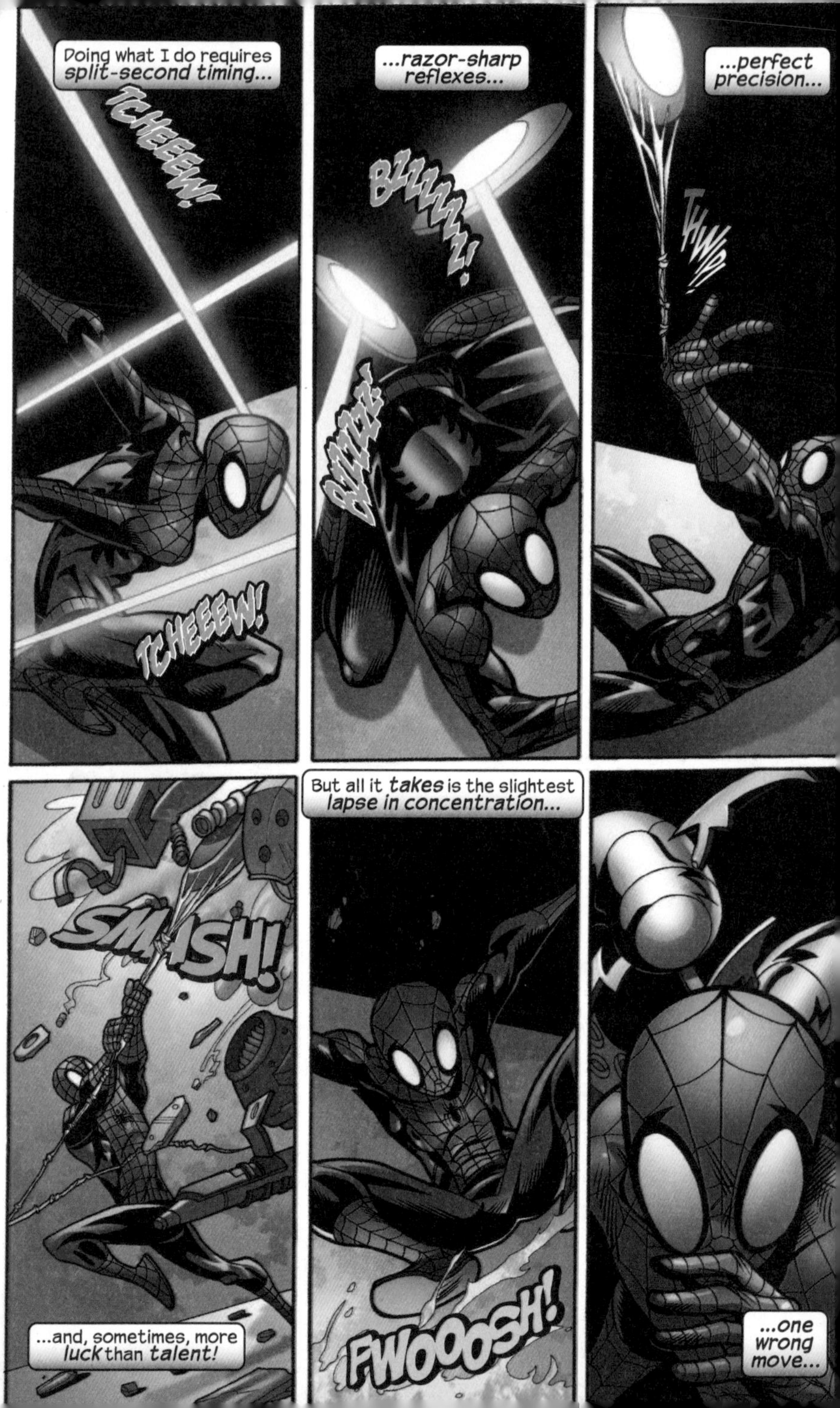

Doing what I do requires split-second timing...
TCHEEEW!
TCHEEEW!
...razor-sharp reflexes...
...perfect precision...
THWIP!
SMASH!
...and, sometimes, more luck than talent!
But all it takes is the slightest lapse in concentration...
FWOOOSH!
...one wrong move...

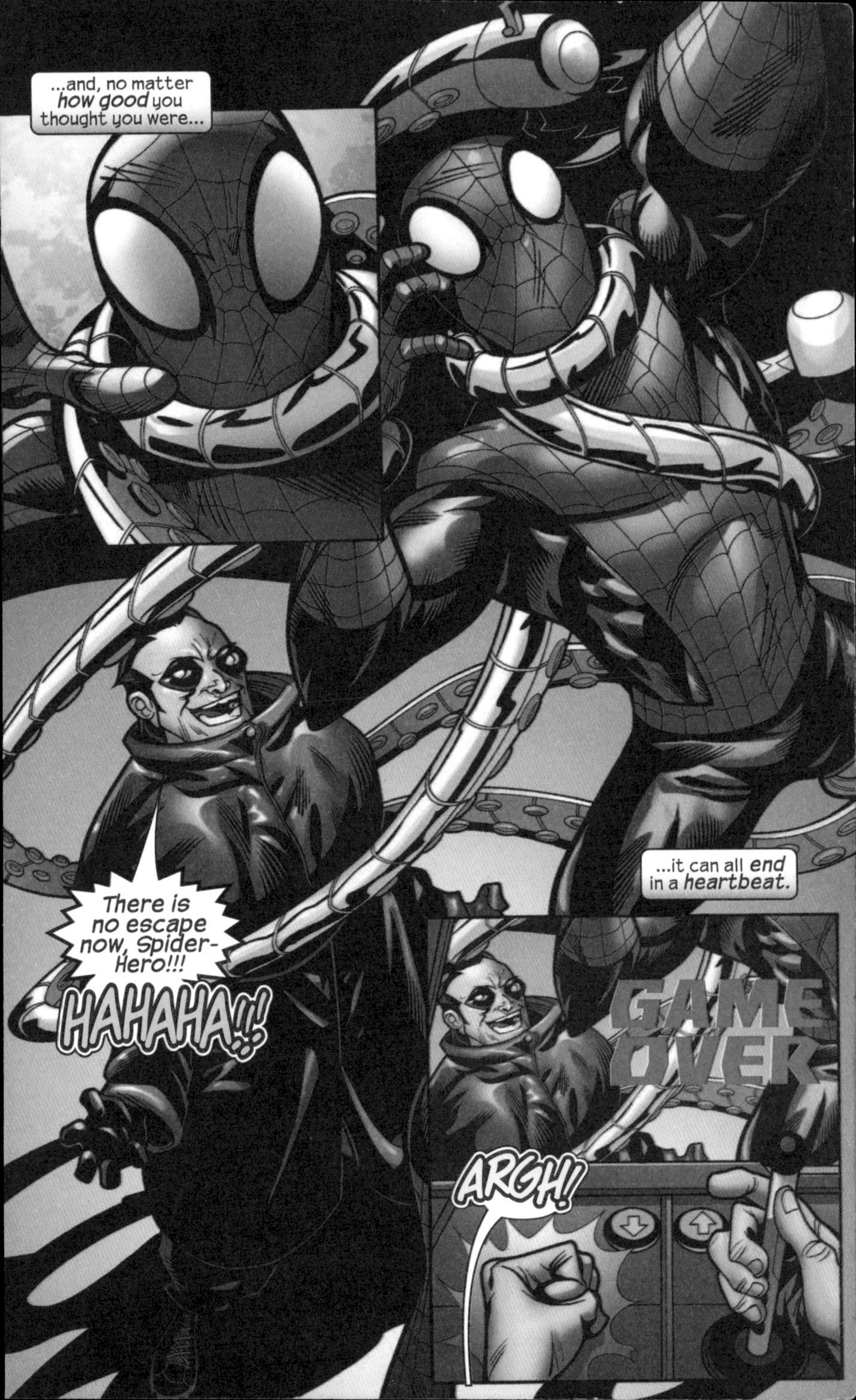
...and, no matter how good you thought you were...
There is no escape now, Spider-Hero!!!
HAHAHA!!!
...it can all end in a heartbeat.
GAME OVER
ARGH!

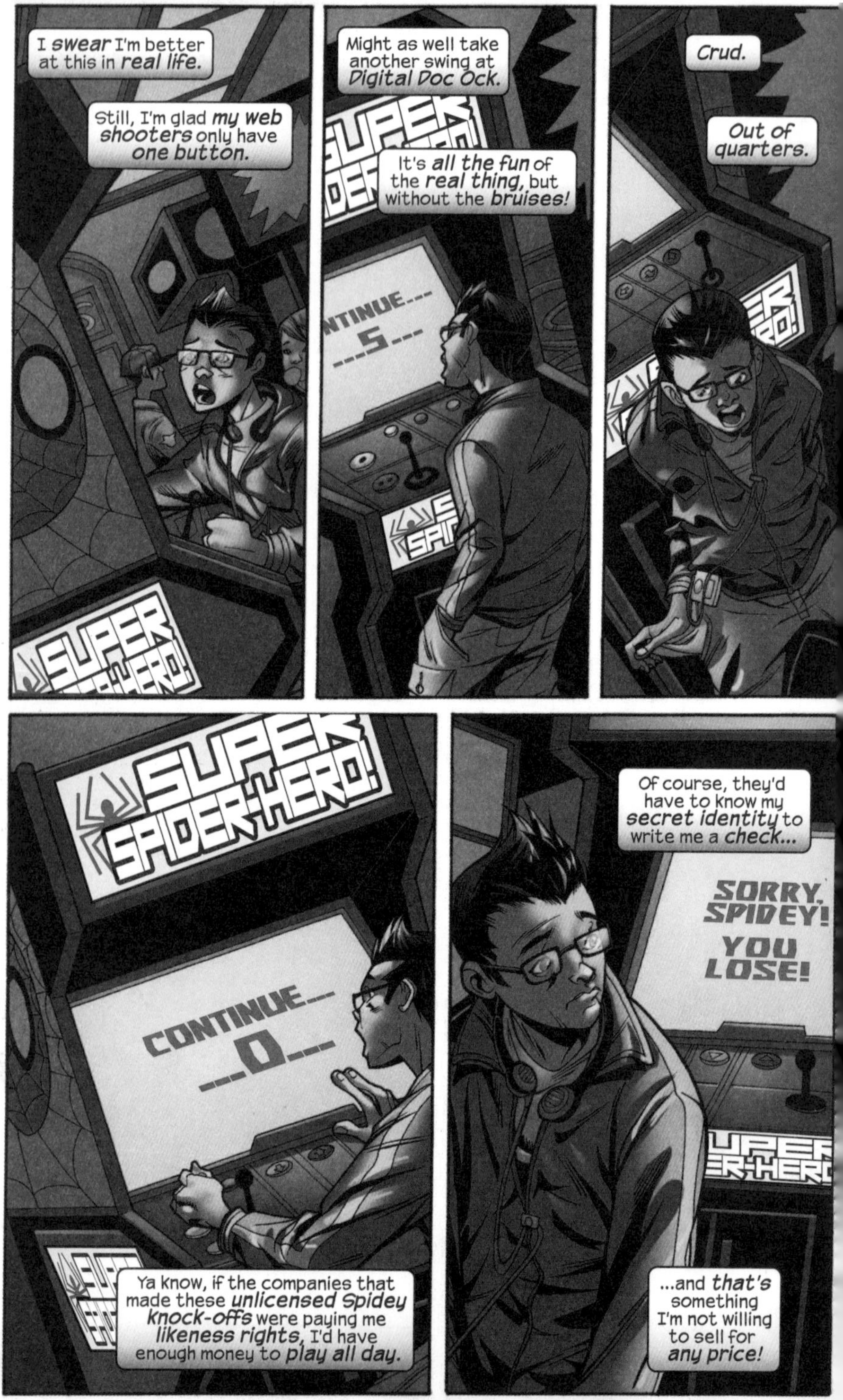

I swear I'm better at this in real life.
Still, I'm glad my web shooters only have one button.
SUPER SPIDER-HERO!
Might as well take another swing at Digital Doc Ock.
It's all the fun of the real thing, but without the bruises!
CONTINUE... ...5...
Crud.
Out of quarters.
SUPER SPIDER-HERO!
CONTINUE... ...0...
Ya know, if the companies that made these unlicensed Spidey knock-offs were paying me likeness rights, I'd have enough money to play all day.
Of course, they'd have to know my secret identity to write me a check...
SORRY, SPIDEY! YOU LOSE!
...and that's something I'm not willing to sell for any price!

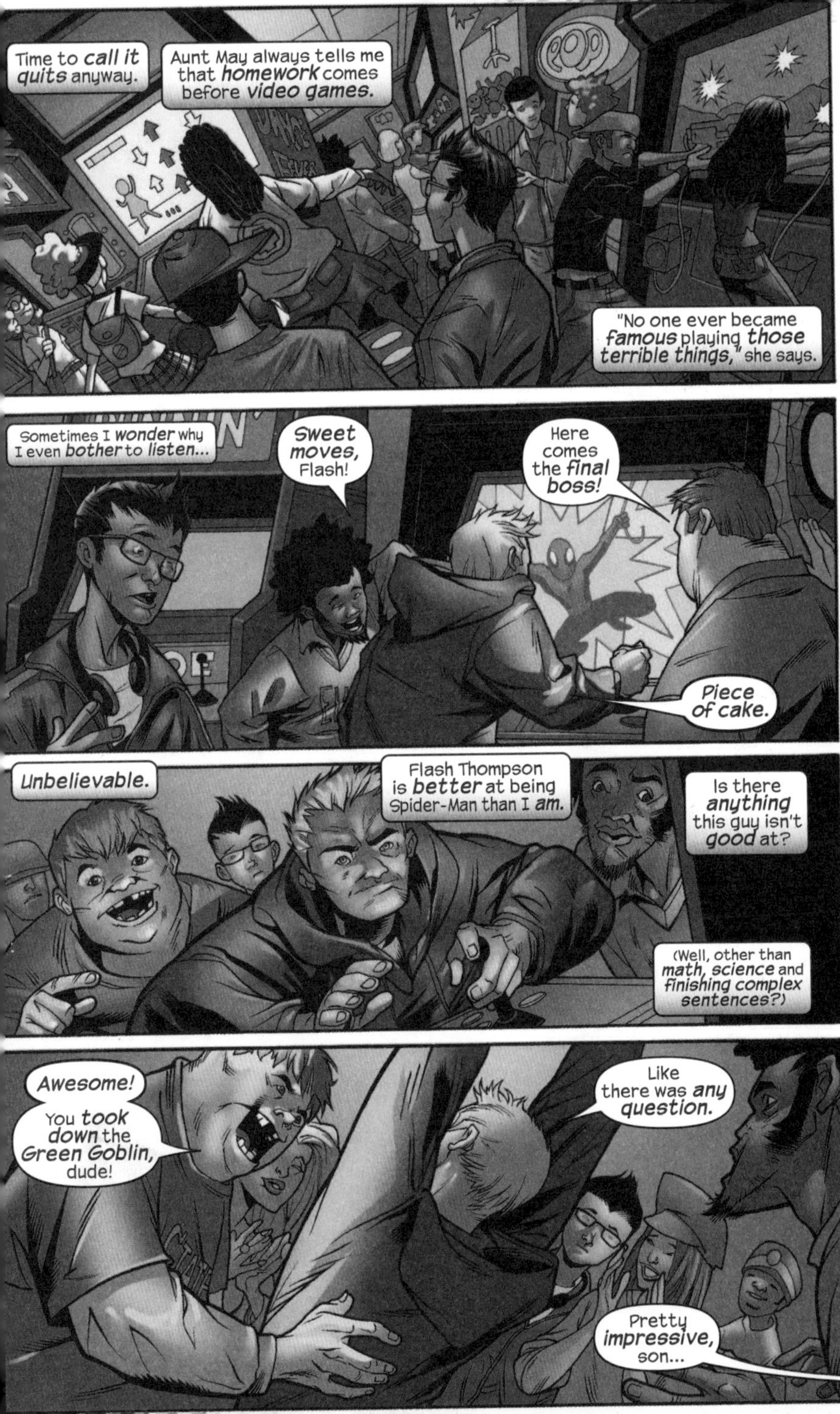
Time to call it quits anyway.
Aunt May always tells me that homework comes before video games.
"No one ever became famous playing those terrible things," she says.
Sometimes I wonder why I even bother to listen...
Sweet moves, Flash!
Here comes the final boss!
Piece of cake.
Unbelievable.
Flash Thompson is better at being Spider-Man than I am.
Is there anything this guy isn't good at?
(Well, other than math, science and finishing complex sentences?)
Awesome!
You took down the Green Goblin, dude!
Like there was any question.
Pretty impressive, son...

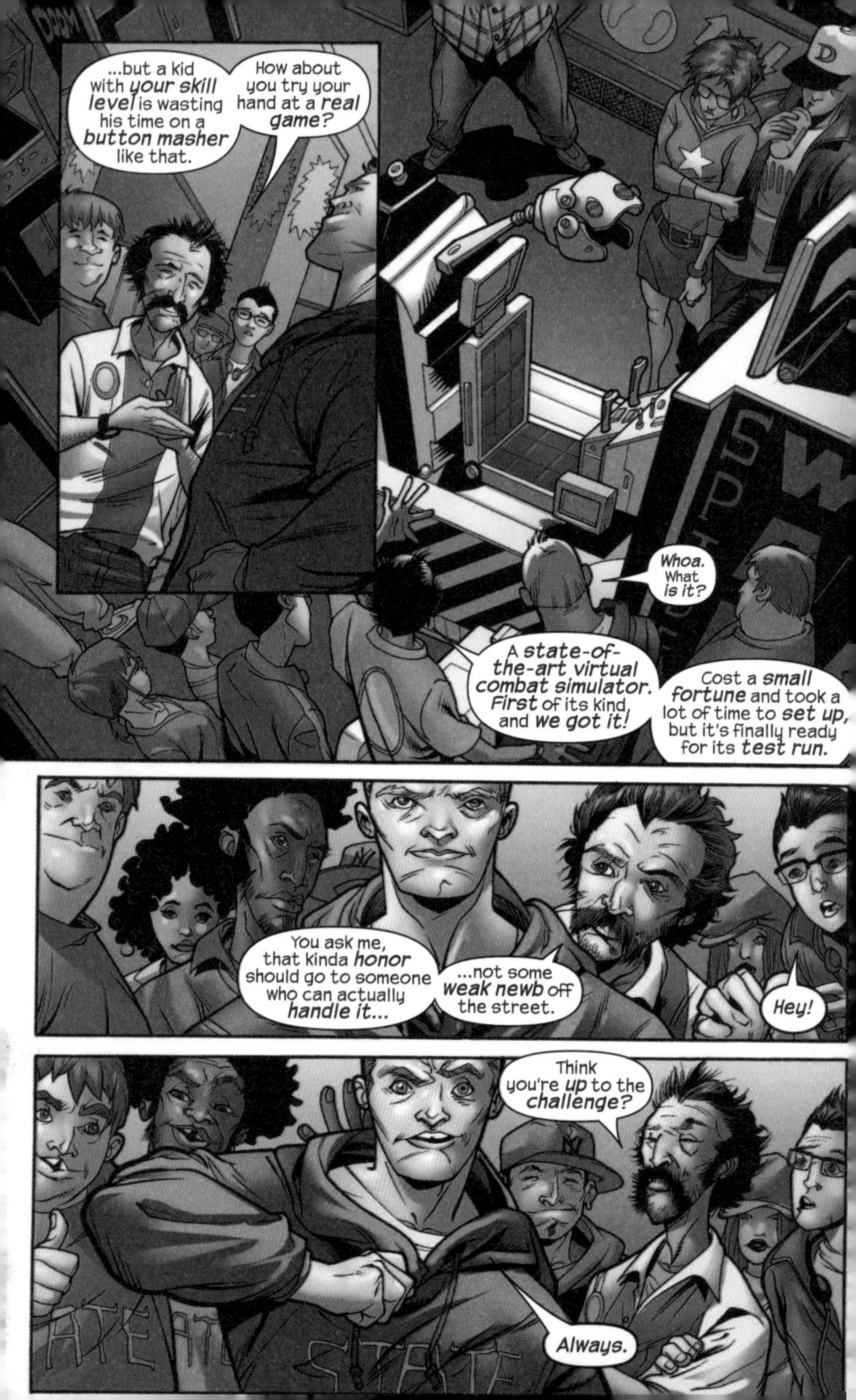
...but a kid with your skill level is wasting his time on a button masher like that.
How about you try your hand at a real game?
Whoa. What is it?
A state-of-the-art virtual combat simulator. First of its kind, and we got it!
Cost a small fortune and took a lot of time to set up, but it's finally ready for its test run.
You ask me, that kinda honor should go to someone who can actually handle it...
...not some weak newb off the street.
Hey!
Think you're up to the challenge?
Always.

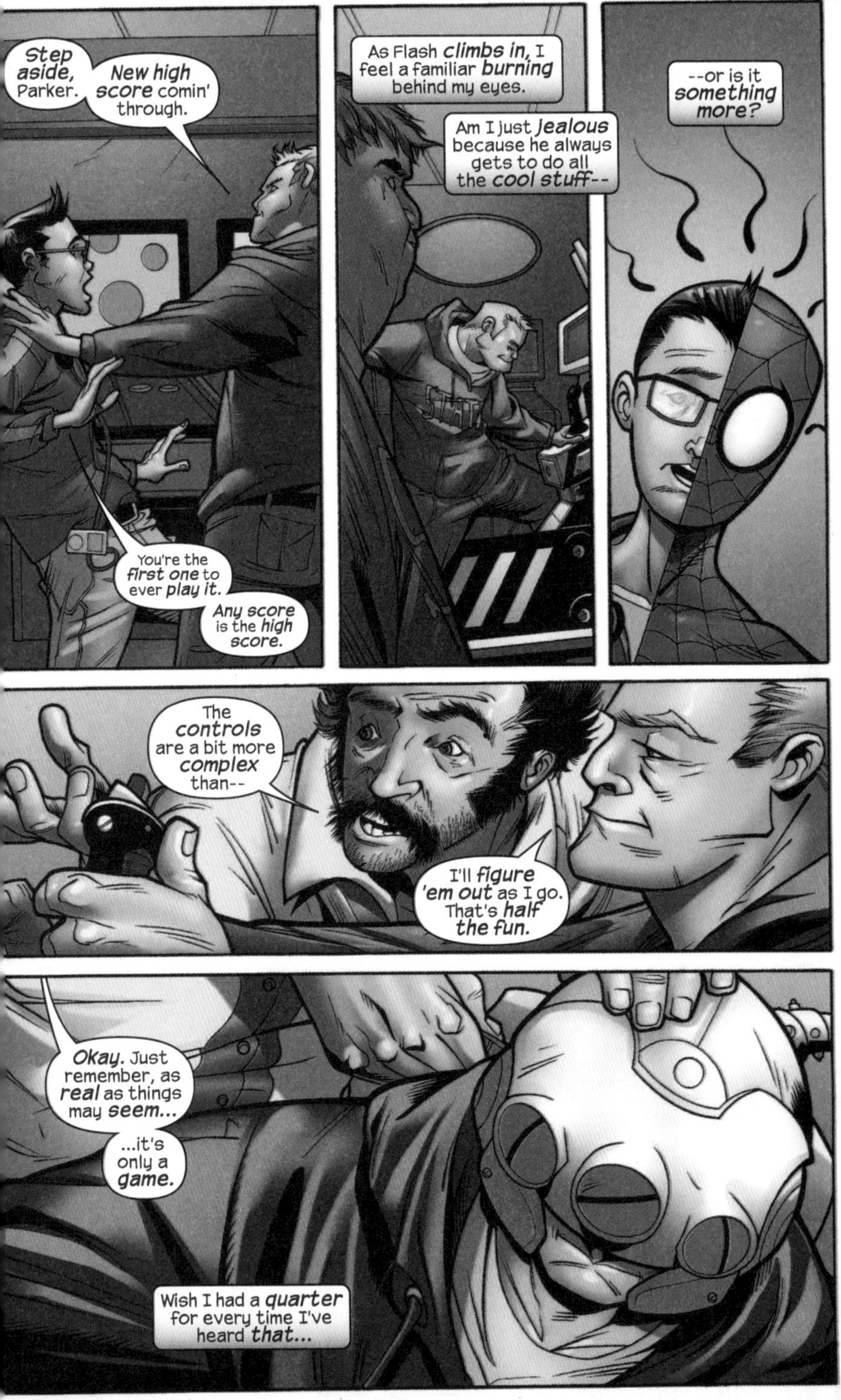
Step aside, Parker.
New high score comin' through.
You're the first one to ever play it.
Any score is the high score.
As Flash climbs in, I feel a familiar burning behind my eyes.
Am I just jealous because he always gets to do all the cool stuff--
--or is it something more?
The controls are a bit more complex than--
I'll figure 'em out as I go. That's half the fun.
Okay. Just remember, as real as things may seem...
...it's only a game.
Wish I had a quarter for every time I've heard that...

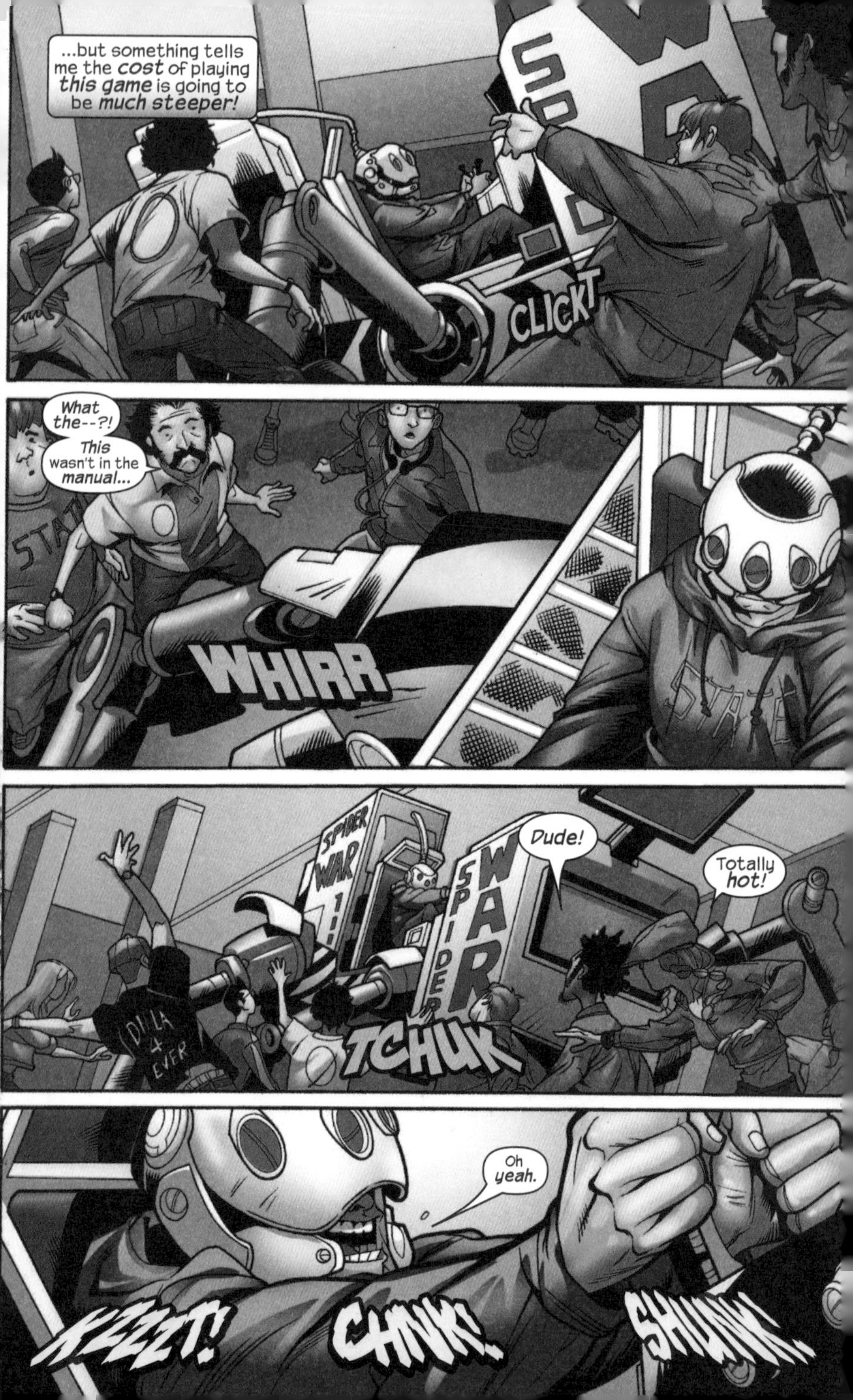

...but something tells me the *cost* of playing *this game* is going to be *much steeper!*
CLICKT
What the--?!
This wasn't in the *manual*...
WHIRR
Dude!
Totally *hot!*
TCHUK
Oh yeah.
KZZZT!
CHNK!
SHUNK!

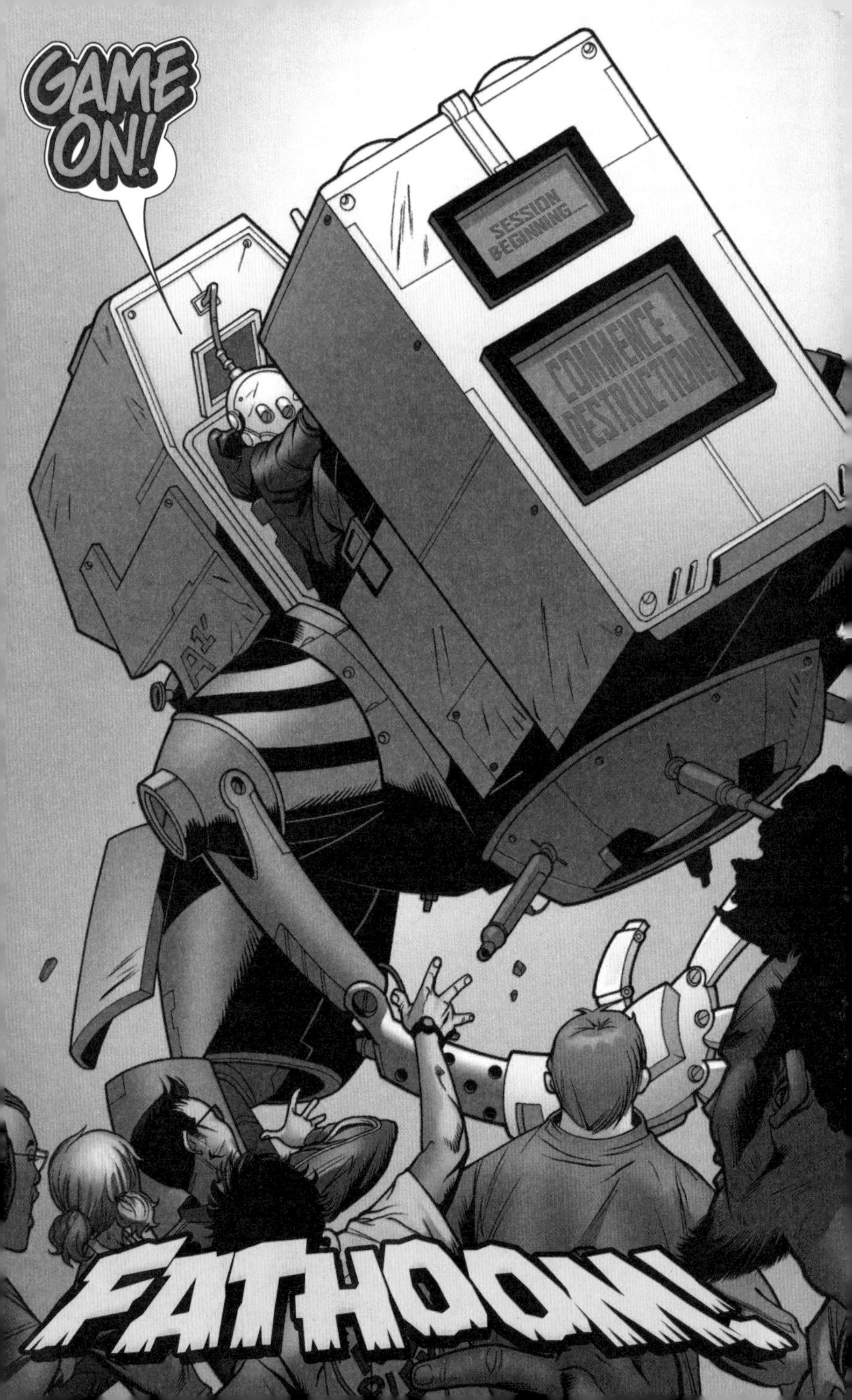
GAME ON!
SESSION BEGINNING...
COMMENCE DESTRUCTION!
FATHOOM!

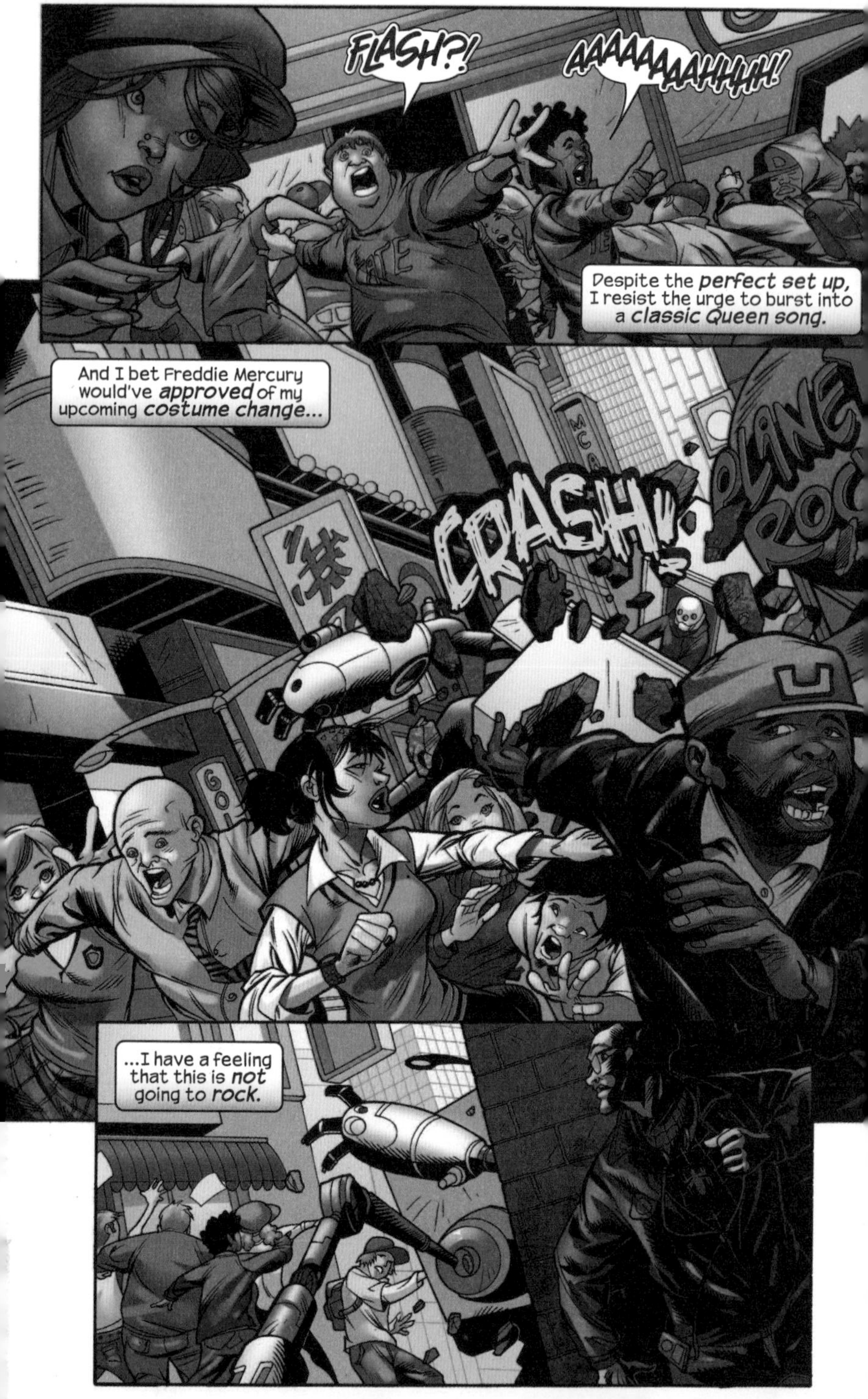
FLASH?!
AAAAAAAAHHHH!
Despite the perfect set up, I resist the urge to burst into a classic Queen song.
And I bet Freddie Mercury would've approved of my upcoming costume change...
CRASH!
PLANET ROCK
...I have a feeling that this is not going to rock.

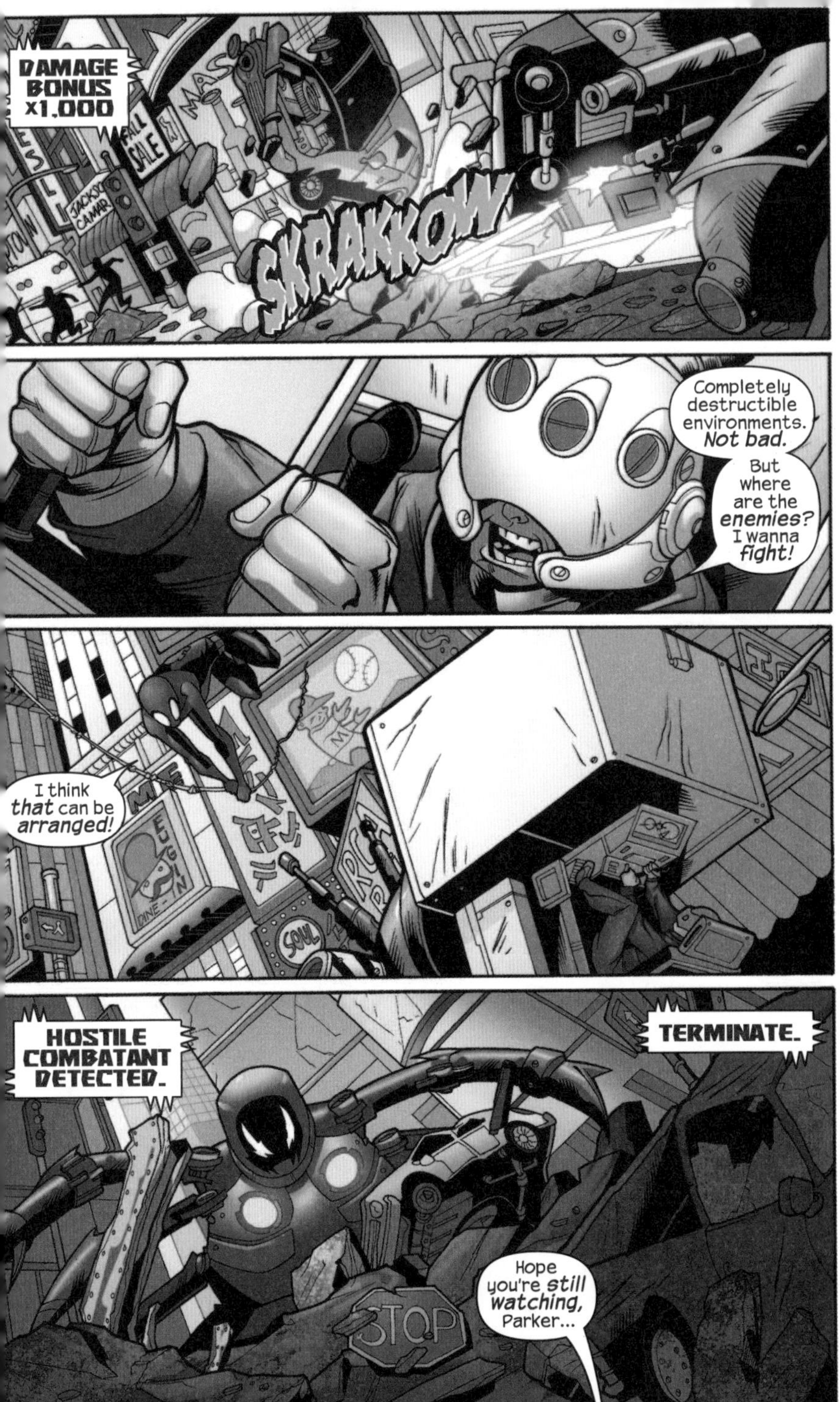
DAMAGE BONUS X1,000
SKRAKKOW
Completely destructible environments. Not bad.
But where are the enemies? I wanna fight!
I think that can be arranged!
HOSTILE COMBATANT DETECTED.
TERMINATE.
Hope you're still watching, Parker...

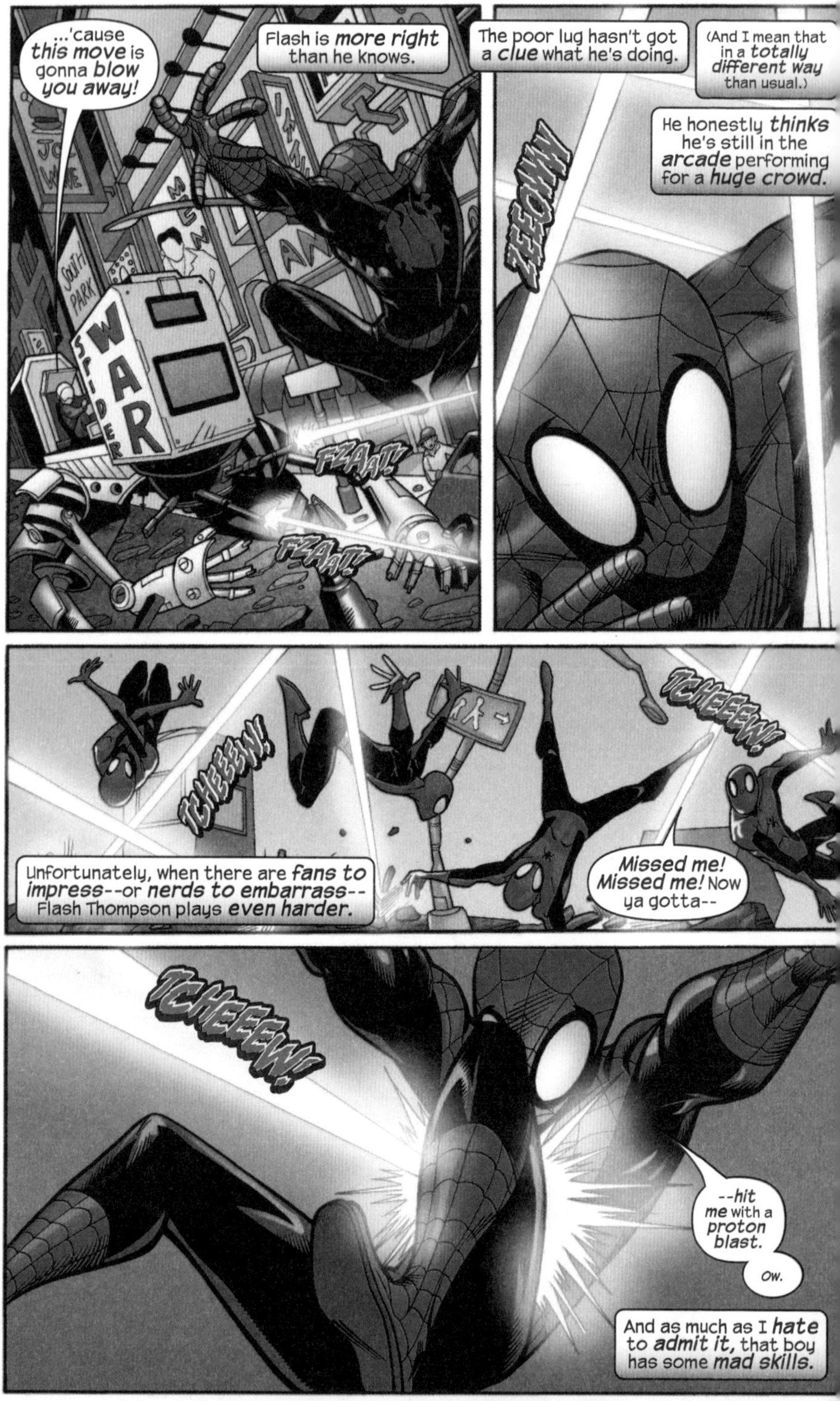
...'cause this move is gonna blow you away!
Flash is more right than he knows.
FZAAAT!
FZAAAT!
The poor lug hasn't got a clue what he's doing.
(And I mean that in a totally different way than usual.)
He honestly thinks he's still in the arcade performing for a huge crowd.
ZEEOWW
TCHEEEW!
TCHEEEW!
Unfortunately, when there are fans to impress--or nerds to embarrass--Flash Thompson plays even harder.
Missed me! Missed me! Now ya gotta--
TCHEEEW!
--hit me with a proton blast.
Ow.
And as much as I hate to admit it, that boy has some mad skills.

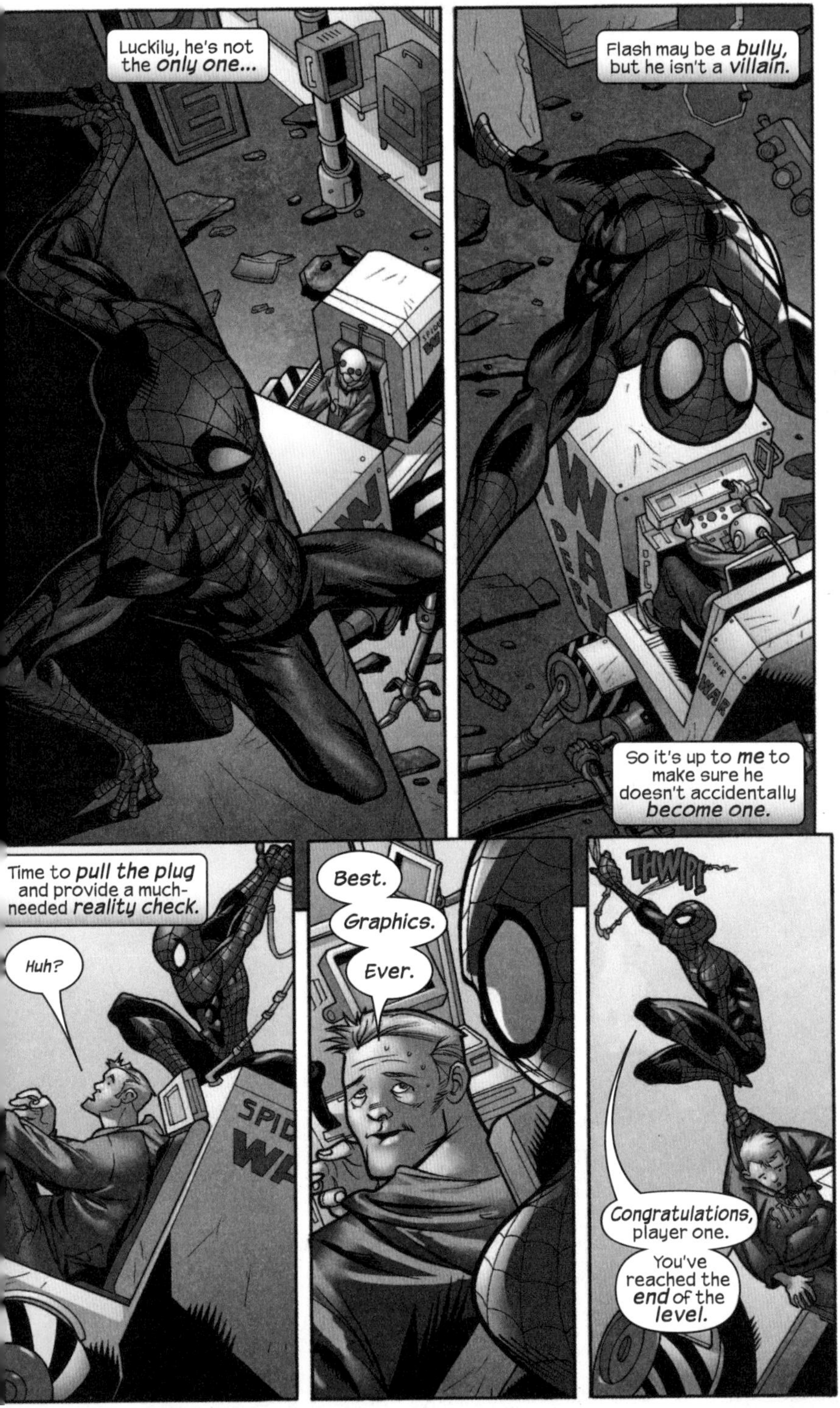

Luckily, he's not the only one...
Flash may be a bully, but he isn't a villain.
So it's up to me to make sure he doesn't accidentally become one.
Time to pull the plug and provide a much-needed reality check.
Huh?
Best.
Graphics.
Ever.
THWIP!
Congratulations, player one.
You've reached the end of the level.

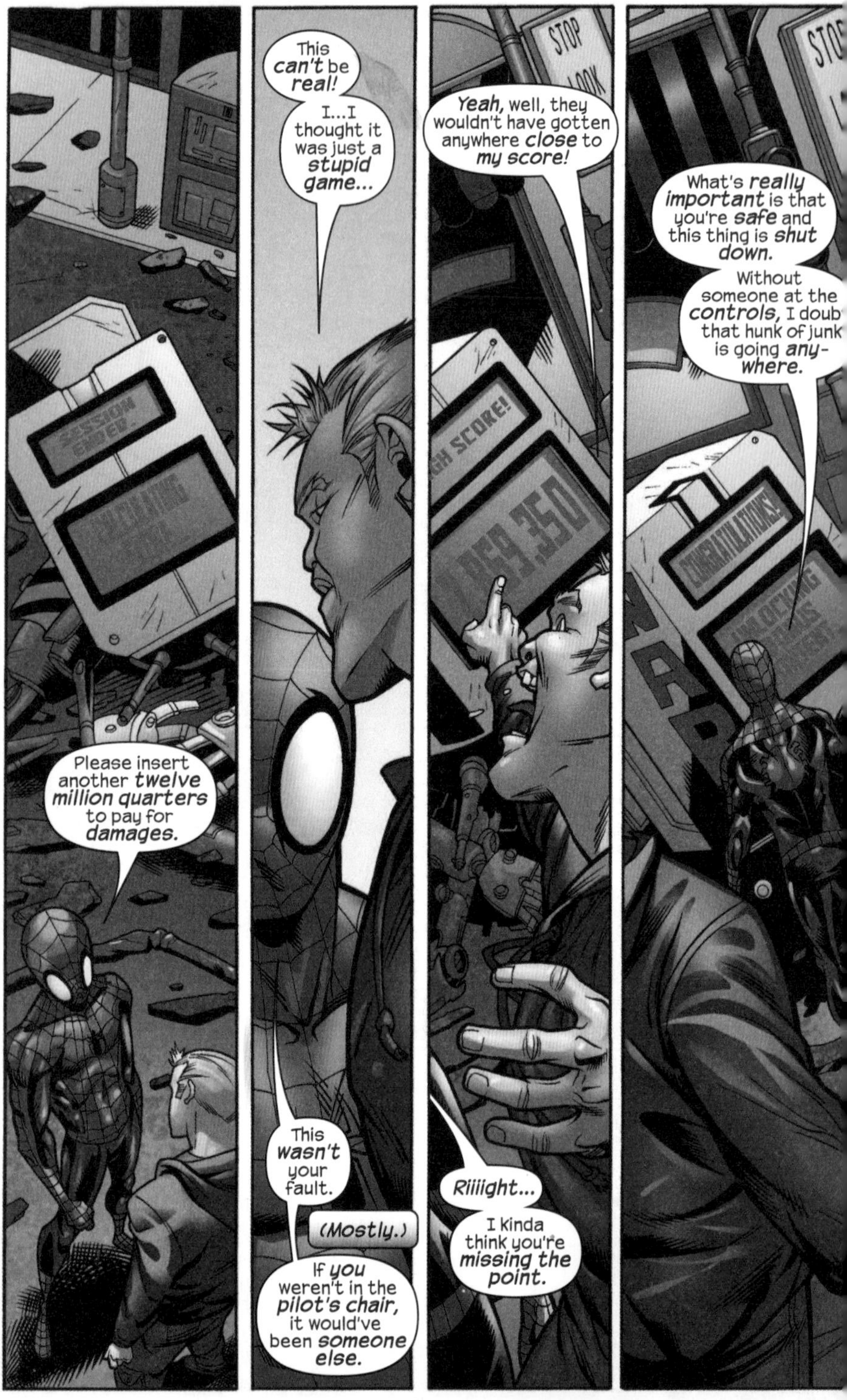

Please insert another twelve million quarters to pay for damages.
This can't be real!
I...I thought it was just a stupid game...
This wasn't your fault.
(Mostly.)
If you weren't in the pilot's chair, it would've been someone else.
Yeah, well, they wouldn't have gotten anywhere close to my score!
Riiight...
I kinda think you're missing the point.
What's really important is that you're safe and this thing is shut down.
Without someone at the controls, I doub that hunk of junk is going any-where.

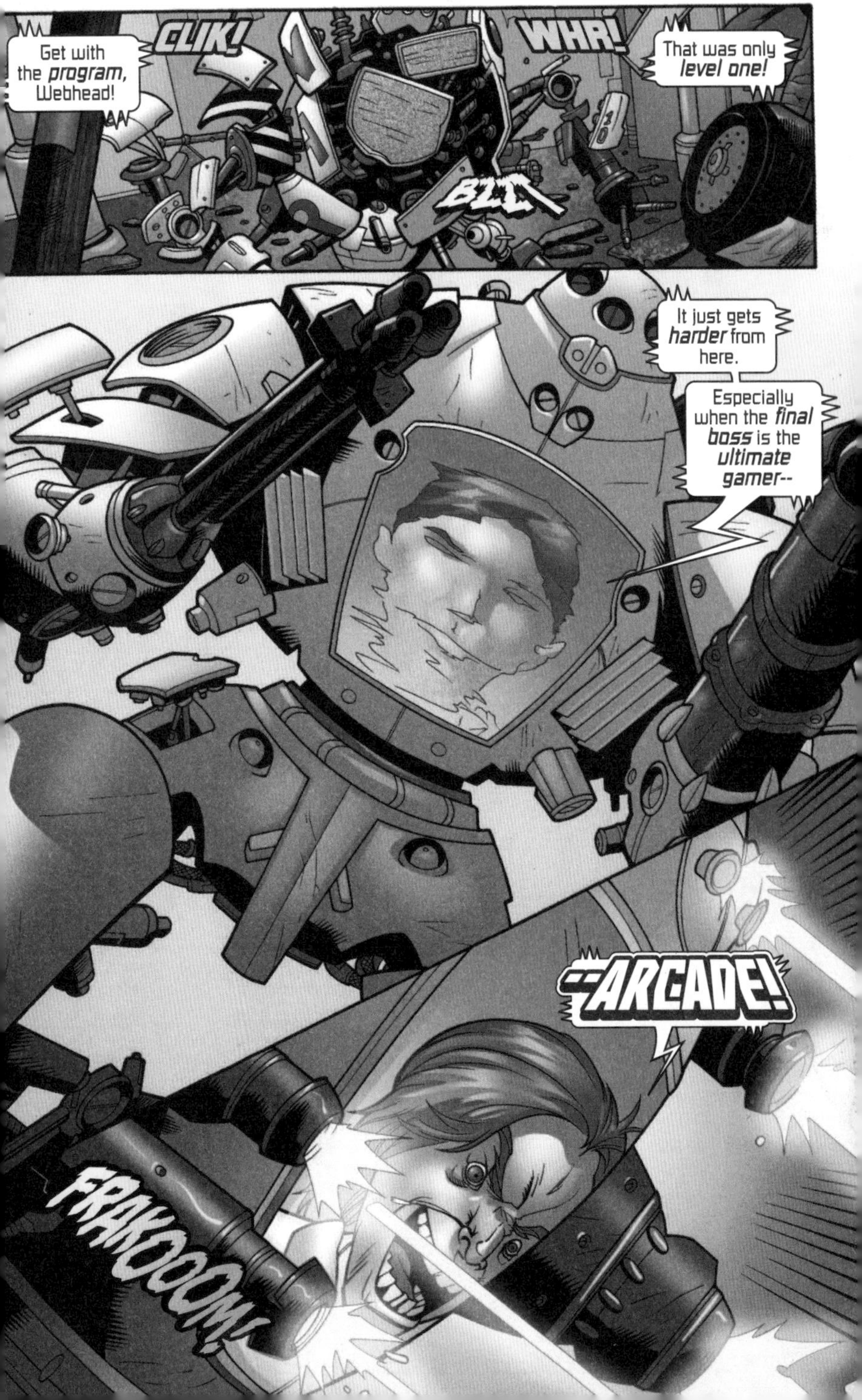
Get with the *program*, Webhead!
CLIK!
WHR!
That was only *level one!*
BZZT
It just gets *harder* from here.
Especially when the *final boss* is the *ultimate gamer--*
--ARCADE!
FRAKOOOM!

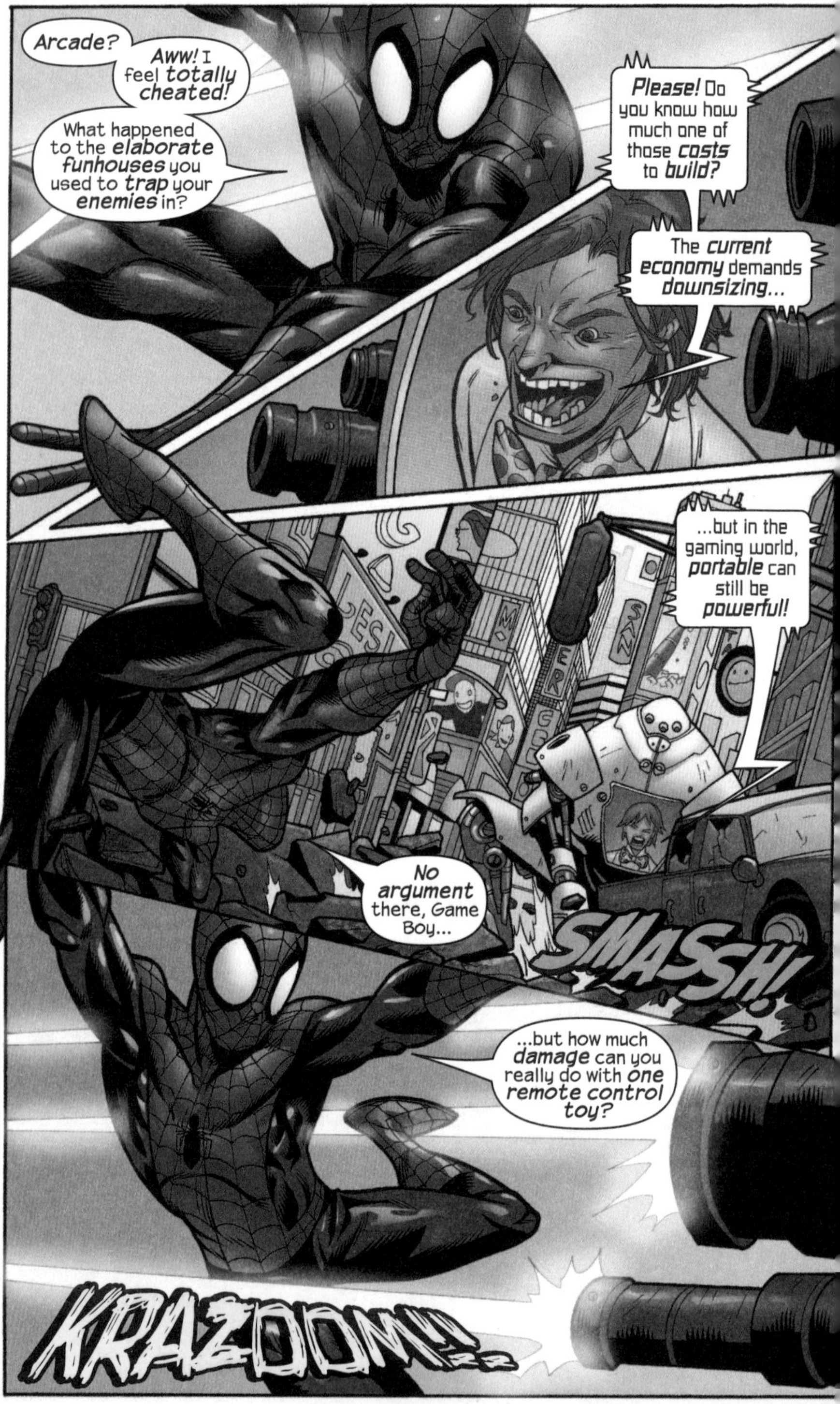
Arcade?
Aww! I feel totally cheated!
What happened to the elaborate funhouses you used to trap your enemies in?
Please! Do you know how much one of those costs to build?
The current economy demands downsizing...
...but in the gaming world, portable can still be powerful!
No argument there, Game Boy...
SMASSH!
...but how much damage can you really do with one remote control toy?
KRAZOOM!!

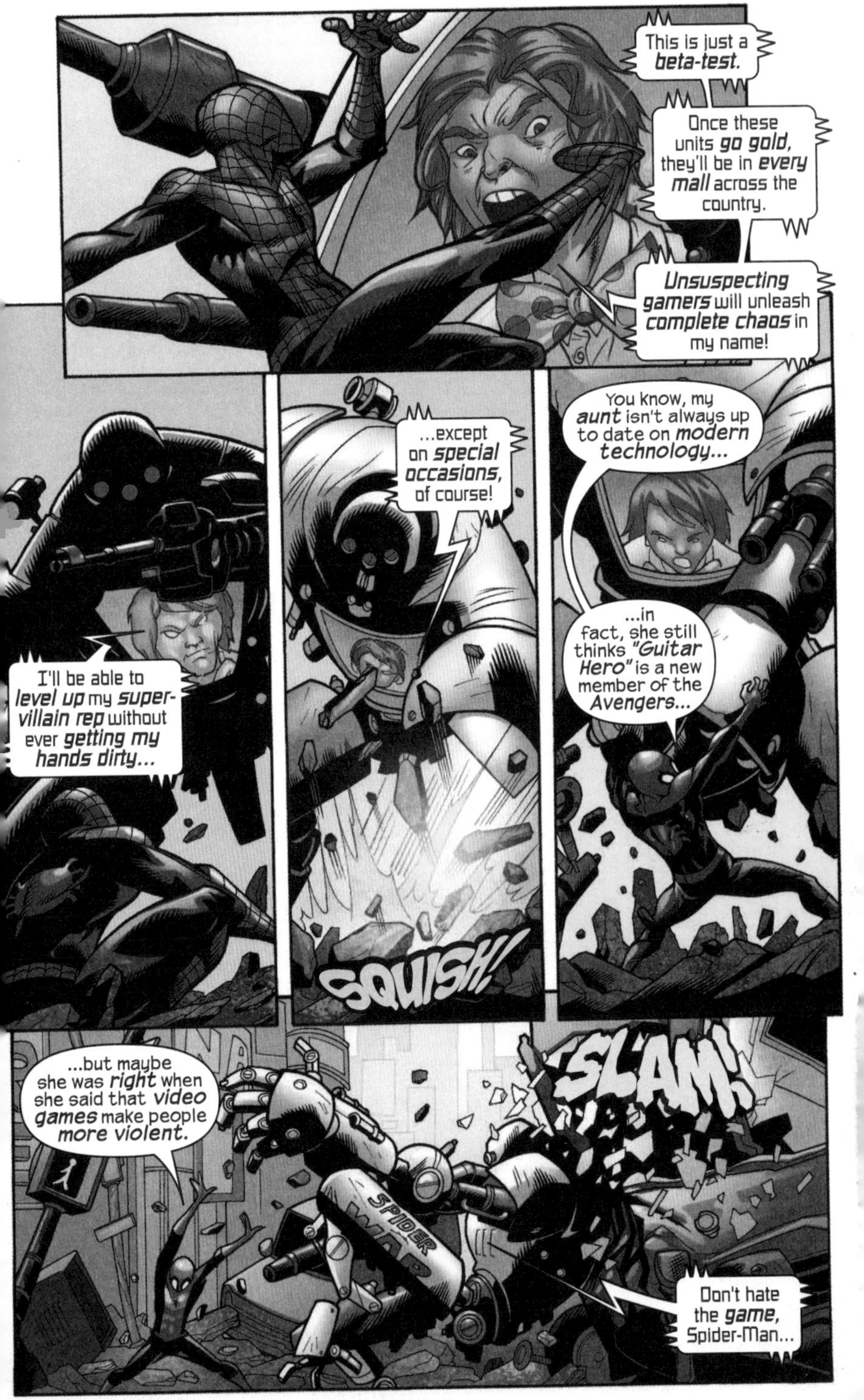
This is just a beta-test.
Once these units go gold, they'll be in every mall across the country.
Unsuspecting gamers will unleash complete chaos in my name!
I'll be able to level up my super-villain rep without ever getting my hands dirty...
...except on special occasions, of course!
SQUISH!
You know, my aunt isn't always up to date on modern technology...
...in fact, she still thinks "Guitar Hero" is a new member of the Avengers...
...but maybe she was right when she said that video games make people more violent.
SLAM!
SPIDER
Don't hate the game, Spider-Man...

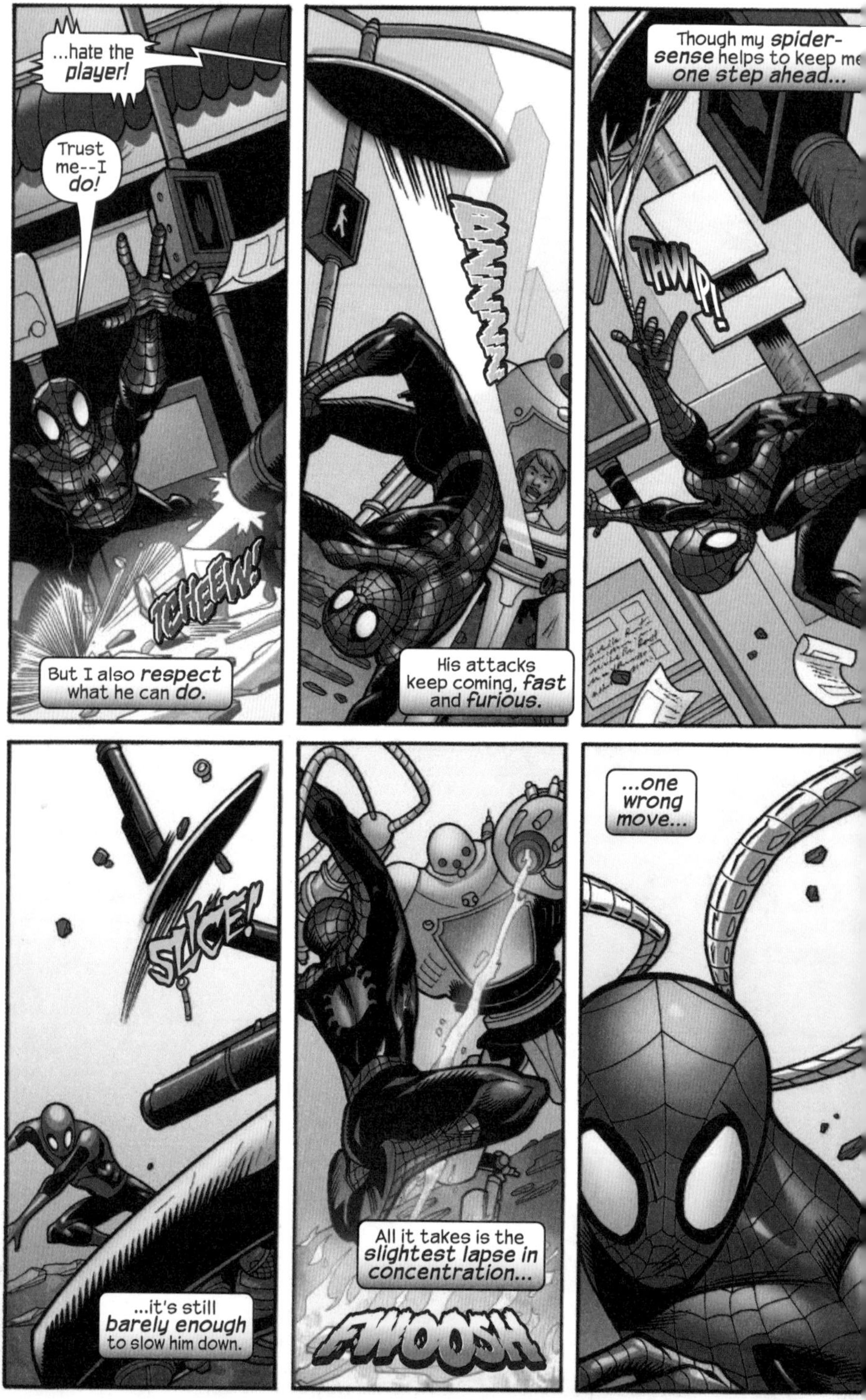
...hate the player!
Trust me--I do!
TCHEEW!
But I also respect what he can do.
BZZZZZ
His attacks keep coming, fast and furious.
Though my spider-sense helps to keep me one step ahead...
THWIP!
SLICE!
...it's still barely enough to slow him down.
All it takes is the slightest lapse in concentration...
FWOOSH
...one wrong move...

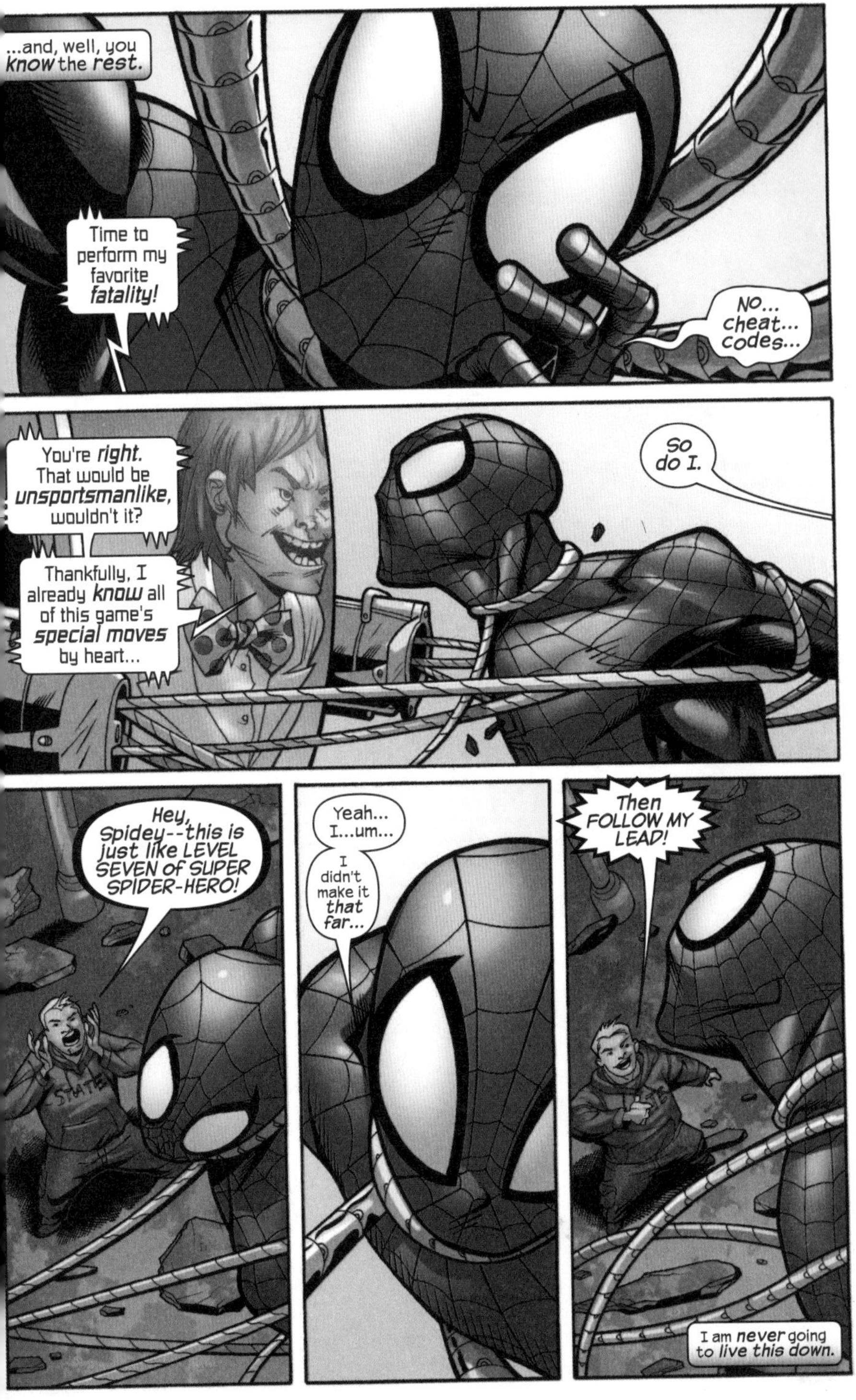
...and, well, you know the rest.
Time to perform my favorite fatality!
NO... cheat... codes...
You're right. That would be unsportsmanlike, wouldn't it?
Thankfully, I already know all of this game's special moves by heart...
So do I.
Hey, Spidey--this is just like LEVEL SEVEN of SUPER SPIDER-HERO!
Yeah... I...um...
I didn't make it that far...
Then FOLLOW MY LEAD!
I am never going to live this down.

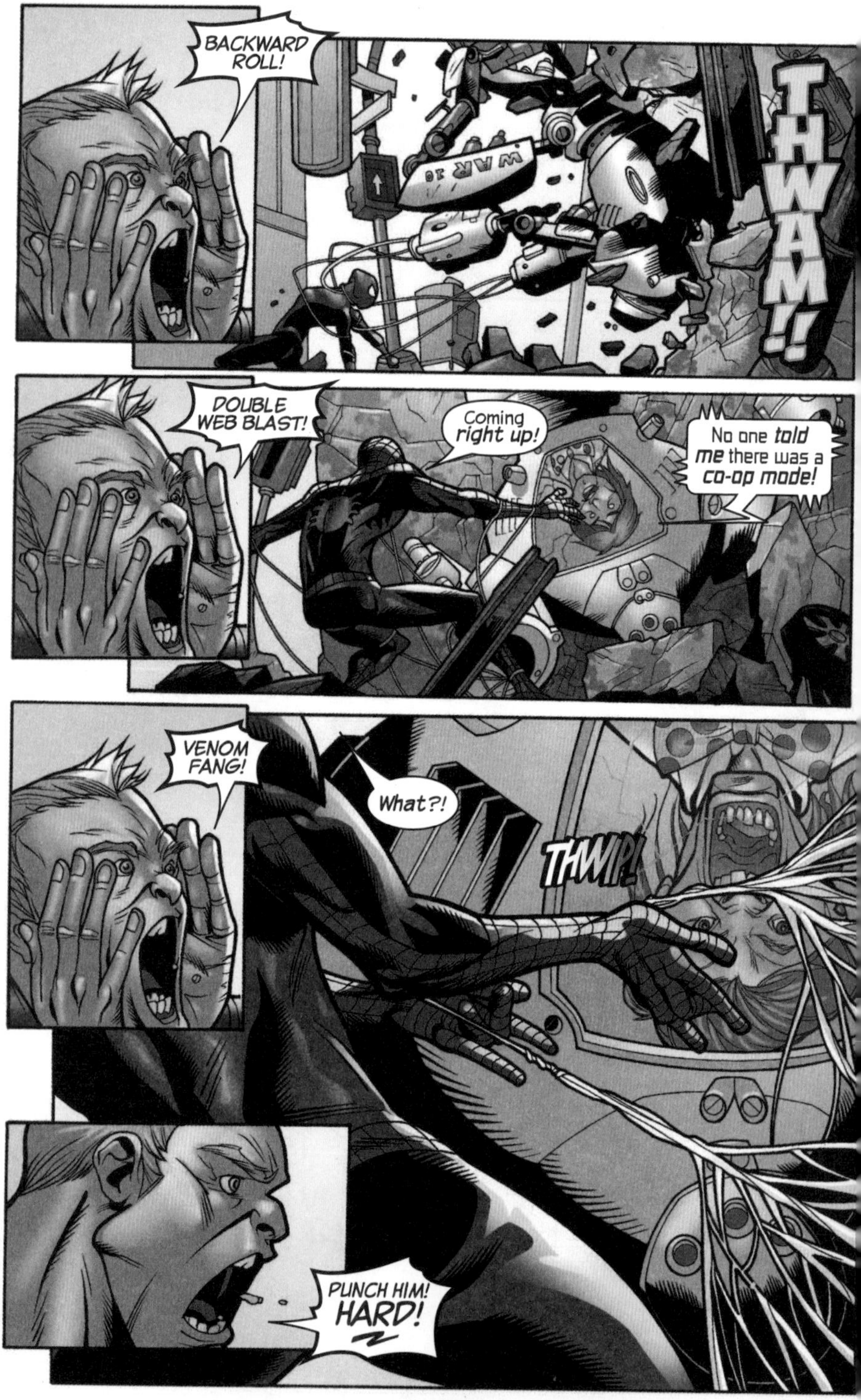
BACKWARD ROLL!
THWAM!!
DOUBLE WEB BLAST!
Coming right up!
No one told me there was a co-op mode!
VENOM FANG!
What?!
THWIP!
PUNCH HIM! HARD!

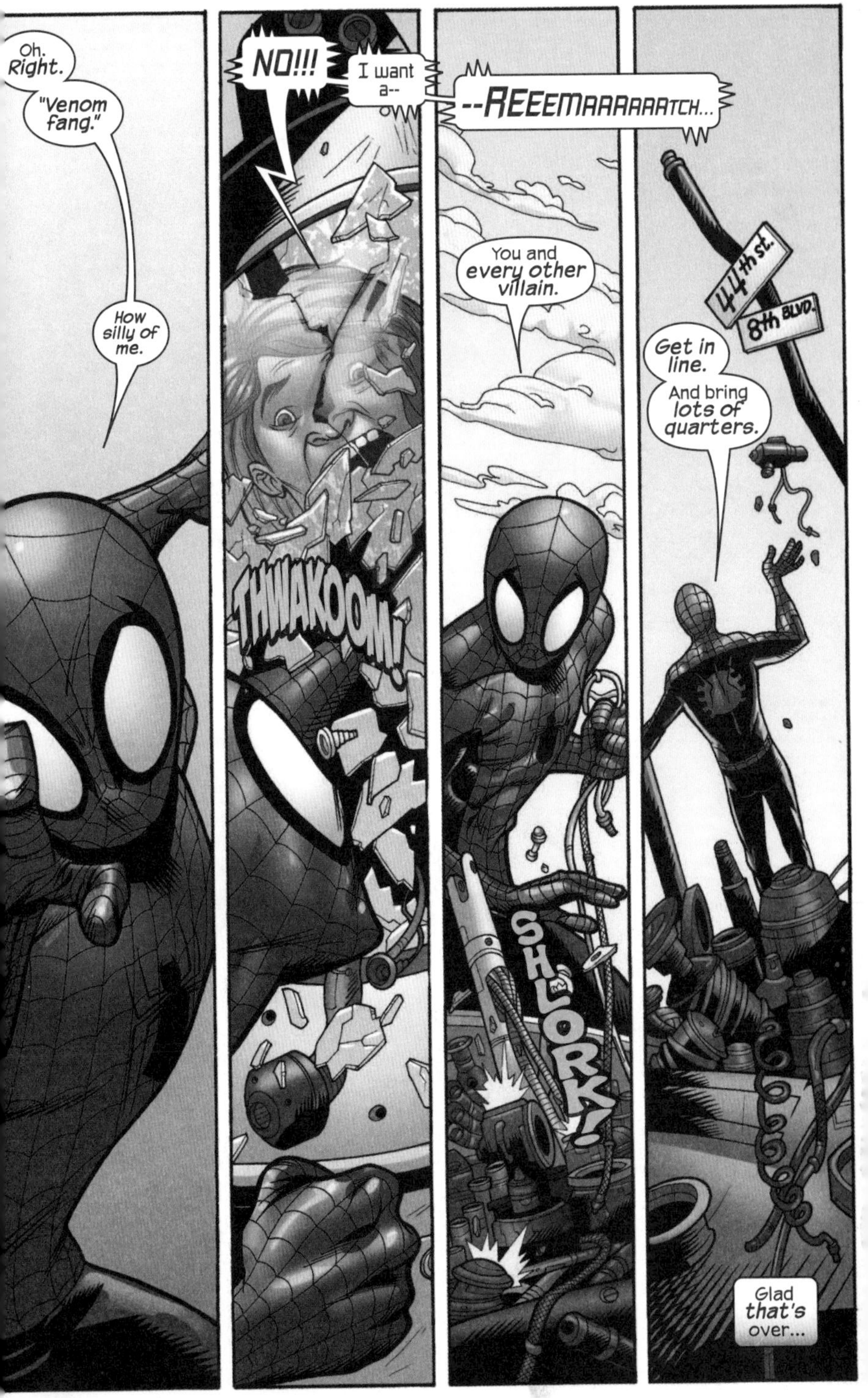
Oh. Right.
"Venom fang."
How silly of me.
NO!!!
I want a--
--REEEMAAAAAAATCH...
THWAKOOM!
You and every other villain.
SHLORK!
44th St.
8th BLVD.
Get in line.
And bring lots of quarters.
Glad that's over...

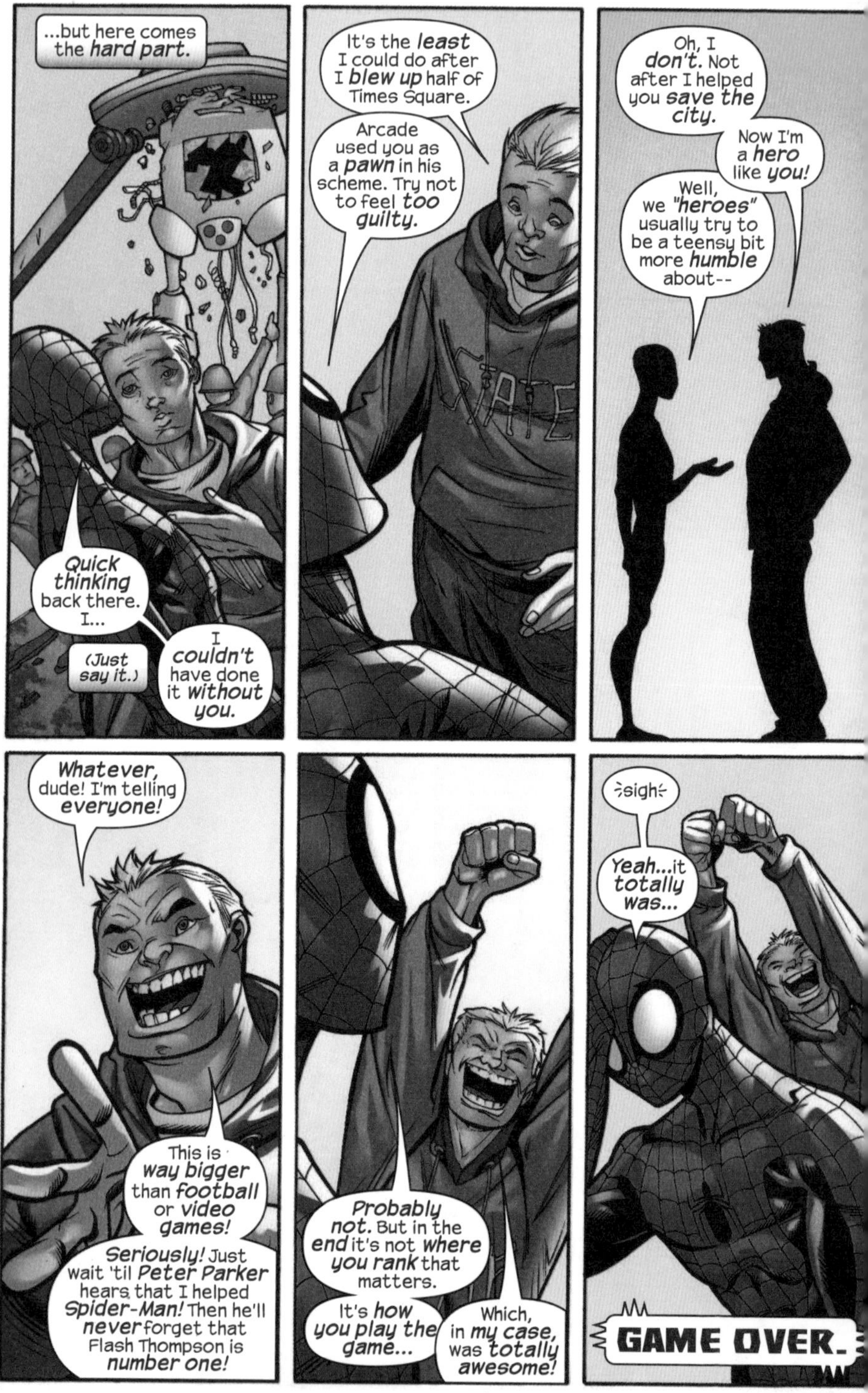
...but here comes the *hard part.*
Quick thinking back there. I...
(Just say it.)
I *couldn't* have done it *without you.*
It's the *least* I could do after I *blew up* half of Times Square.
Arcade used you as a *pawn* in his scheme. Try not to feel *too guilty.*
Oh, I *don't.* Not after I helped you *save the city.*
Now I'm a *hero* like *you!*
Well, we *"heroes"* usually try to be a teensy bit more *humble* about--
Whatever, dude! I'm telling *everyone!*
This is *way bigger* than *football* or *video games!*
Seriously! Just wait 'til *Peter Parker* hears that I helped *Spider-Man!* Then he'll *never* forget that Flash Thompson is *number one!*
Probably not. But in the *end* it's not *where you rank* that matters.
It's *how you play the game...*
Which, in *my case,* was *totally awesome!*
sigh
Yeah...it totally was...
GAME OVER.

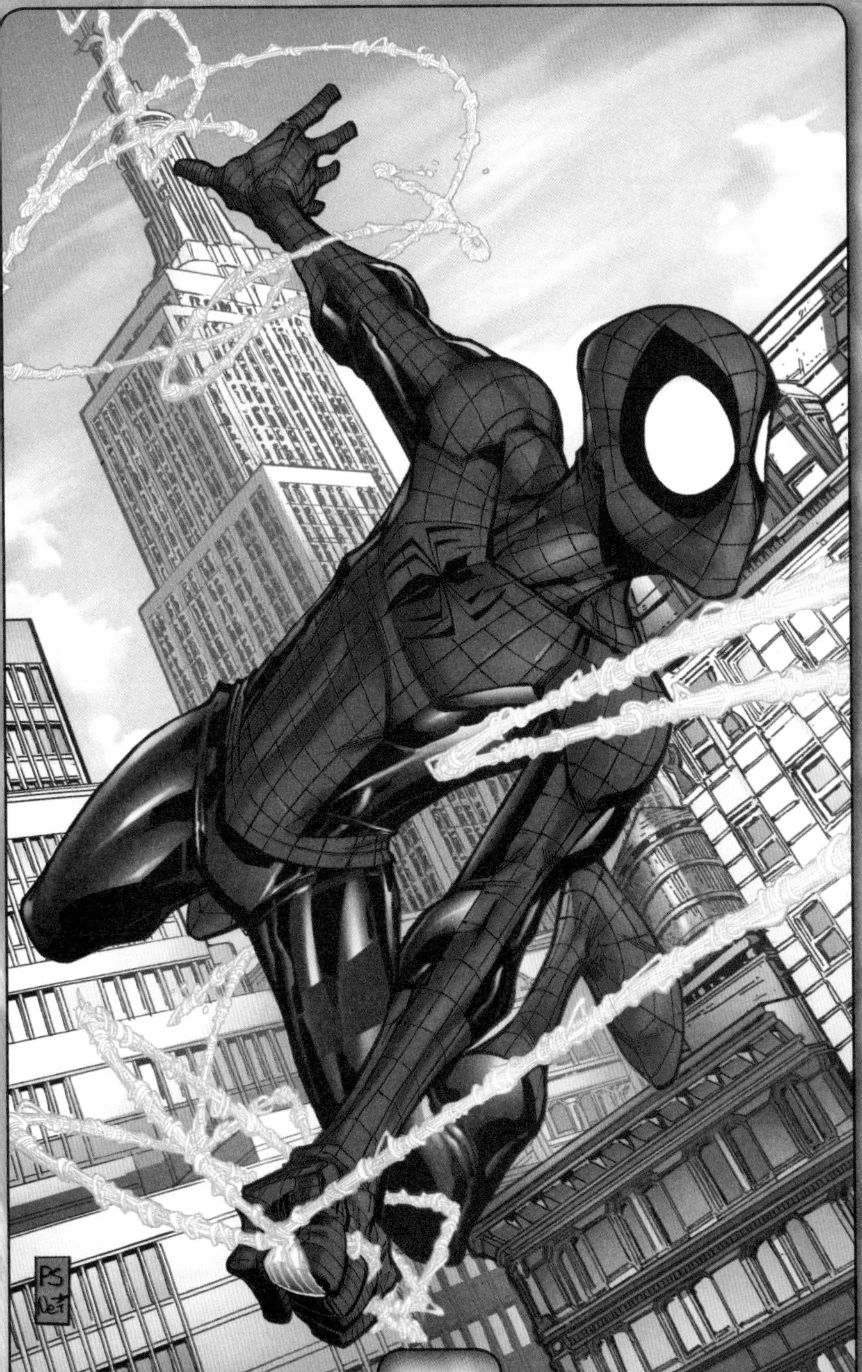

#50

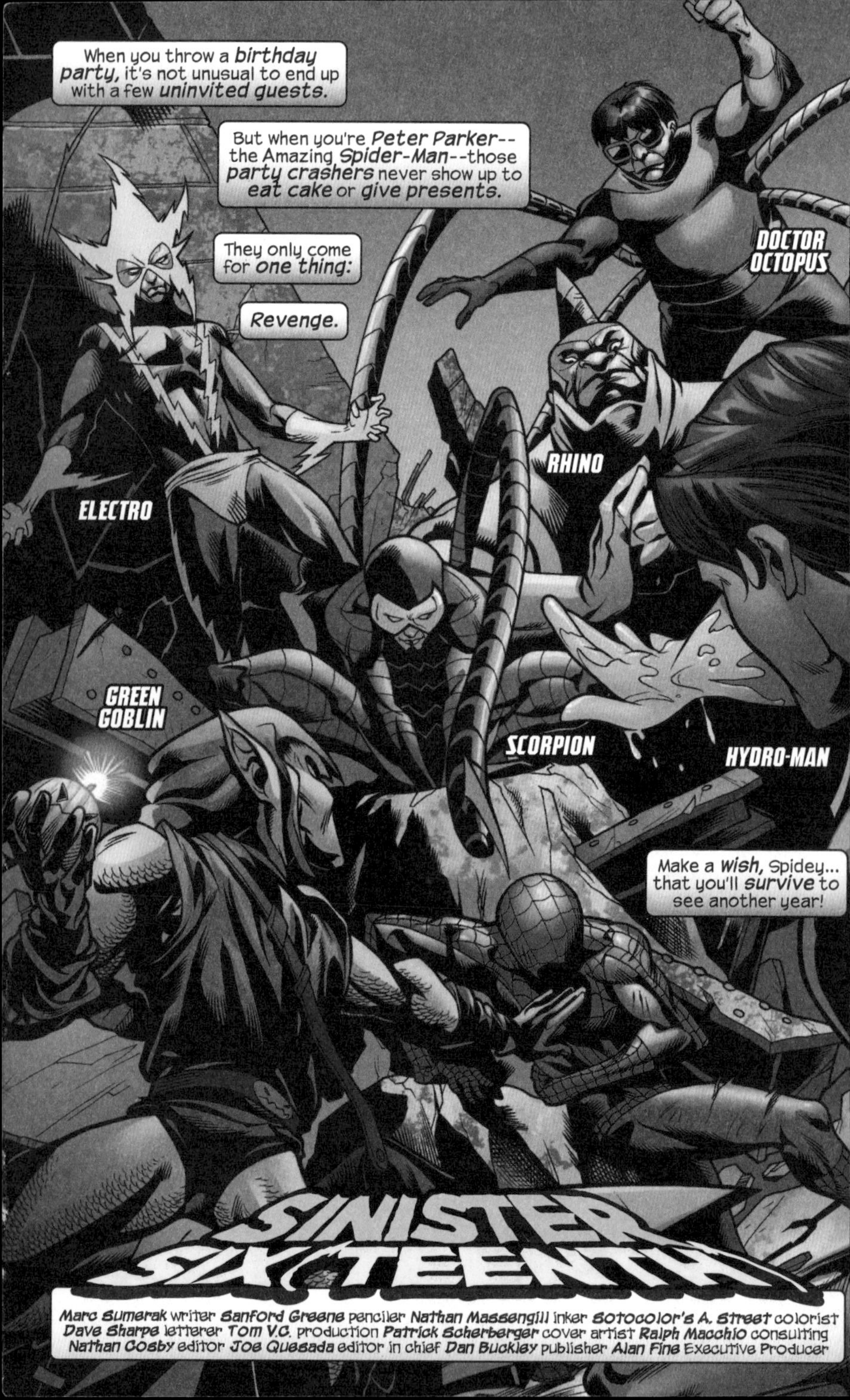
When you throw a birthday party, it's not unusual to end up with a few uninvited guests.
But when you're Peter Parker--the Amazing Spider-Man--those party crashers never show up to eat cake or give presents.
They only come for one thing:
Revenge.
DOCTOR OCTOPUS
ELECTRO
RHINO
GREEN GOBLIN
SCORPION
HYDRO-MAN
Make a wish, Spidey... that you'll survive to see another year!
SINISTER SIX(TEENTH)
Marc Sumerak writer Sanford Greene penciler Nathan Massengill inker Sotocolor's A. Street colorist Dave Sharpe letterer Tom V.C. production Patrick Scherberger cover artist Ralph Macchio consulting Nathan Cosby editor Joe Quesada editor in chief Dan Buckley publisher Alan Fine Executive Producer

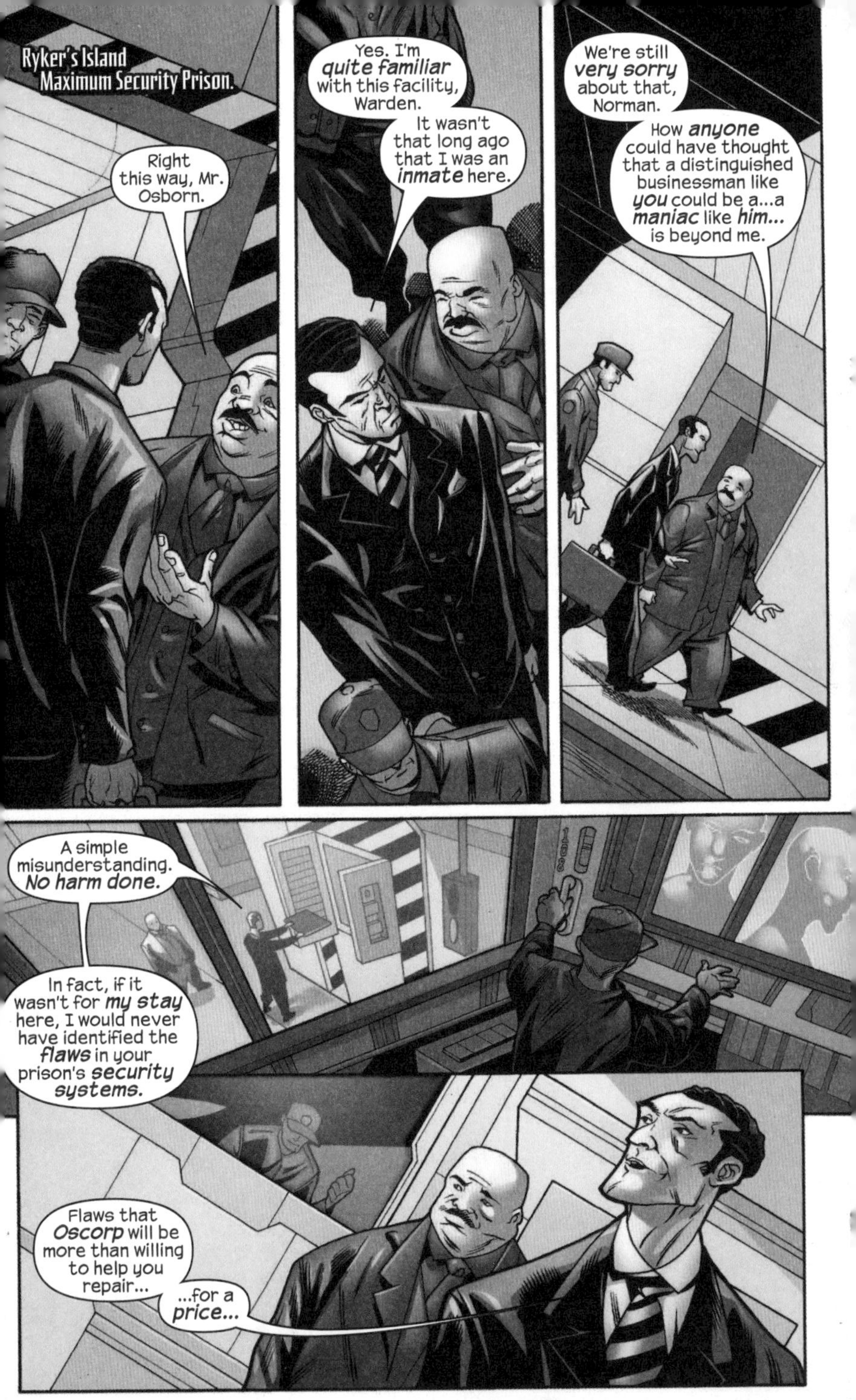
Ryker's Island
Maximum Security Prison.
Right this way, Mr. Osborn.
Yes. I'm *quite familiar* with this facility, Warden.
It wasn't that long ago that I was an *inmate* here.
We're still *very sorry* about that, Norman.
How *anyone* could have thought that a distinguished businessman like *you* could be a...a *maniac* like *him...* is beyond me.
A simple misunderstanding. *No harm done.*
In fact, if it wasn't for *my stay* here, I would never have identified the *flaws* in your prison's *security systems.*
Flaws that *Oscorp* will be more than willing to help you repair...
...for a *price...*

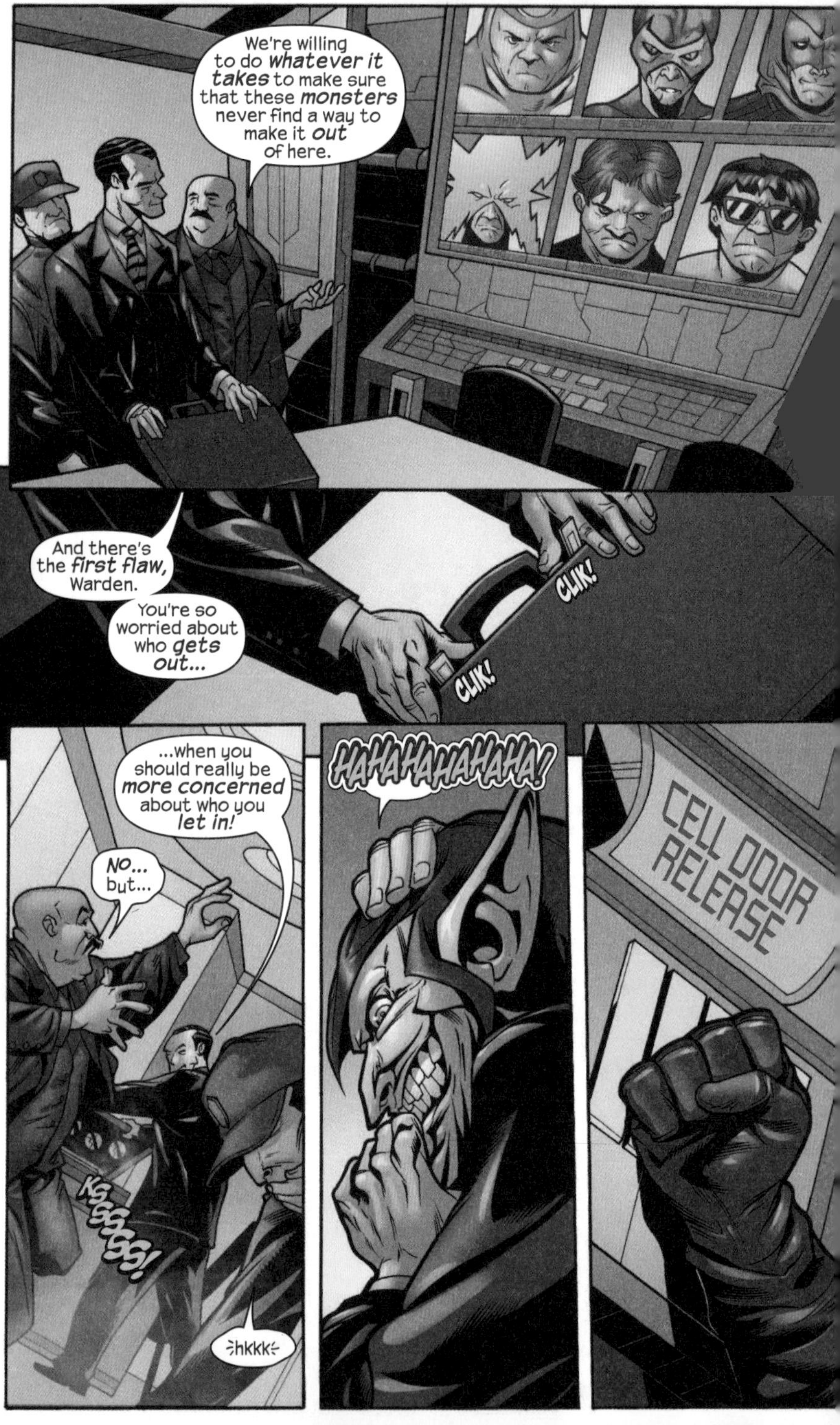

We're willing to do *whatever it takes* to make sure that these *monsters* never find a way to make it *out* of here.
And there's the *first flaw,* Warden.
You're so worried about who *gets out*...
CLIK!
CLIK!
...when you should really be *more concerned* about who you *let in!*
NO... but...
KSSSSS!
hkkk
HAHAHAHAHAHA!
CELL DOOR RELEASE

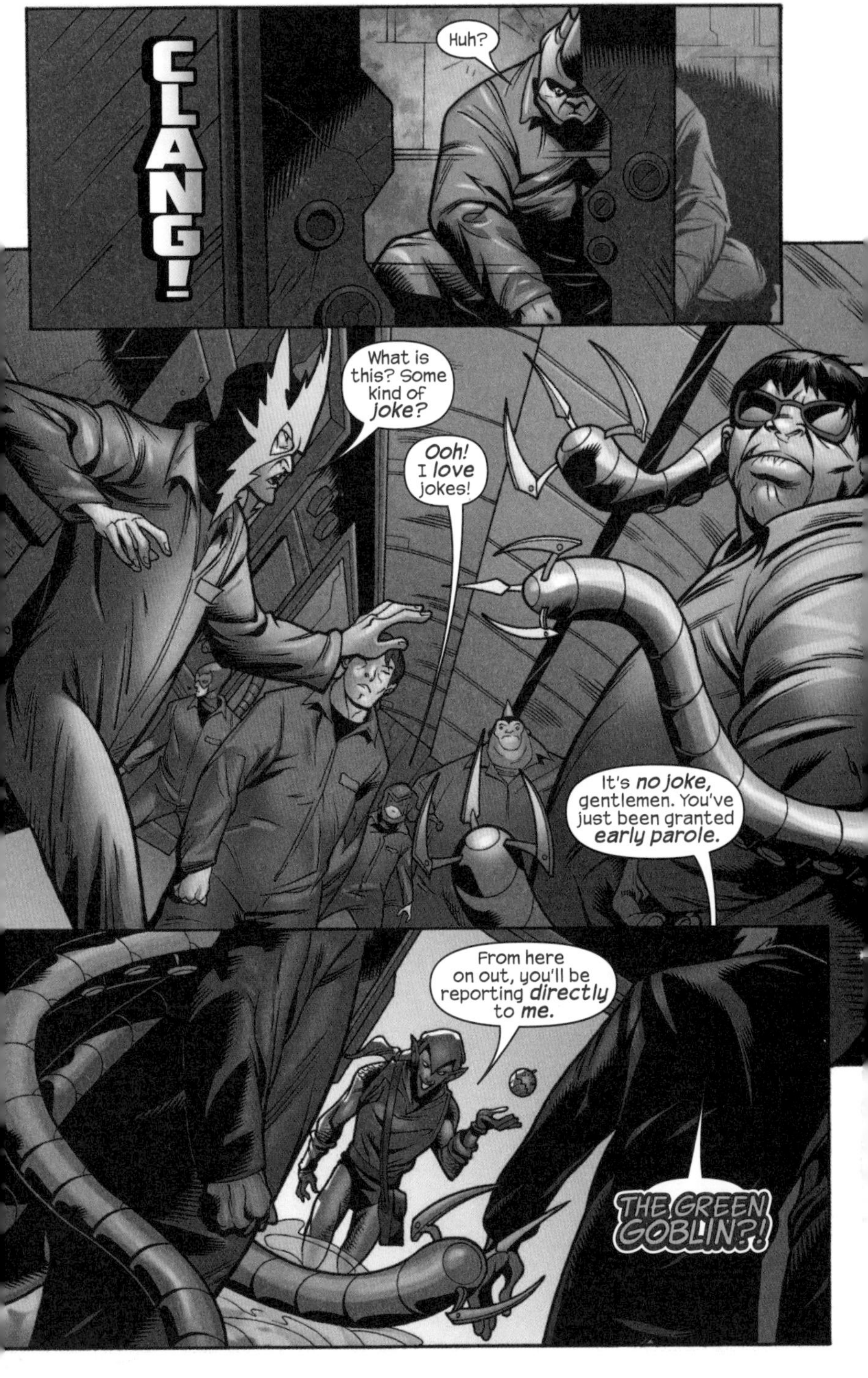
CLANG!
Huh?
What is this? Some kind of *joke?*
Ooh! I *love* jokes!
It's *no joke,* gentlemen. You've just been granted *early parole.*
From here on out, you'll be reporting *directly* to *me.*
THE GREEN GOBLIN?!

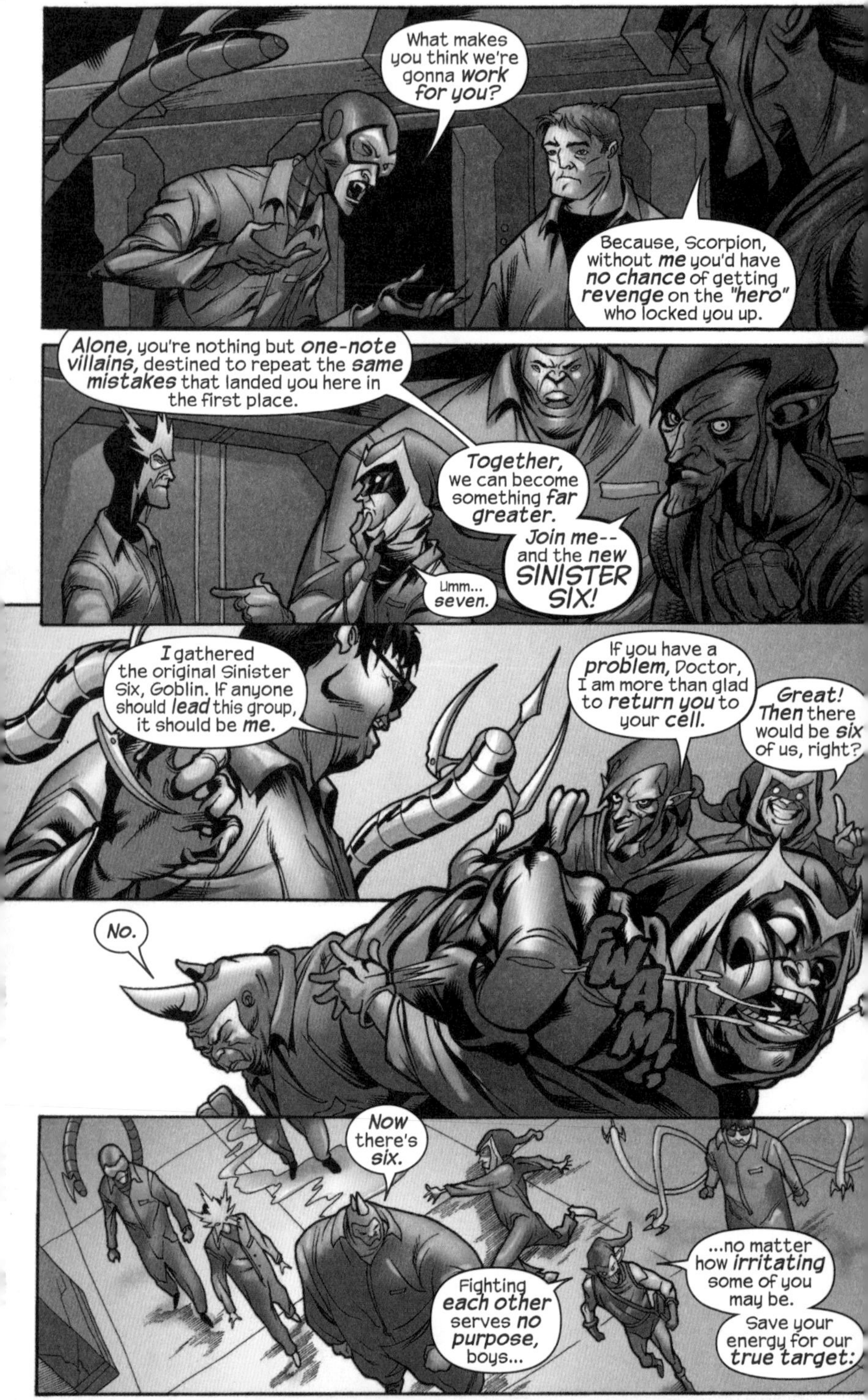

What makes you think we're gonna *work* for you?
Because, Scorpion, without *me* you'd have *no chance* of getting *revenge* on the *"hero"* who locked you up.
Alone, you're nothing but *one-note villains*, destined to repeat the *same mistakes* that landed you here in the first place.
Together, we can become something *far greater*.
Join me-- and the *new* SINISTER SIX!
Umm... *seven*.
I gathered the original Sinister Six, Goblin. If anyone should *lead* this group, it should be *me*.
If you have a *problem*, Doctor, I am more than glad to *return you* to your *cell*.
Great! Then there would be *six* of us, right?
No.
FWAM!
Now there's *six*.
Fighting *each other* serves *no purpose*, boys...
...no matter how *irritating* some of you may be.
Save your energy for our *true target:*

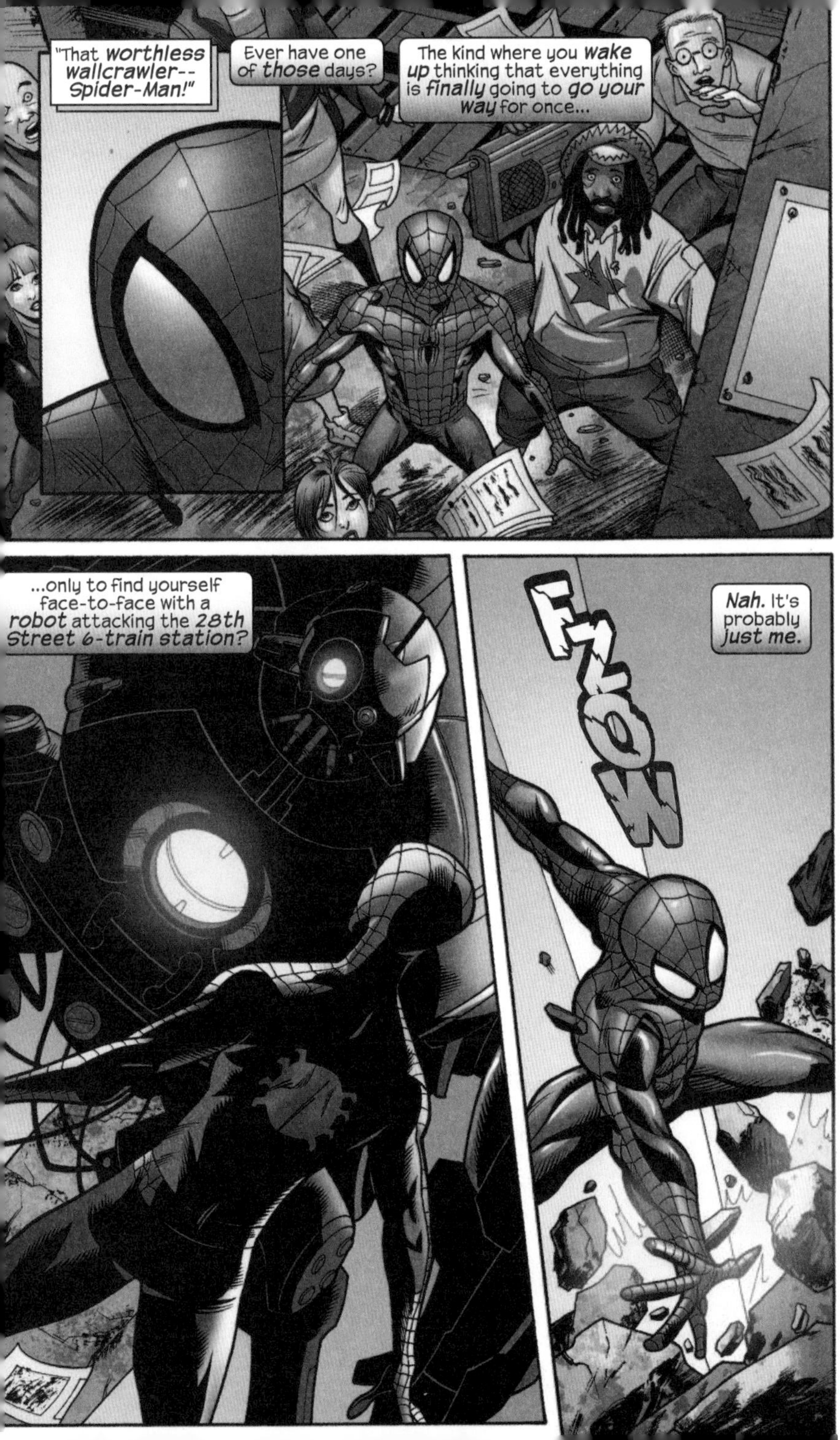
"That worthless wallcrawler-- Spider-Man!"
Ever have one of those days?
The kind where you wake up thinking that everything is finally going to go your way for once...
...only to find yourself face-to-face with a robot attacking the 28th Street 6-train station?
FZOW
Nah. It's probably just me.

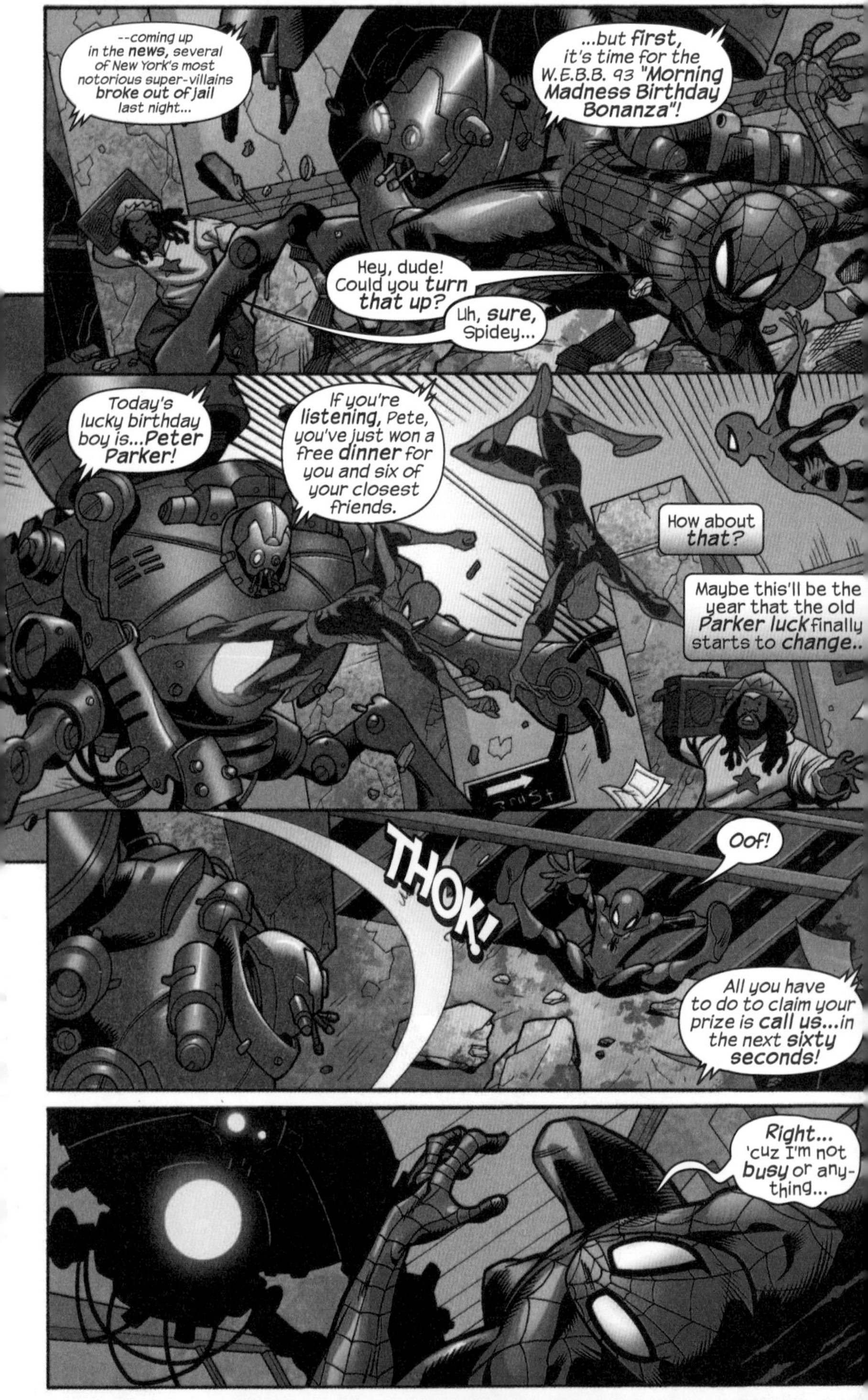
--coming up in the news, several of New York's most notorious super-villains broke out of jail last night...
...but first, it's time for the W.E.B.B. 93 "Morning Madness Birthday Bonanza"!
Hey, dude! Could you turn that up?
Uh, sure, Spidey...
Today's lucky birthday boy is...Peter Parker!
If you're listening, Pete, you've just won a free dinner for you and six of your closest friends.
How about that?
Maybe this'll be the year that the old Parker luck finally starts to change..
THOK!
Oof!
All you have to do to claim your prize is call us...in the next sixty seconds!
Right... 'cuz I'm not busy or any-thing...

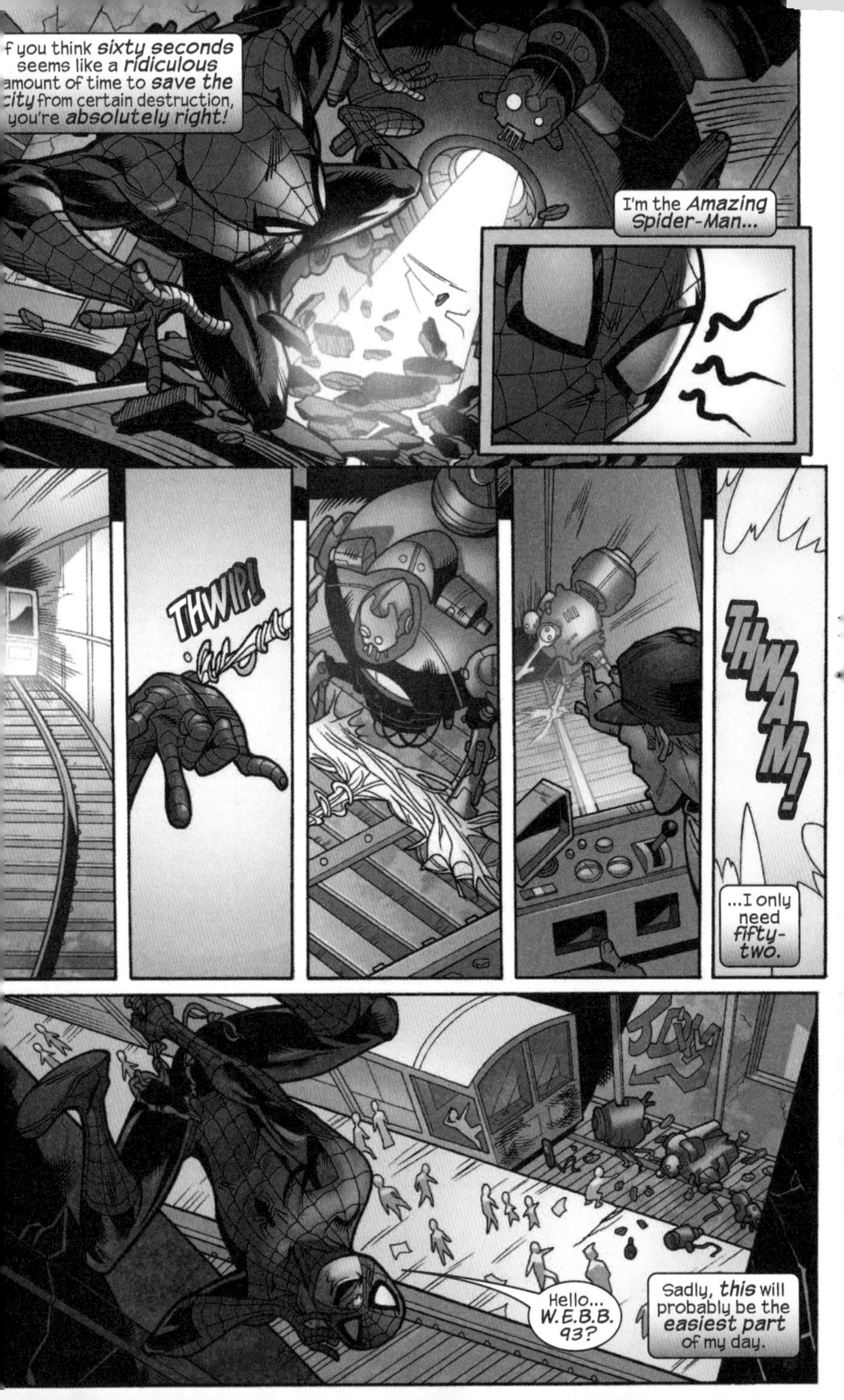

f you think sixty seconds seems like a ridiculous amount of time to save the city from certain destruction, you're absolutely right!
I'm the Amazing Spider-Man...
THWIP!
THWAM!
...I only need fifty-two.
Hello... W.E.B.B. 93?
Sadly, this will probably be the easiest part of my day.

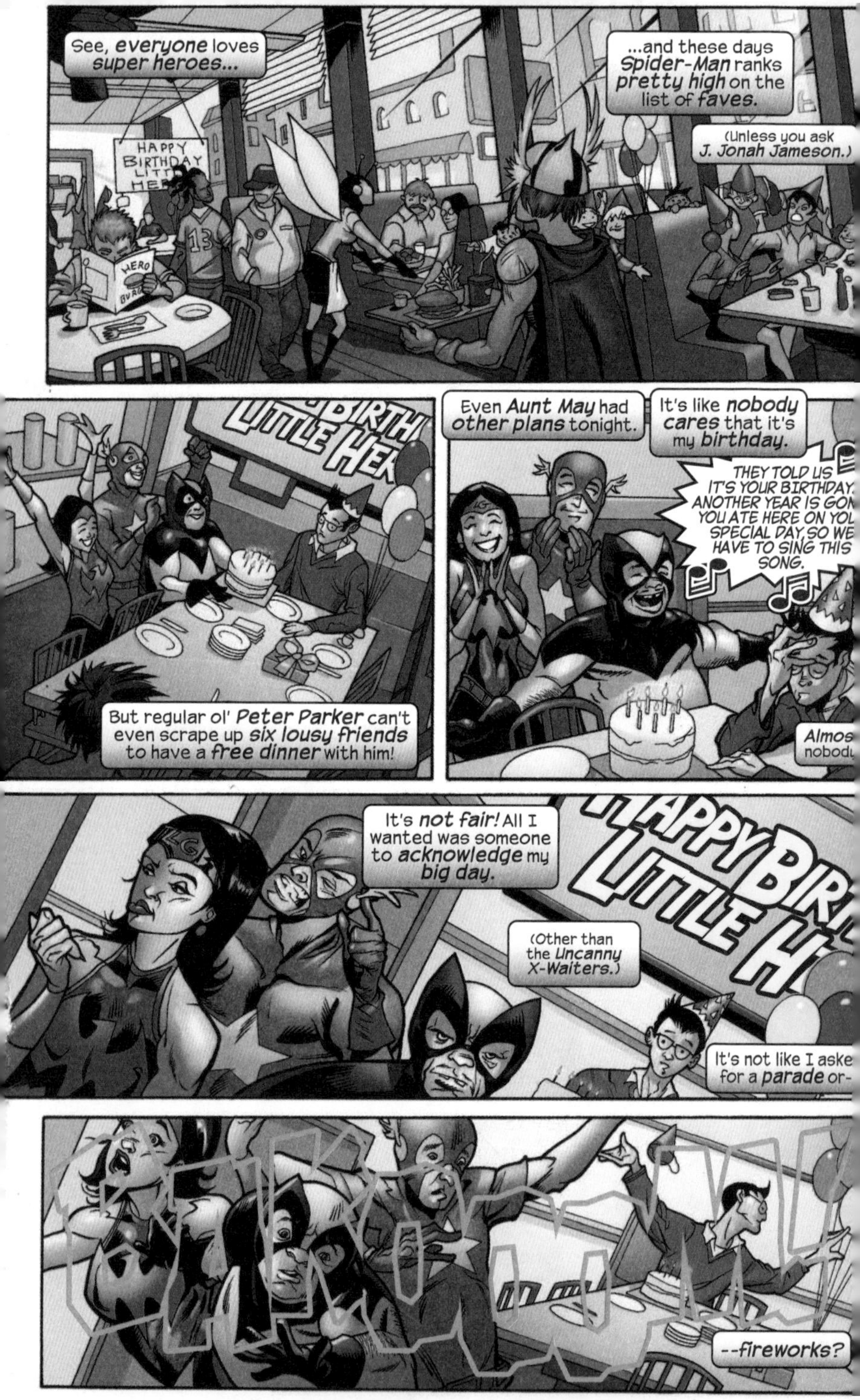
See, everyone loves super heroes...
...and these days Spider-Man ranks pretty high on the list of faves.
(Unless you ask J. Jonah Jameson.)
HAPPY BIRTHDAY
Even Aunt May had other plans tonight.
It's like nobody cares that it's my birthday.
But regular ol' Peter Parker can't even scrape up six lousy friends to have a free dinner with him!
THEY TOLD US IT'S YOUR BIRTHDAY. ANOTHER YEAR IS GON YOU ATE HERE ON YOU SPECIAL DAY, SO WE HAVE TO SING THIS SONG.
Almos nobody
It's not fair! All I wanted was someone to acknowledge my big day.
(Other than the Uncanny X-Waiters.)
It's not like I aske for a parade or-
--fireworks?

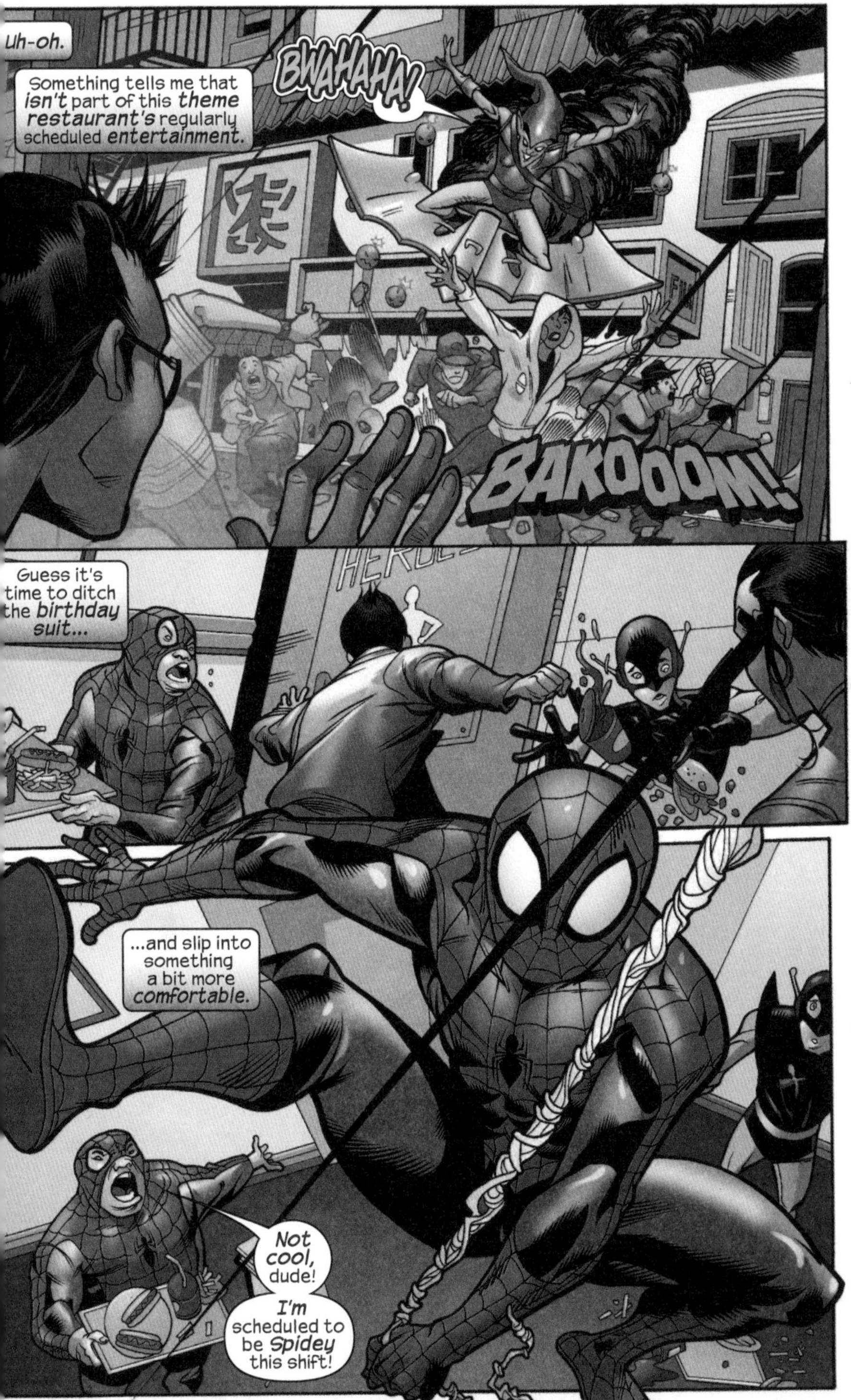
Uh-oh.
Something tells me that isn't part of this theme restaurant's regularly scheduled entertainment.
BWAHAHA!
BAKOOOM!
Guess it's time to ditch the birthday suit...
...and slip into something a bit more comfortable.
Not cool, dude!
I'm scheduled to be Spidey this shift!

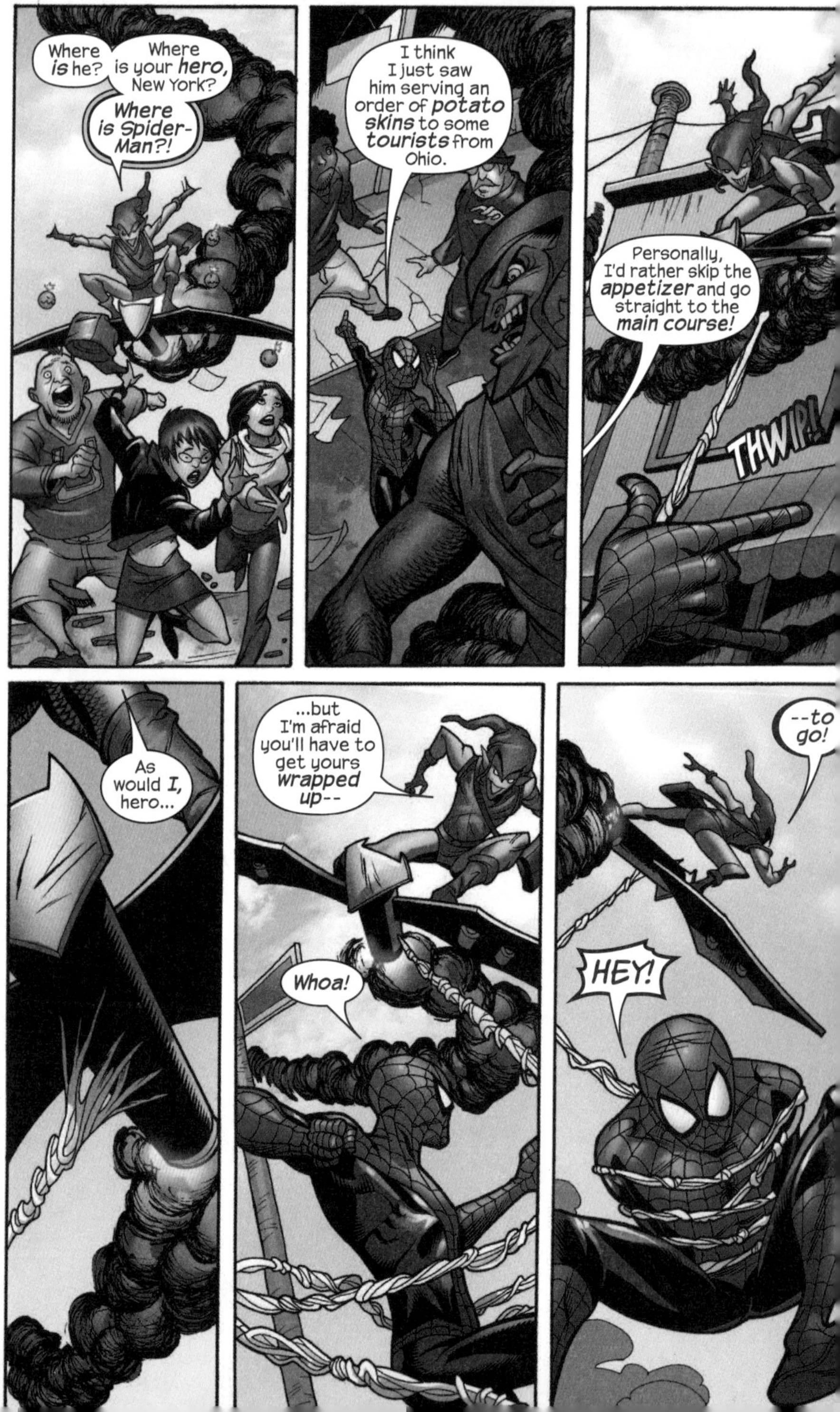
Where is he?
Where is your hero, New York?
Where is Spider-Man?!
I think I just saw him serving an order of potato skins to some tourists from Ohio.
Personally, I'd rather skip the appetizer and go straight to the main course!
THWIP!
As would I, hero...
...but I'm afraid you'll have to get yours wrapped up--
Whoa!
--to go!
HEY!

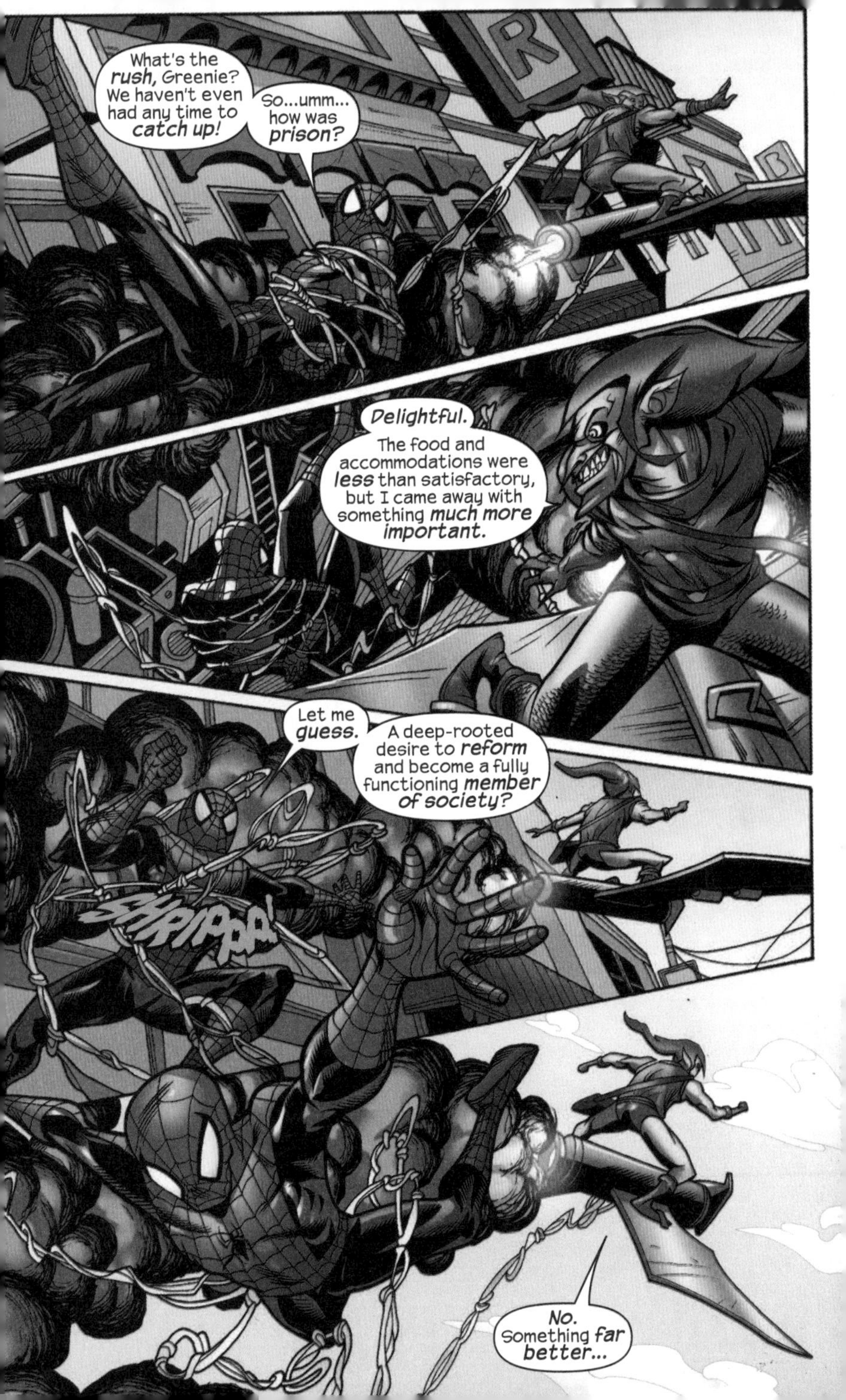
What's the *rush,* Greenie? We haven't even had any time to *catch up!*
So...umm... how was *prison?*
Delightful.
The food and accommodations were *less* than satisfactory, but I came away with something *much more important.*
Let me *guess.*
A deep-rooted desire to *reform* and become a fully functioning *member of society?*
SHHPPPA!
No. Something *far* better...

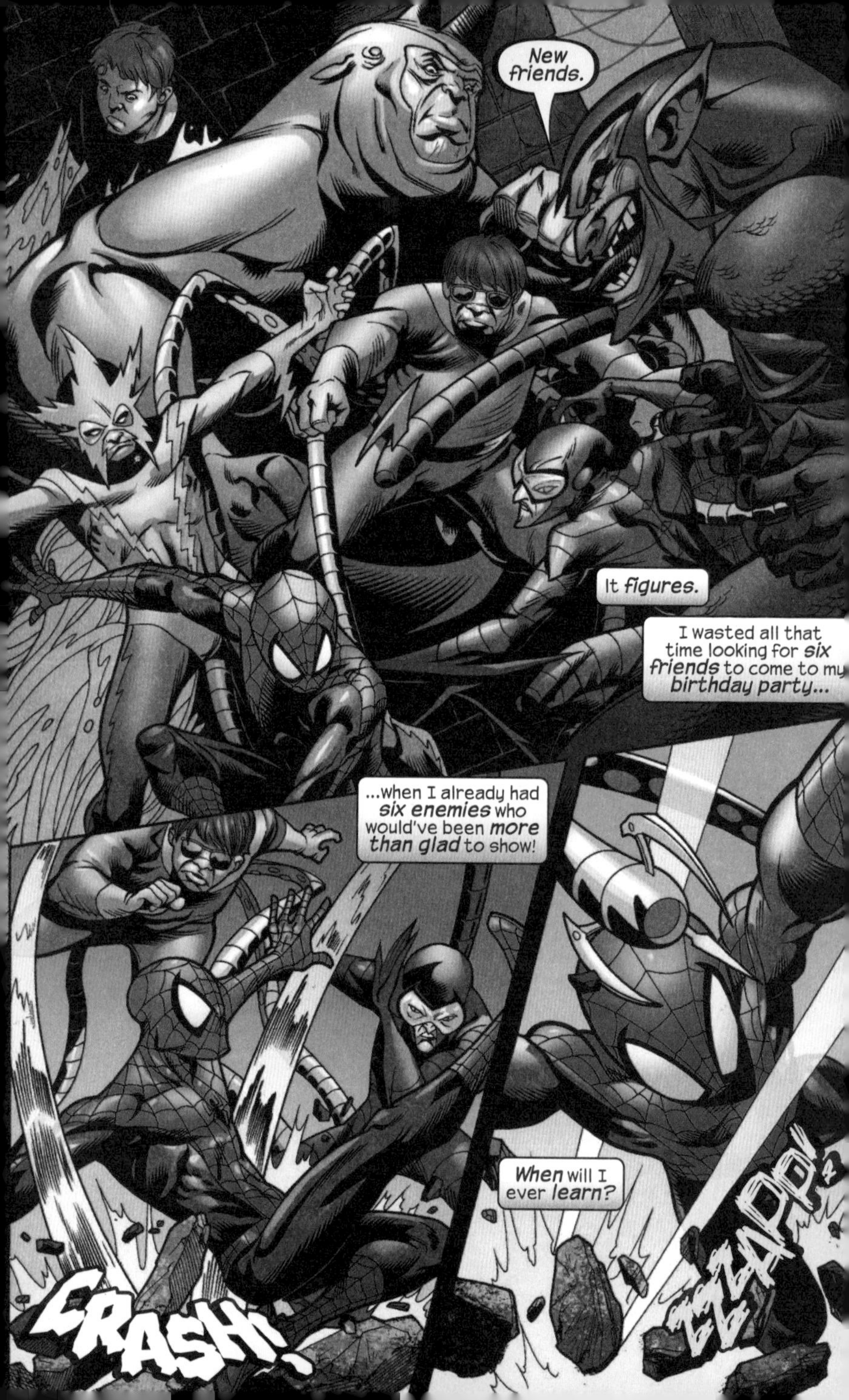
New friends.
It figures.
I wasted all that time looking for six friends to come to my birthday party...
...when I already had six enemies who would've been more than glad to show!
CRASH!
When will I ever learn?

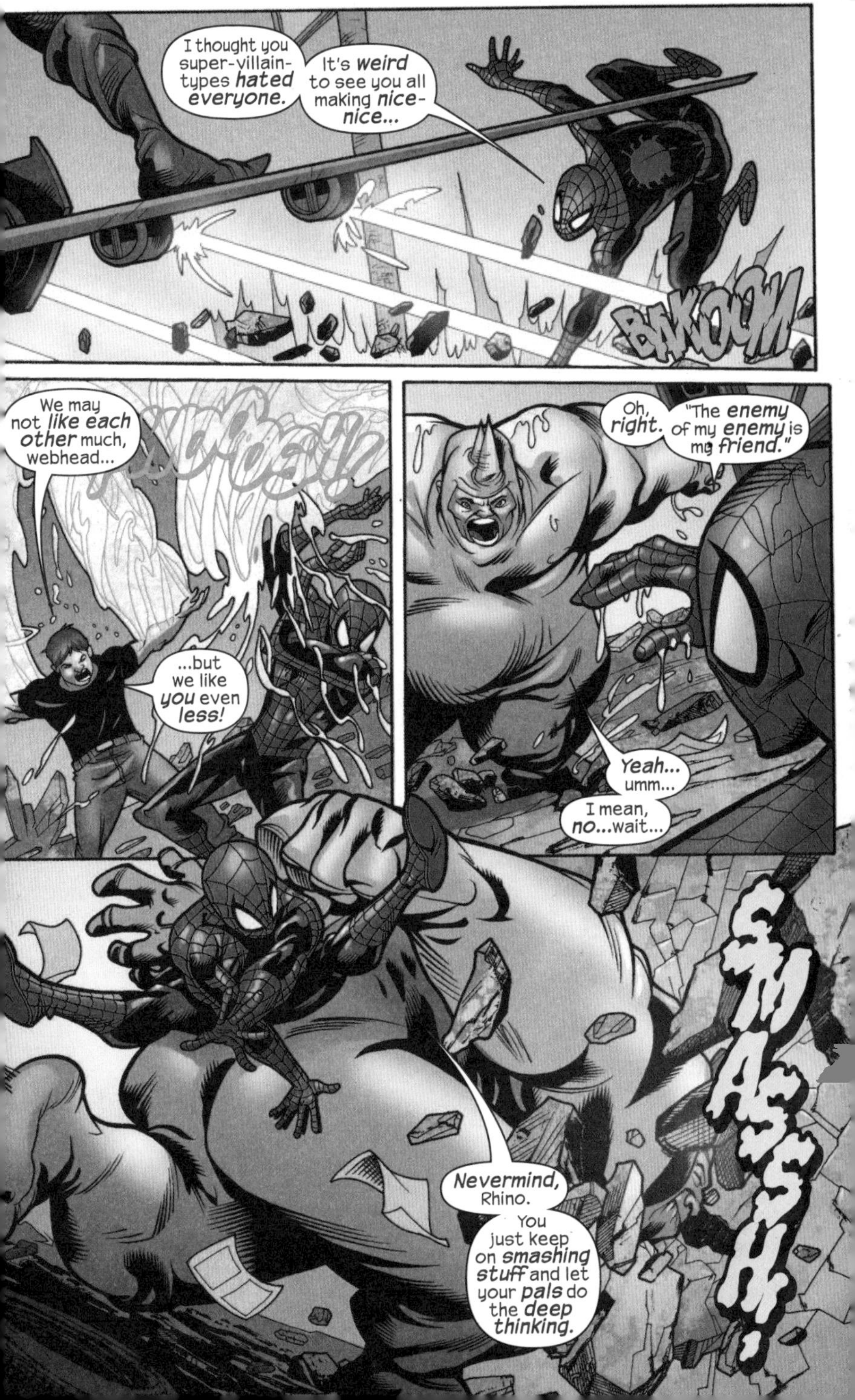
I thought you super-villain-types hated everyone.
It's weird to see you all making nice-nice...
BAKOOM
We may not like each other much, webhead...
...but we like you even less!
Oh, right.
"The enemy of my enemy is my friend."
Yeah... umm...
I mean, no...wait...
SMASSH!
Nevermind, Rhino.
You just keep on smashing stuff and let your pals do the deep thinking.

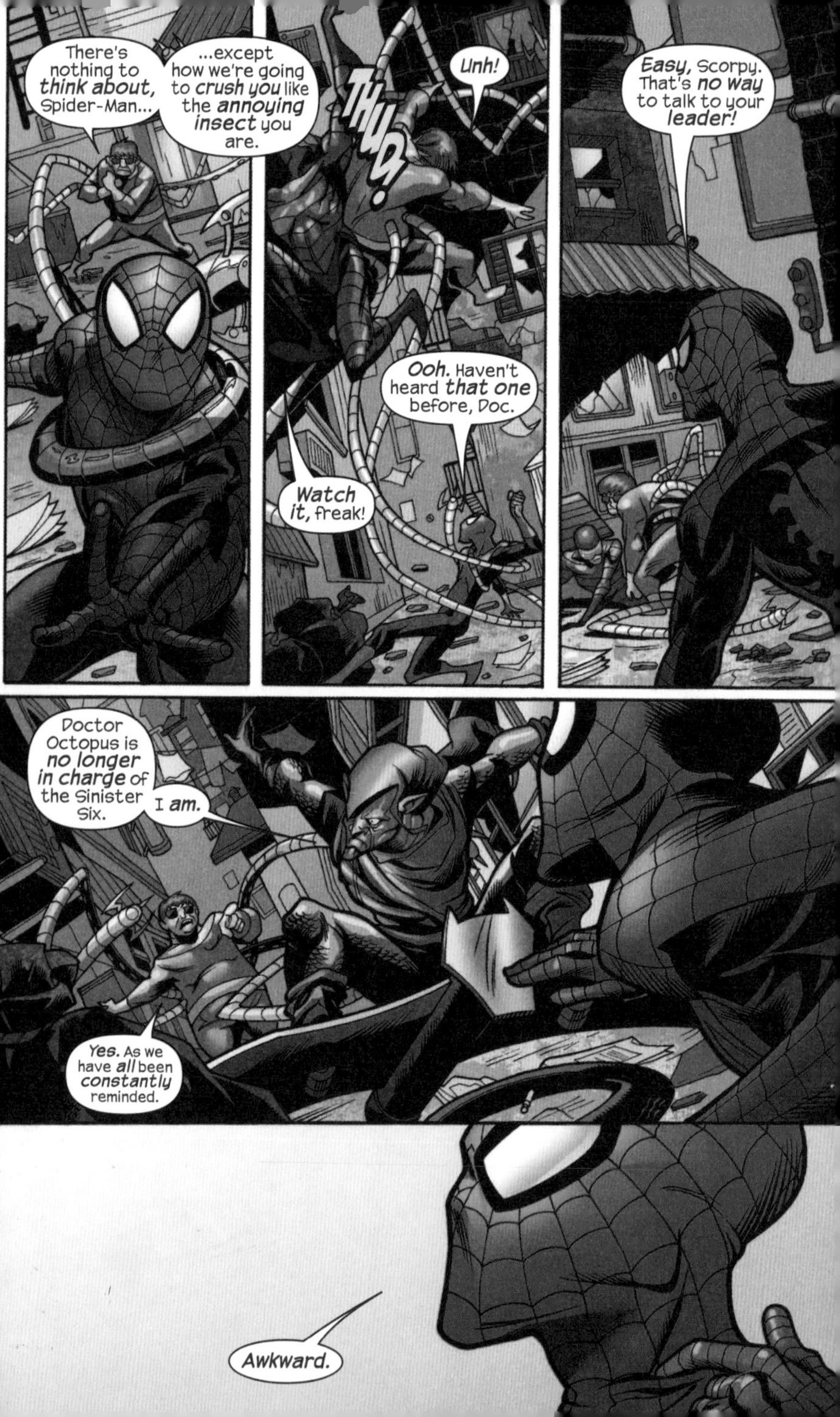
There's nothing to think about, Spider-Man...
...except how we're going to crush you like the annoying insect you are.
THUD!
Unh!
Watch it, freak!
Ooh. Haven't heard that one before, Doc.
Easy, Scorpy. That's no way to talk to your leader!
Doctor Octopus is no longer in charge of the Sinister Six.
I am.
Yes. As we have all been constantly reminded.
Awkward.

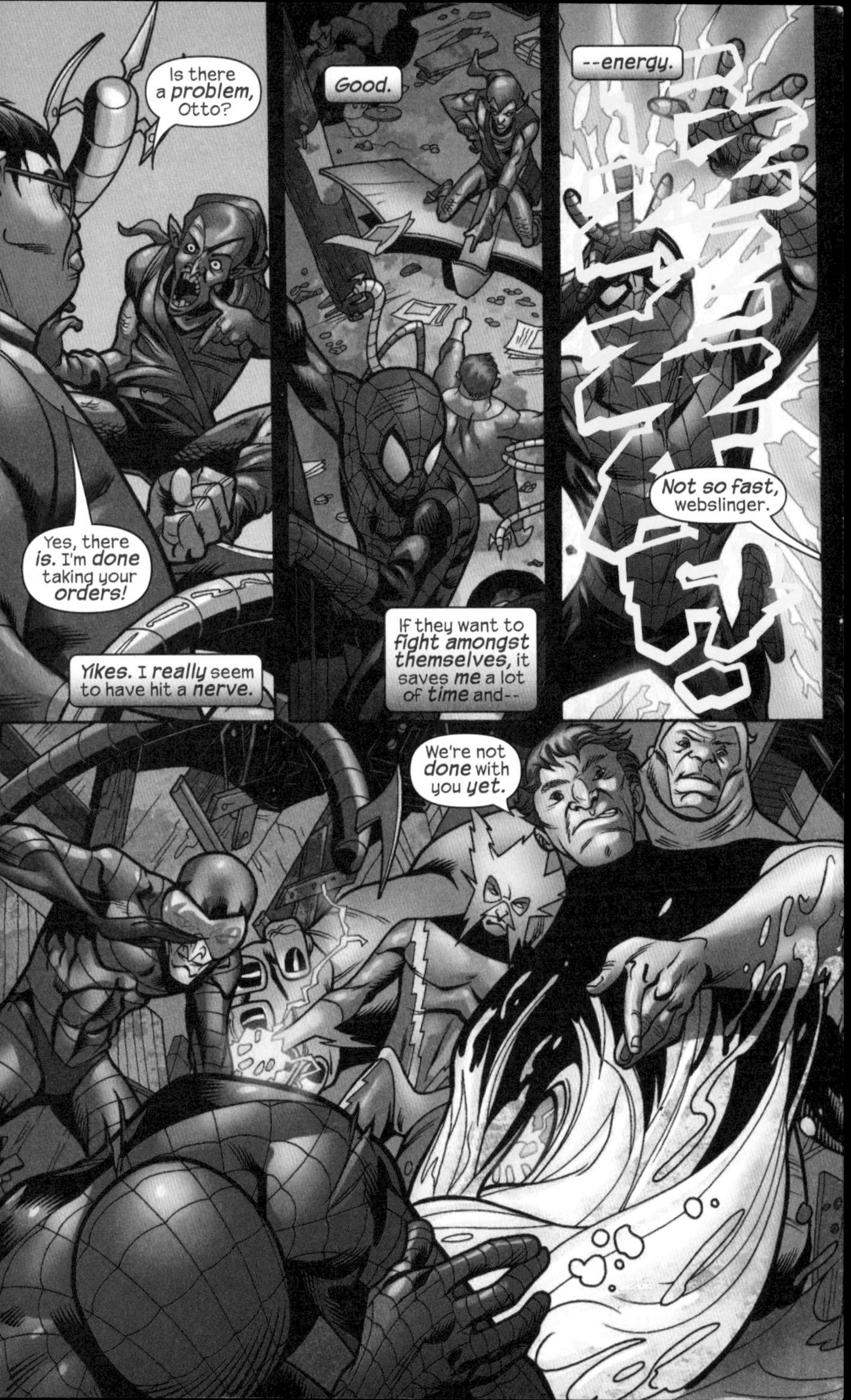
Is there a problem, Otto?
Yes, there is. I'm done taking your orders!
Yikes. I really seem to have hit a nerve.
Good.
If they want to fight amongst themselves, it saves me a lot of time and--
--energy.
Not so fast, webslinger.
We're not done with you yet.

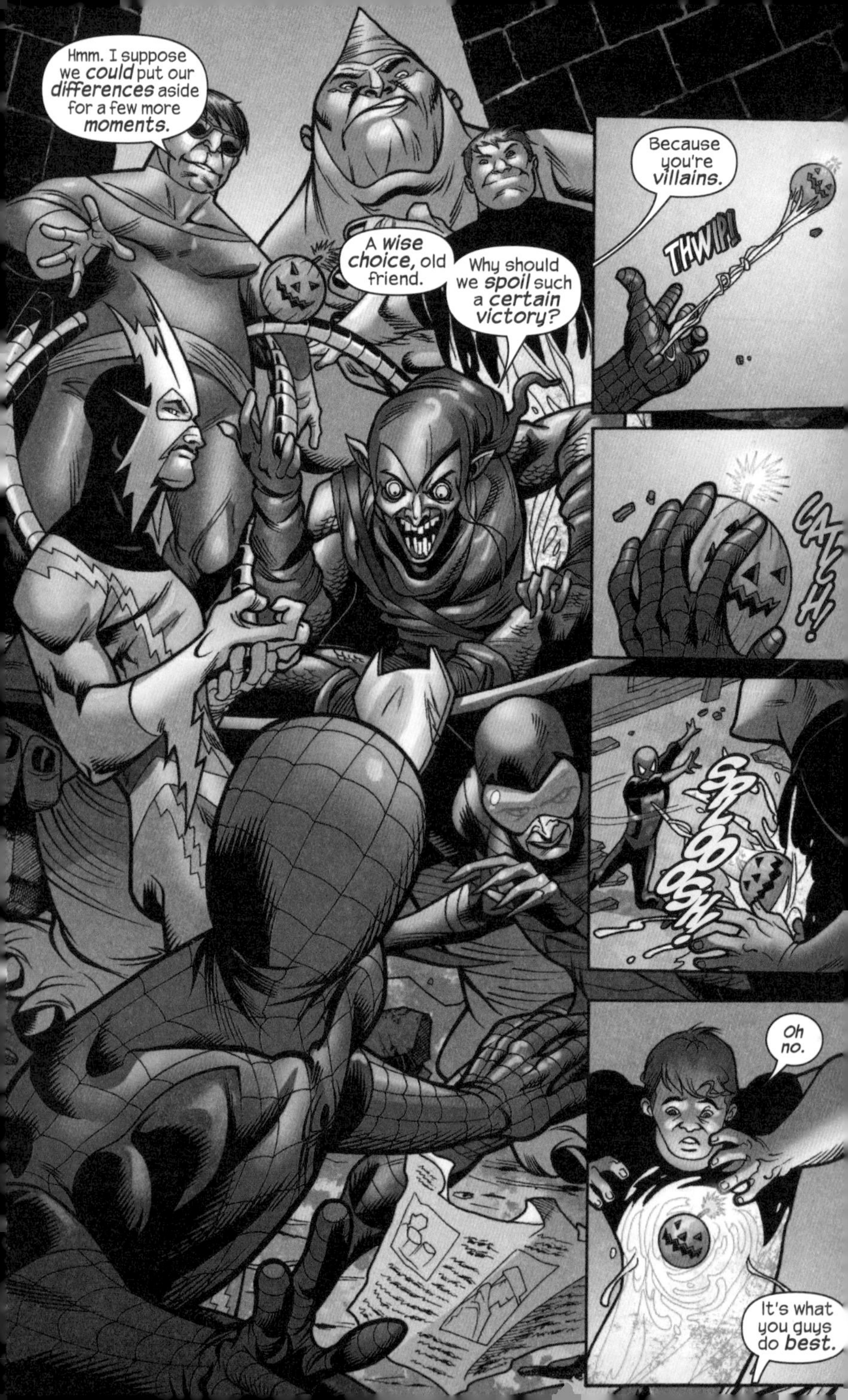

Hmm. I suppose we could put our differences aside for a few more moments.
A wise choice, old friend.
Why should we spoil such a certain victory?
Because you're villains.
THWIP!
CATCH!
SPLOOOSH!
Oh no.
It's what you guys do best.

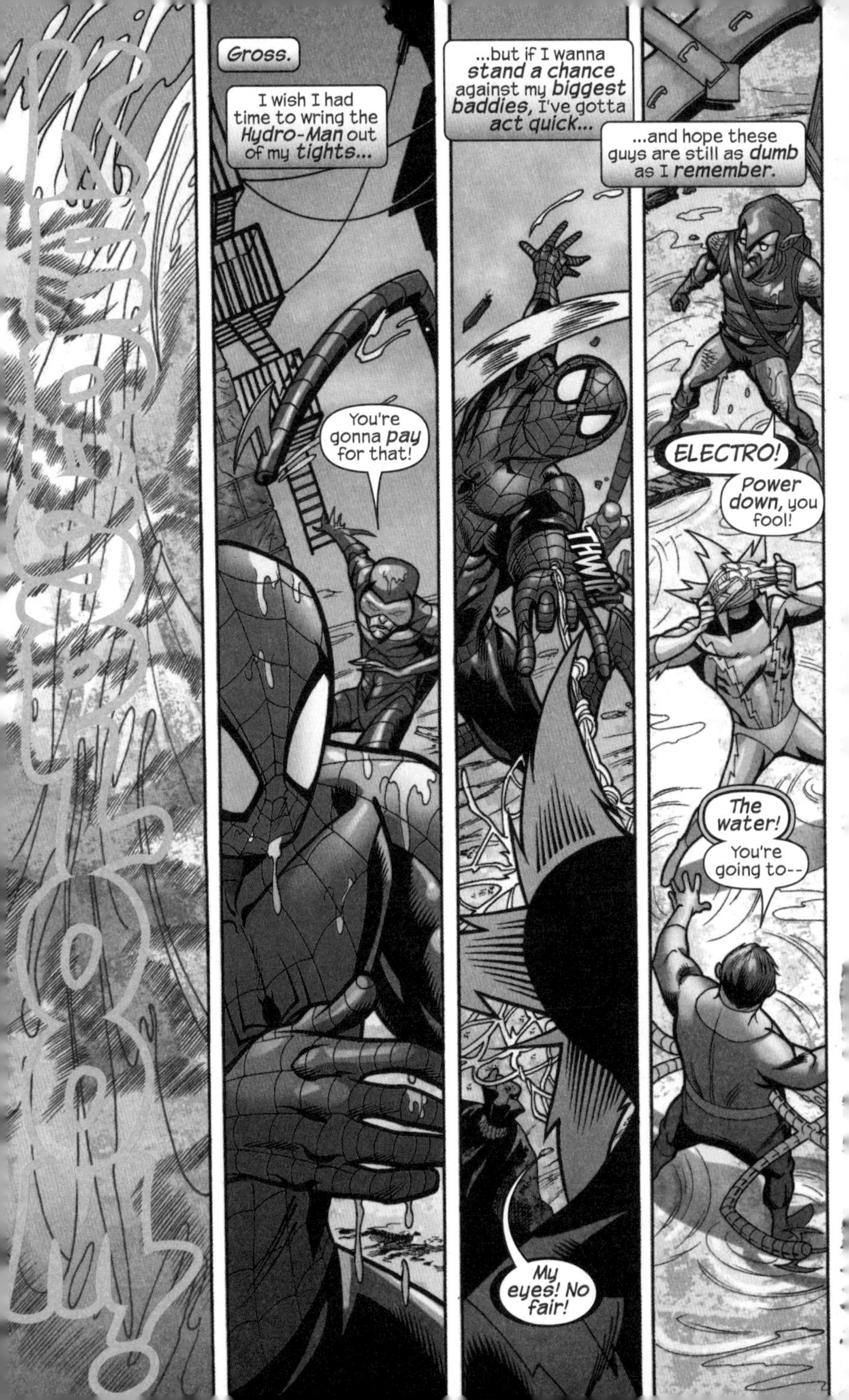
Gross.
I wish I had time to wring the Hydro-Man out of my tights...
You're gonna pay for that!
...but if I wanna stand a chance against my biggest baddies, I've gotta act quick...
THWIP!
My eyes! No fair!
...and hope these guys are still as dumb as I remember.
ELECTRO!
Power down, you fool!
The water!
You're going to--

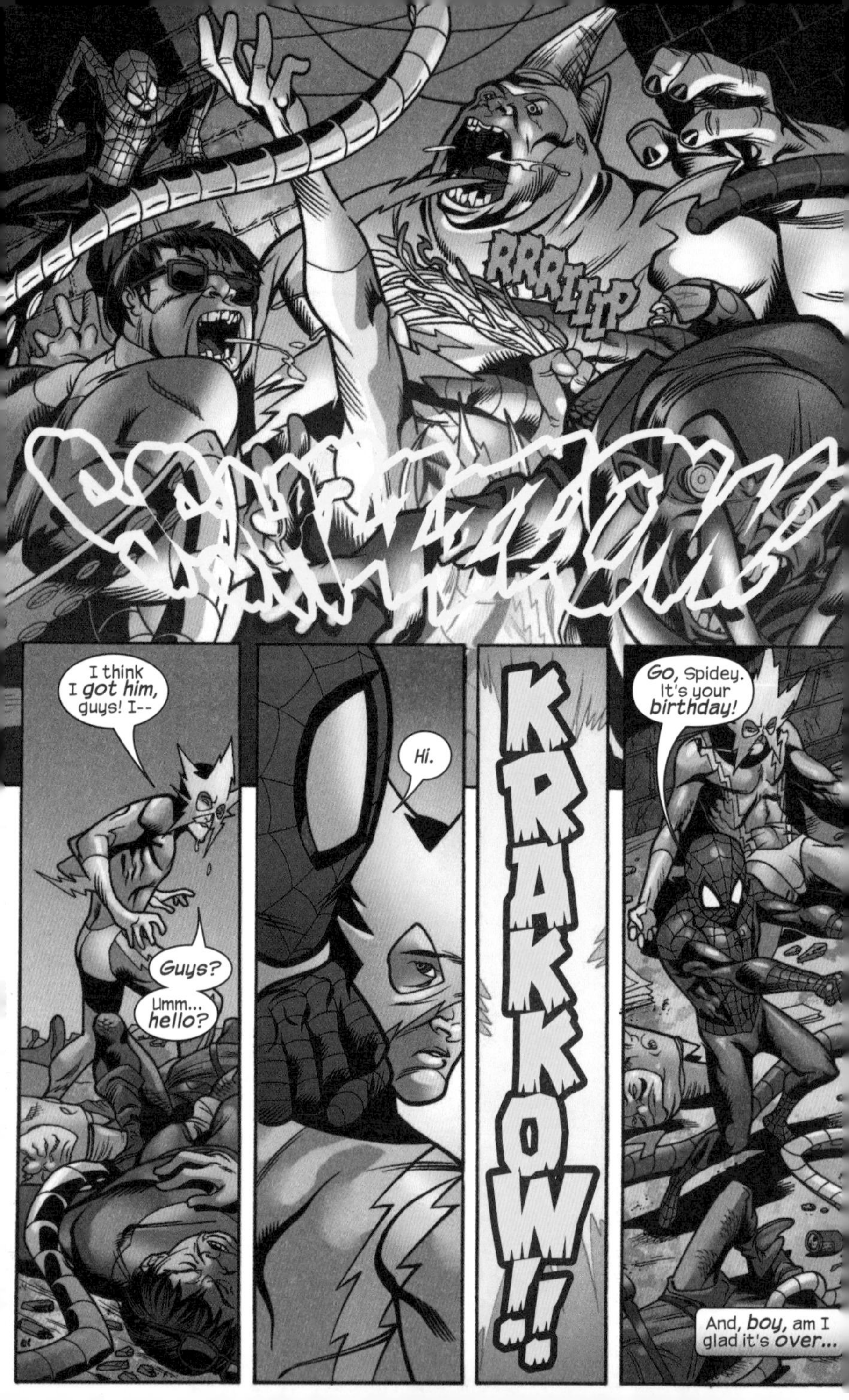
RRRIIIP
I think I got him, guys! I--
Guys?
Umm... hello?
Hi.
KRAKOW!!
Go, Spidey. It's your birthday!
And, boy, am I glad it's over...

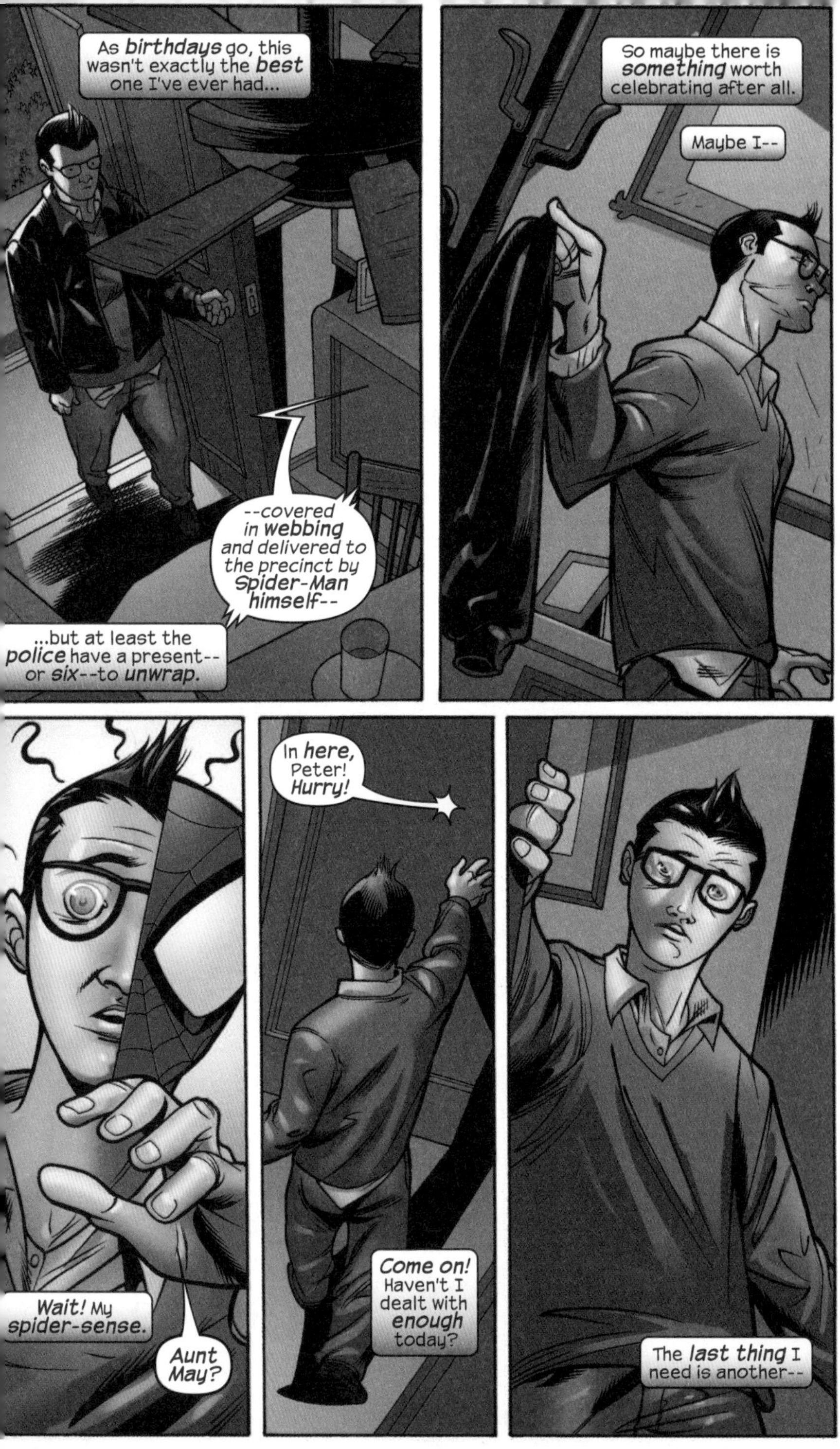
As birthdays go, this wasn't exactly the best one I've ever had...
--covered in webbing and delivered to the precinct by Spider-Man himself--
...but at least the police have a present--or six--to unwrap.
So maybe there is something worth celebrating after all.
Maybe I--
Wait! My spider-sense.
Aunt May?
In here, Peter! Hurry!
Come on! Haven't I dealt with enough today?
The last thing I need is another--

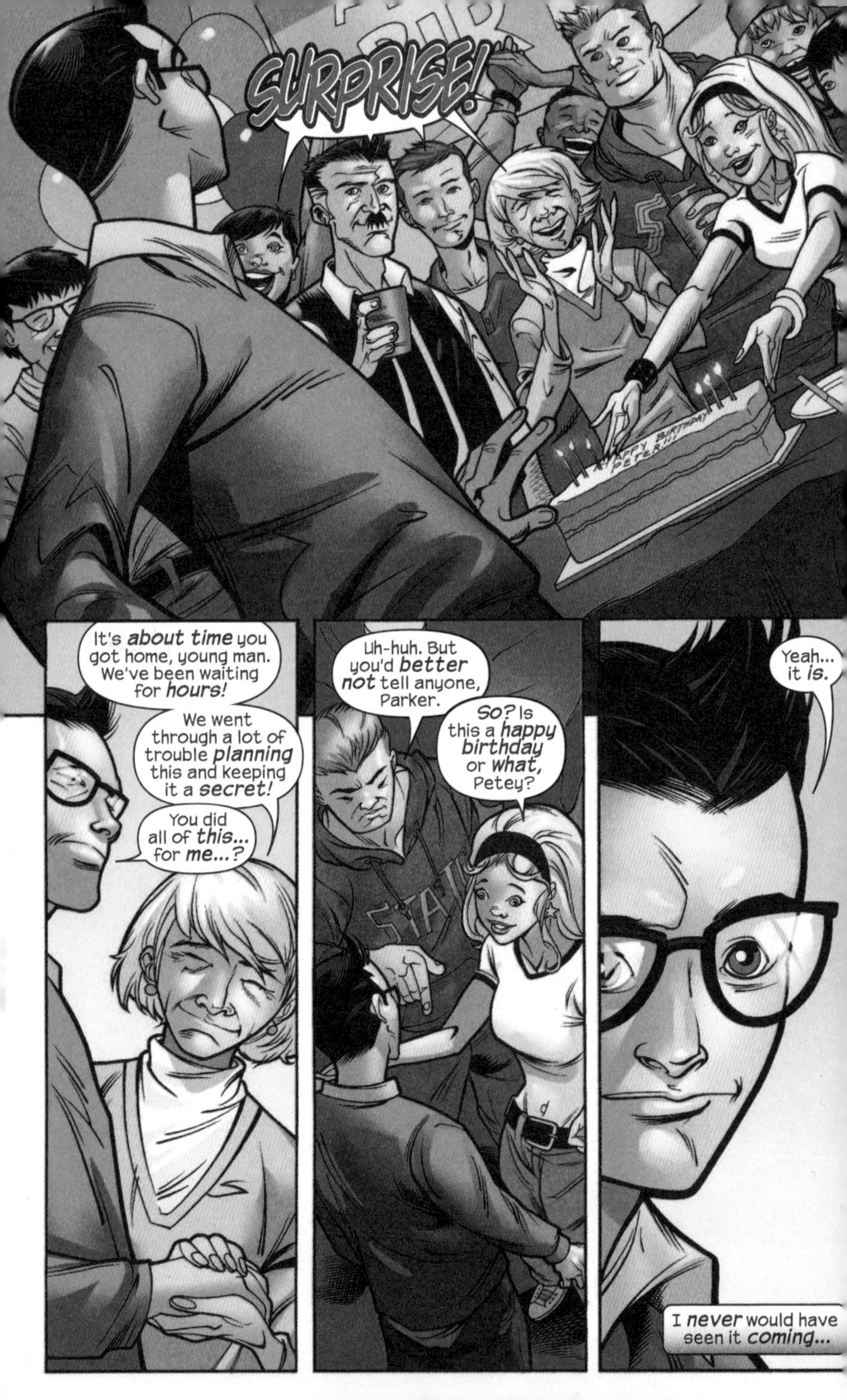
SURPRISE!
HAPPY BIRTHDAY PETER!!!
It's about time you got home, young man. We've been waiting for hours!
We went through a lot of trouble planning this and keeping it a secret!
You did all of this... for me...?
Uh-huh. But you'd better not tell anyone, Parker.
So? Is this a happy birthday or what, Petey?
Yeah... it is.
I never would have seen it coming...

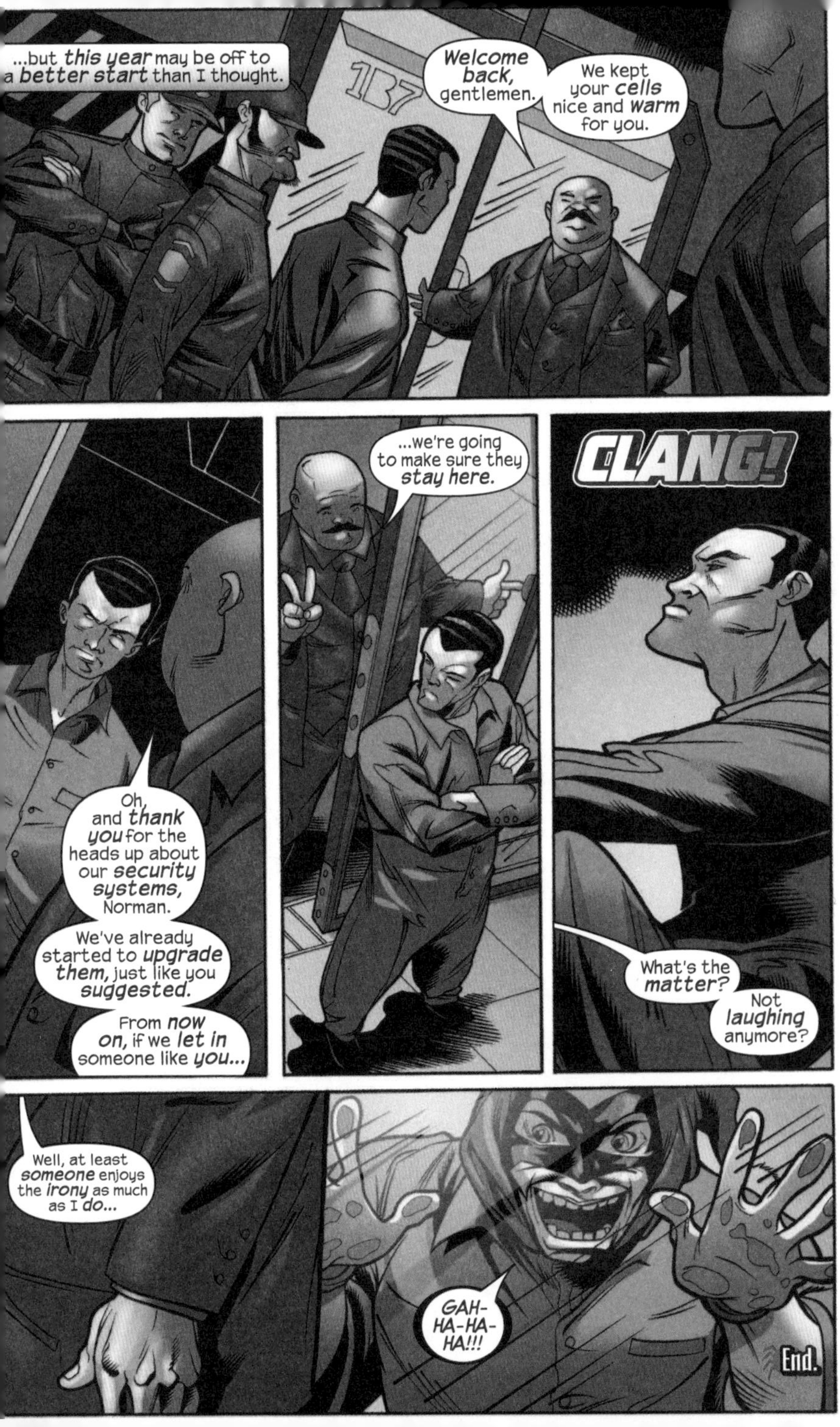
...but this year may be off to a better start than I thought.
Welcome back, gentlemen.
We kept your cells nice and warm for you.
137
Oh, and thank you for the heads up about our security systems, Norman.
We've already started to upgrade them, just like you suggested.
From now on, if we let in someone like you...
...we're going to make sure they stay here.
CLANG!
What's the matter?
Not laughing anymore?
Well, at least someone enjoys the irony as much as I do...
GAH-HA-HA-HA!!!
End.

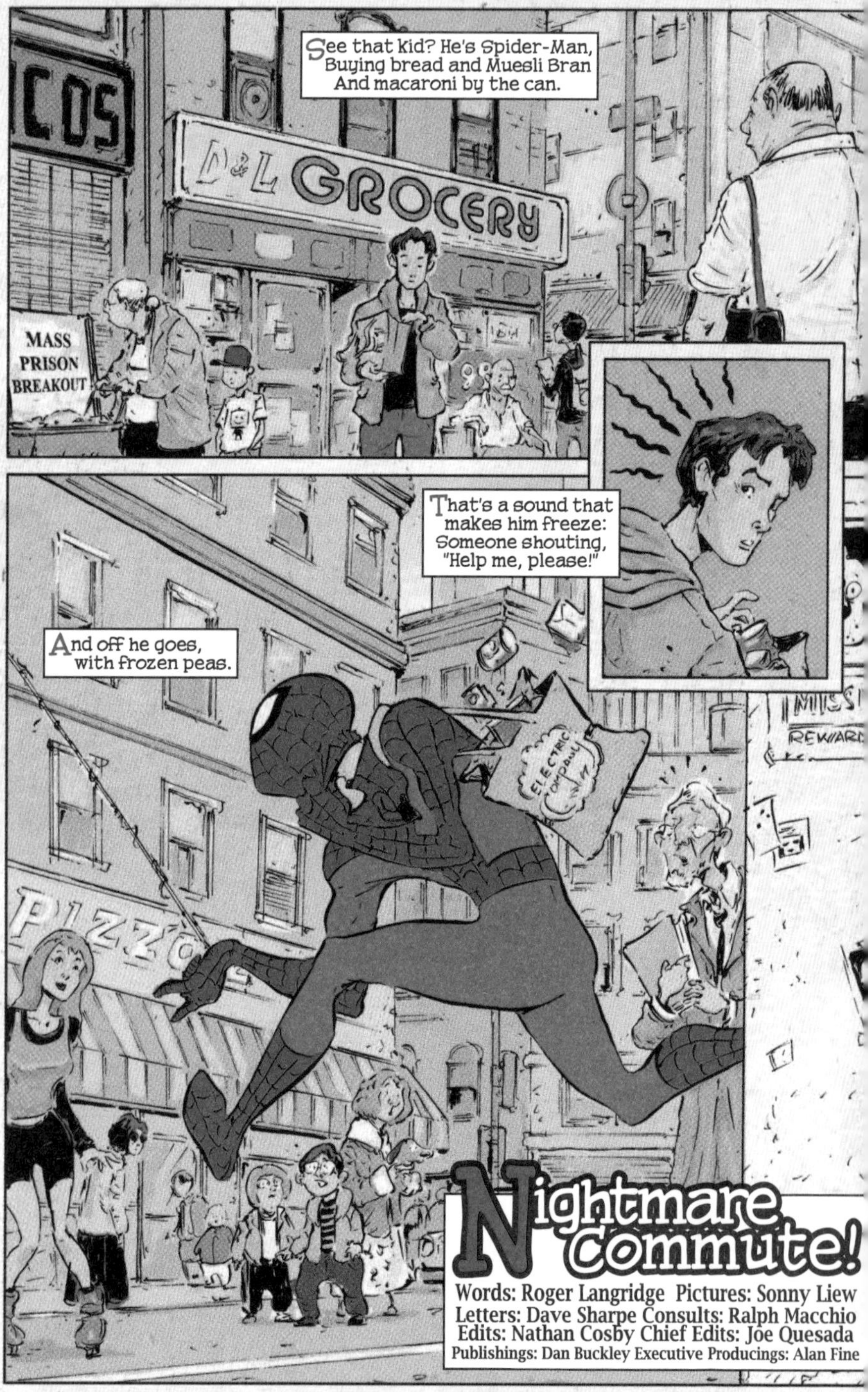
See that kid? He's Spider-Man,
Buying bread and Muesli Bran
And macaroni by the can.
COS
D&L GROCERY
MASS PRISON BREAKOUT
That's a sound that makes him freeze:
Someone shouting, "Help me, please!"
And off he goes, with frozen peas.
ELECTRIC COMPANY
PIZZ
REWARD
Nightmare Commute!
Words: Roger Langridge Pictures: Sonny Liew
Letters: Dave Sharpe Consults: Ralph Macchio
Edits: Nathan Cosby Chief Edits: Joe Quesada
Publishings: Dan Buckley Executive Producings: Alan Fine

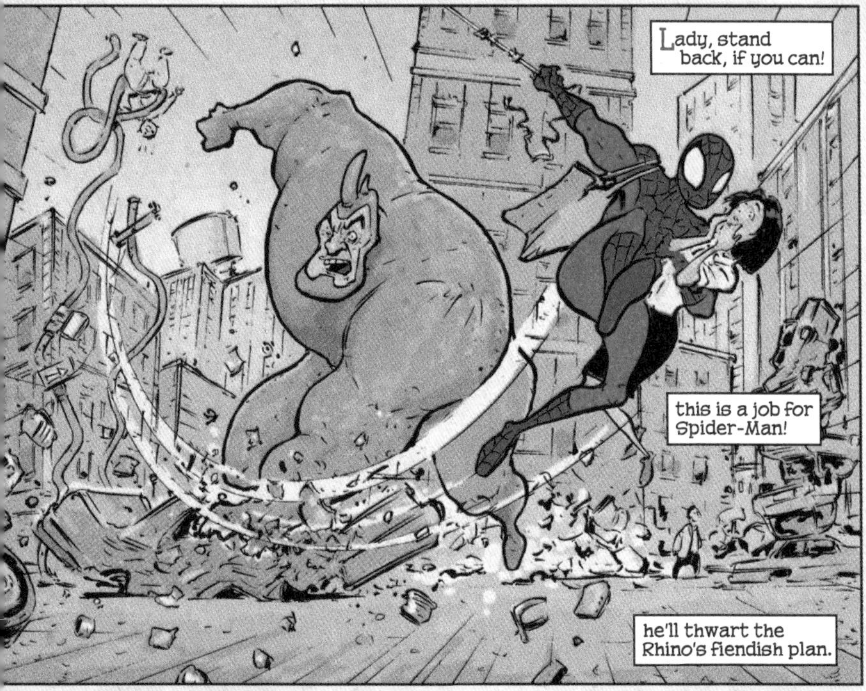
Lady, stand back, if you can!
this is a job for Spider-Man!
he'll thwart the Rhino's fiendish plan.

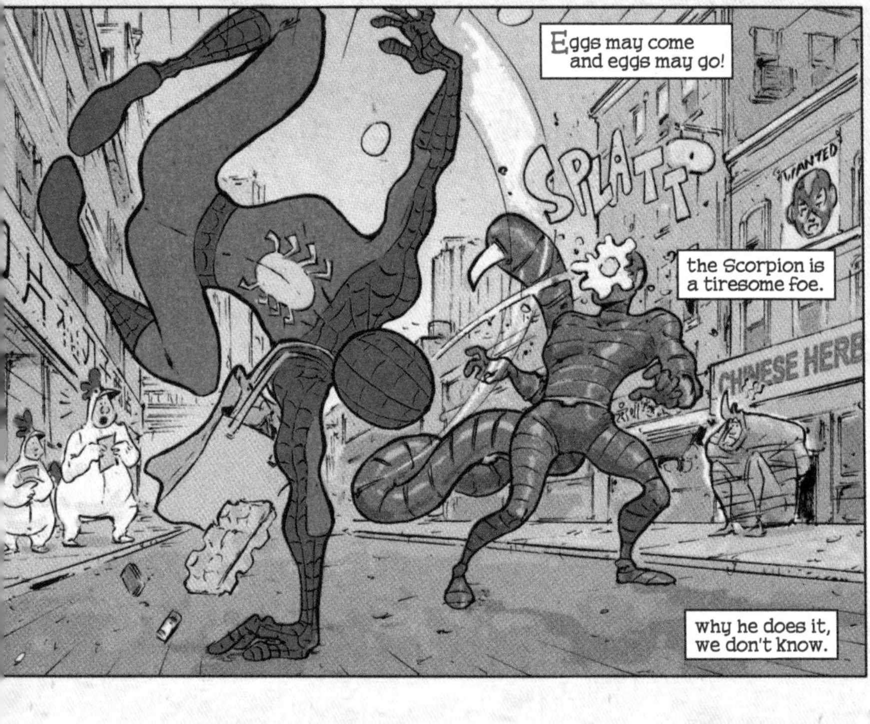
Eggs may come and eggs may go!
SPLATT
WANTED
the Scorpion is a tiresome foe.
CHINESE HERB
why he does it, we don't know.

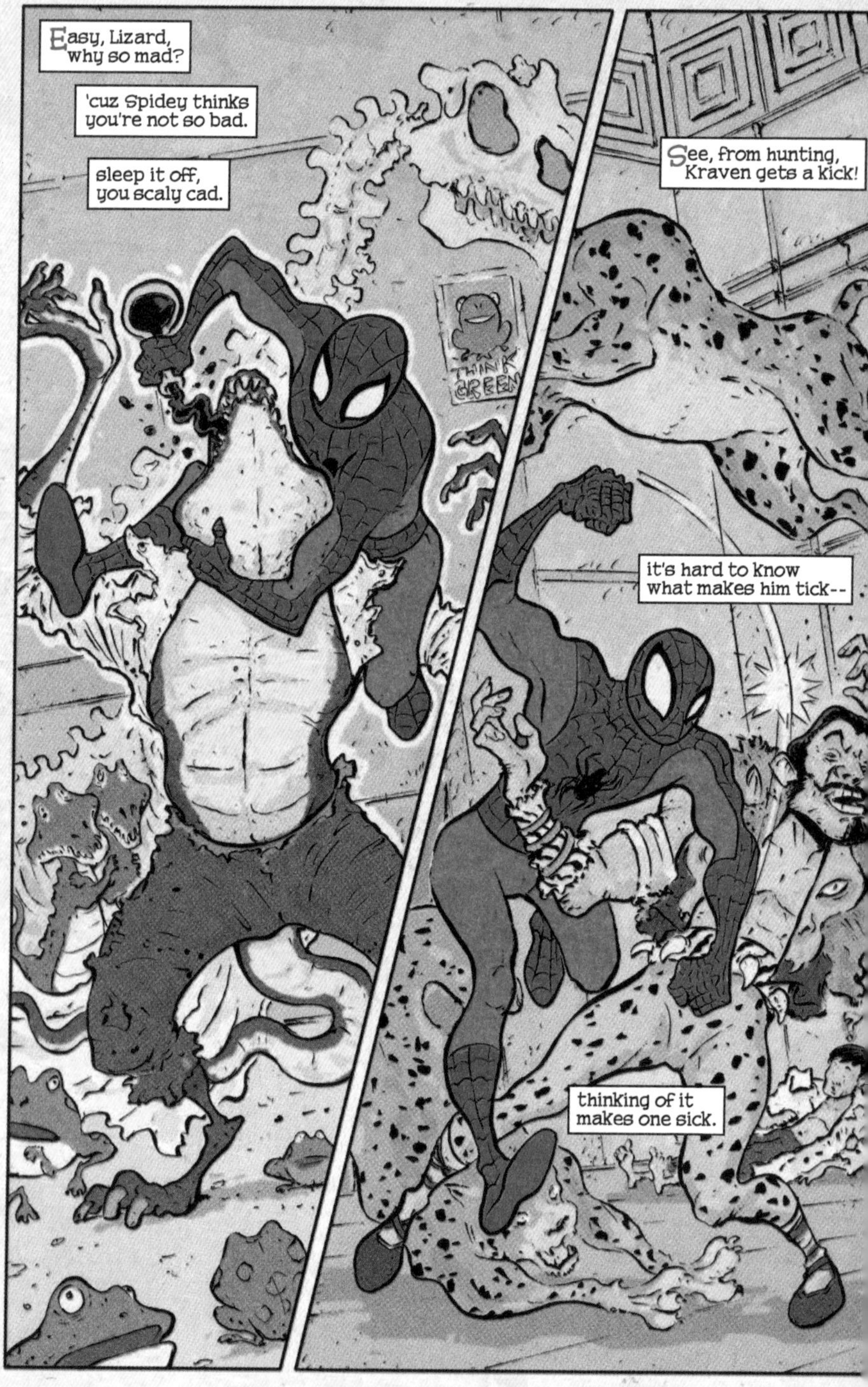
Easy, Lizard, why so mad?
'cuz Spidey thinks you're not so bad.
sleep it off, you scaly cad.
THINK GREEN
See, from hunting, Kraven gets a kick!
it's hard to know what makes him tick--
thinking of it makes one sick.

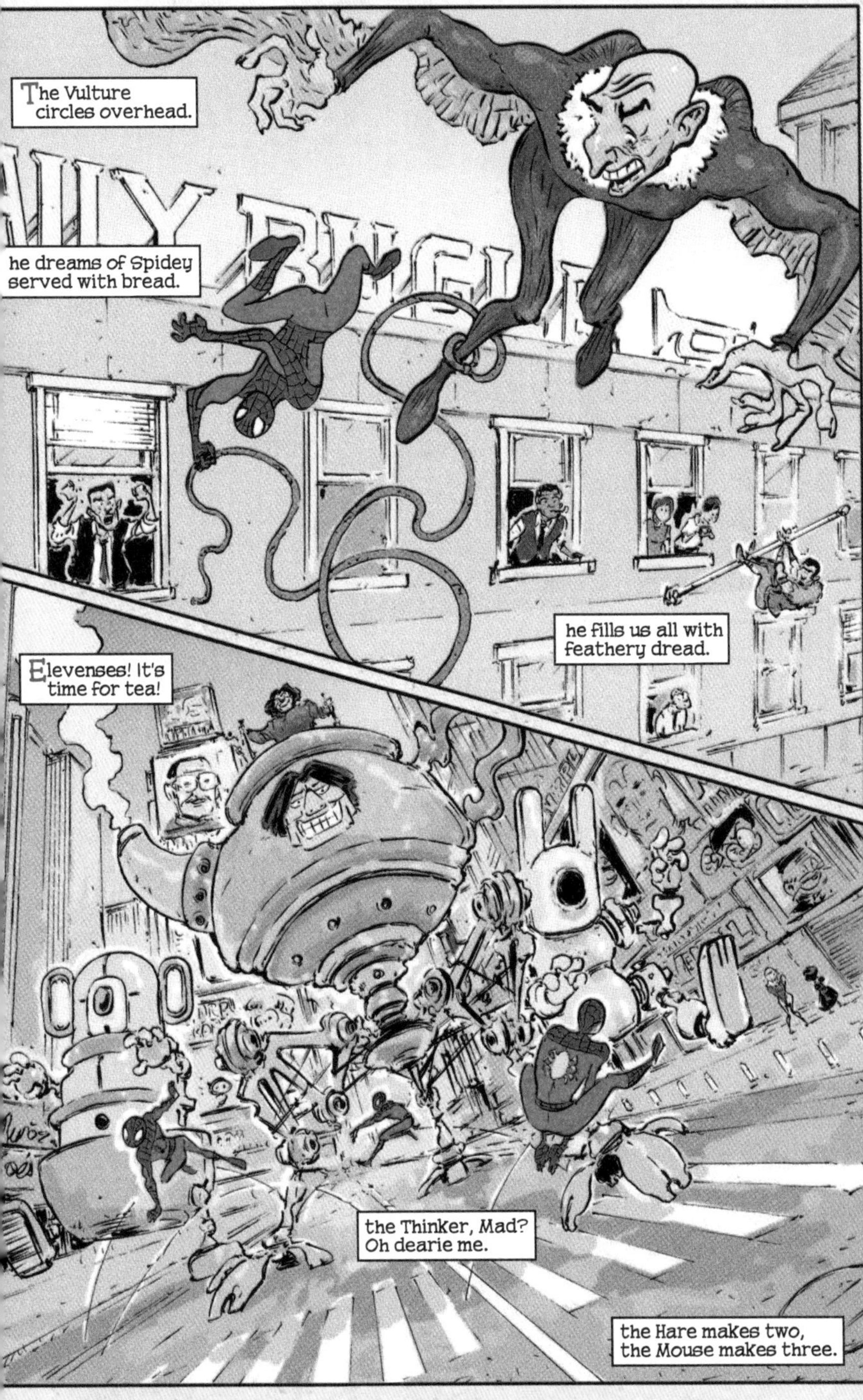
The Vulture circles overhead.
he dreams of Spidey served with bread.
he fills us all with feathery dread.
Elevenses! It's time for tea!
the Thinker, Mad? Oh dearie me.
the Hare makes two, the Mouse makes three.

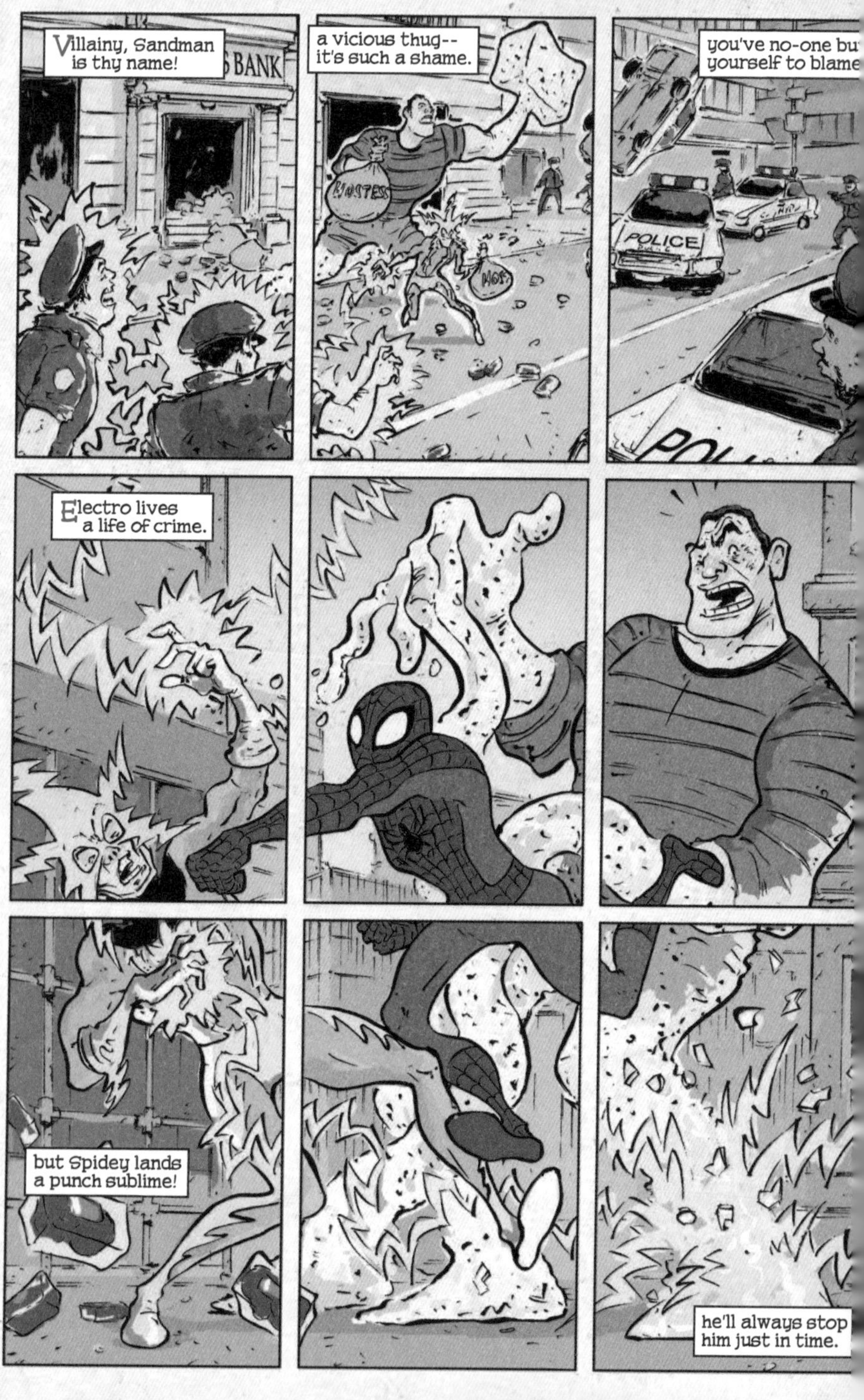
Villainy, Sandman is thy name!
$ BANK
a vicious thug-- it's such a shame.
HOSTESS
you've no-one bu yourself to blame
POLICE
Electro lives a life of crime.
but Spidey lands a punch sublime!
he'll always stop him just in time.

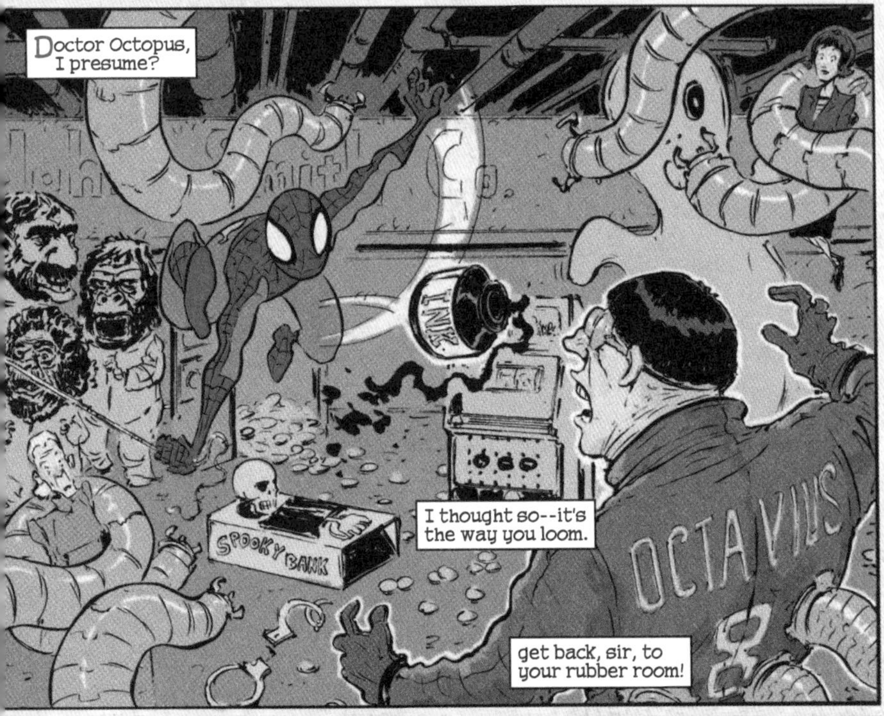
Doctor Octopus, I presume?
INK
SPOOKY BANK
I thought so--it's the way you loom.
OCTAVIUS
8
get back, sir, to your rubber room!

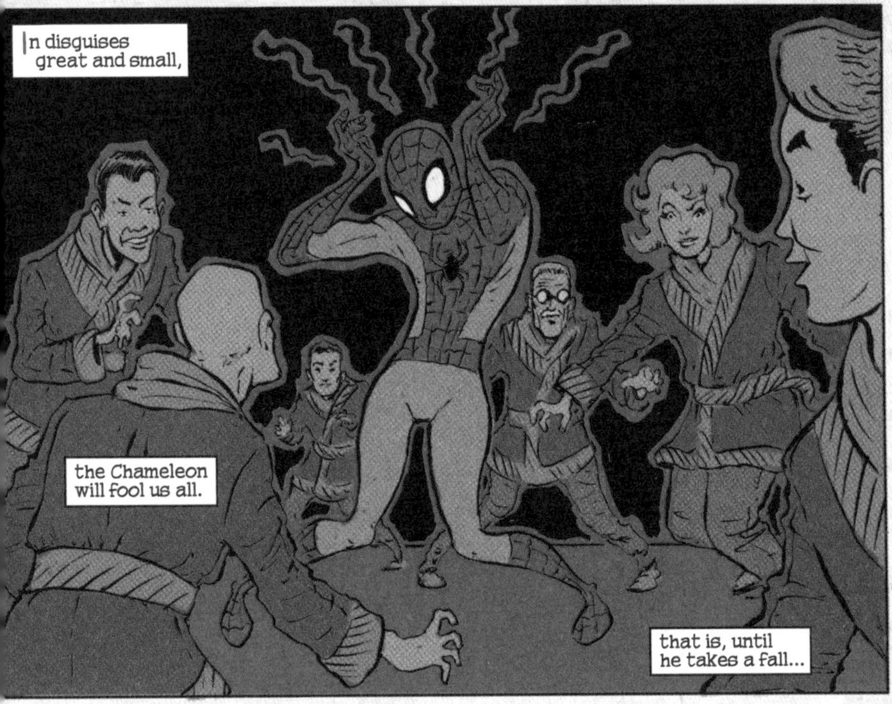
In disguises great and small,
the Chameleon will fool us all.
that is, until he takes a fall...

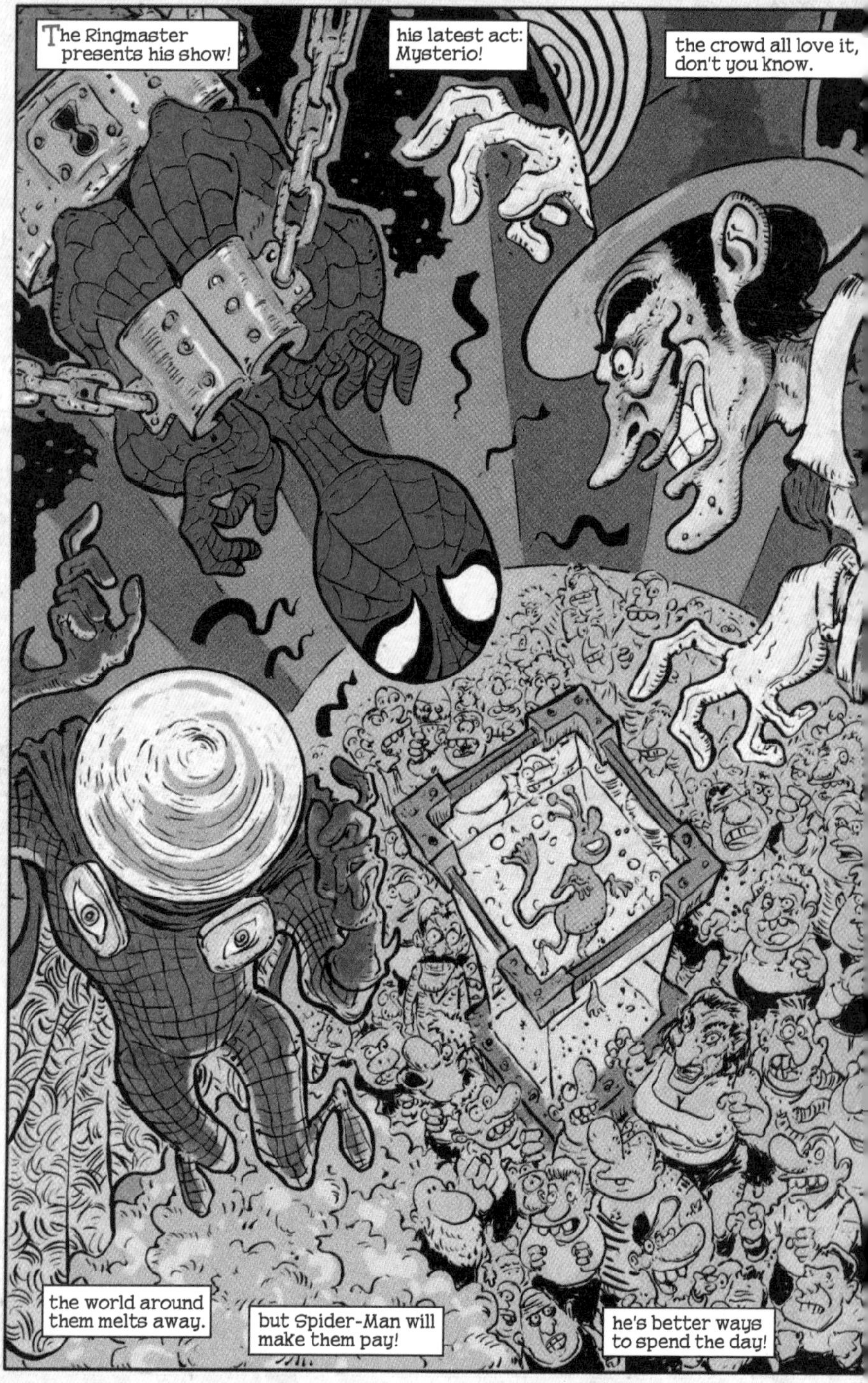
The Ringmaster presents his show!
his latest act: Mysterio!
the crowd all love it, don't you know.
the world around them melts away.
but Spider-Man will make them pay!
he's better ways to spend the day!

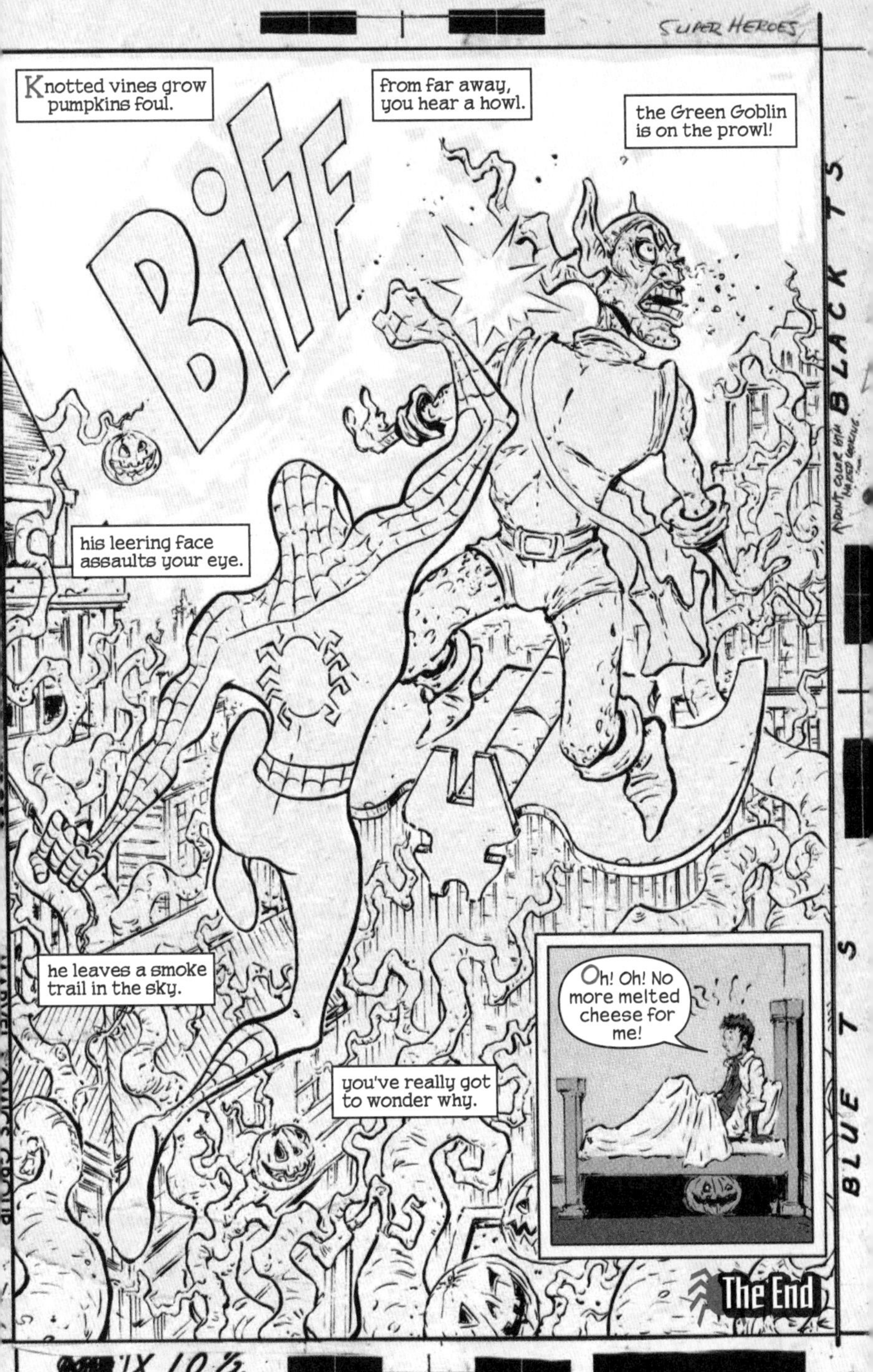
SUPER HEROES
Knotted vines grow pumpkins foul.
from far away, you hear a howl.
the Green Goblin is on the prowl!
BIFF
his leering face assaults your eye.
he leaves a smoke trail in the sky.
you've really got to wonder why.
Oh! Oh! No more melted cheese for me!
The End
BLACK TS
BLUE TS
IX 10 1/2

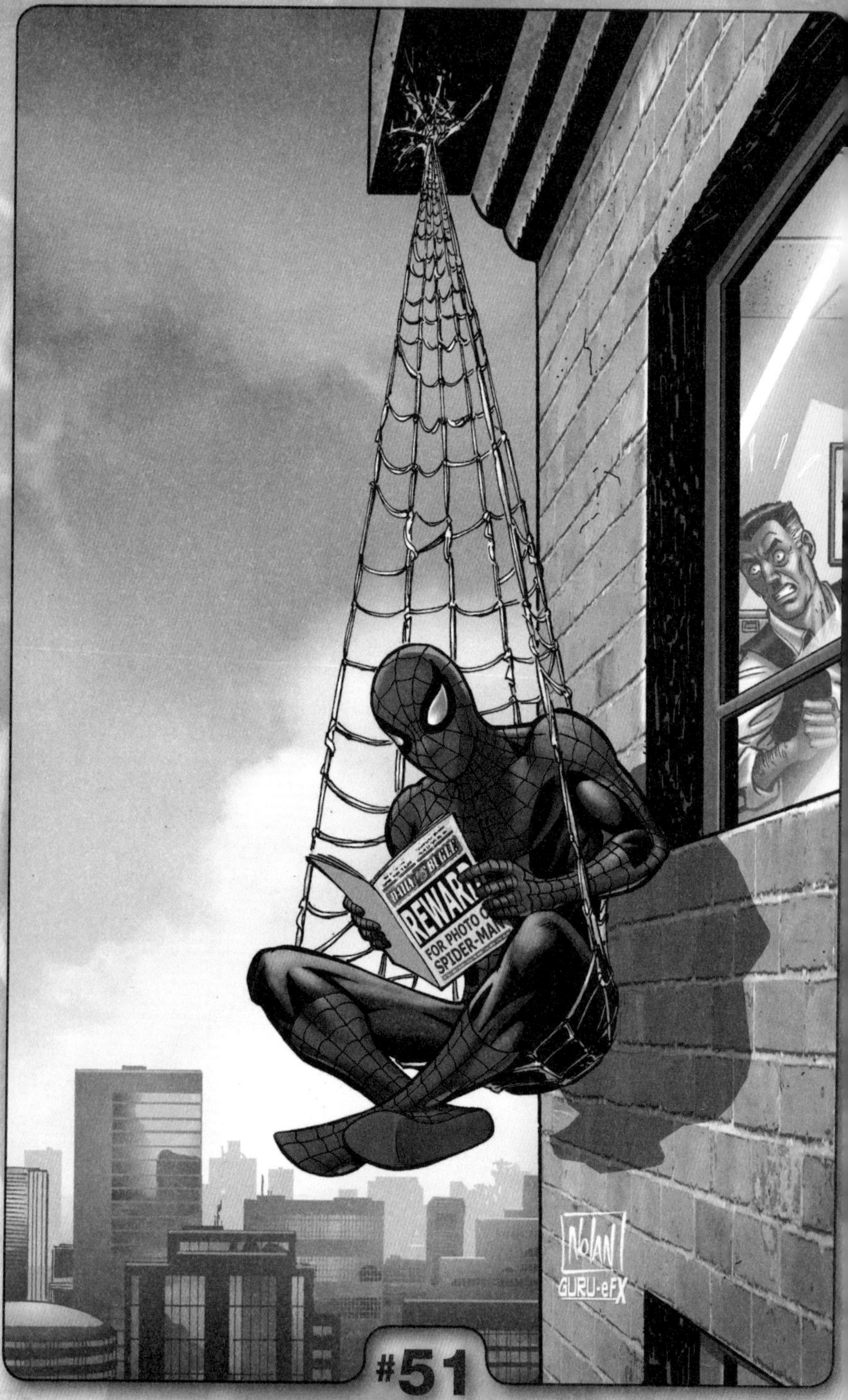
REWAR
FOR PHOTO O
SPIDER-MA
NOLAN
GURU-eFX

#51

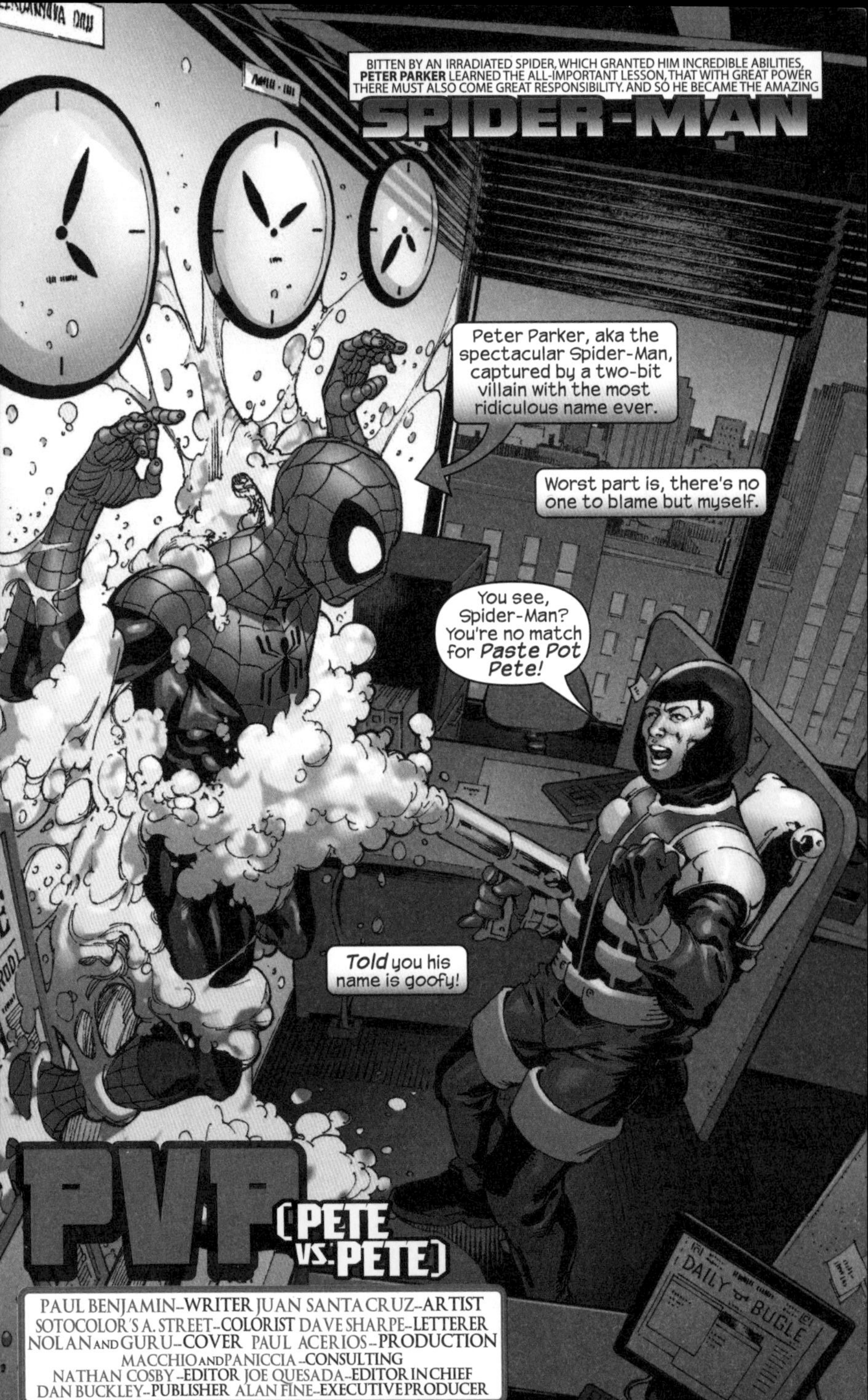

BITTEN BY AN IRRADIATED SPIDER, WHICH GRANTED HIM INCREDIBLE ABILITIES, PETER PARKER LEARNED THE ALL-IMPORTANT LESSON, THAT WITH GREAT POWER THERE MUST ALSO COME GREAT RESPONSIBILITY. AND SO HE BECAME THE AMAZING
SPIDER-MAN
Peter Parker, aka the spectacular Spider-Man, captured by a two-bit villain with the most ridiculous name ever.
Worst part is, there's no one to blame but myself.
You see, Spider-Man? You're no match for Paste Pot Pete!
Told you his name is goofy!
PVP (PETE VS. PETE)
PAUL BENJAMIN--WRITER JUAN SANTA CRUZ--ARTIST
SOTOCOLOR'S A. STREET--COLORIST DAVE SHARPE--LETTERER
NOLAN AND GURU--COVER PAUL ACERIOS--PRODUCTION
MACCHIO AND PANICCIA--CONSULTING
NATHAN COSBY--EDITOR JOE QUESADA--EDITOR IN CHIEF
DAN BUCKLEY--PUBLISHER ALAN FINE--EXECUTIVE PRODUCER
DAILY BUGLE

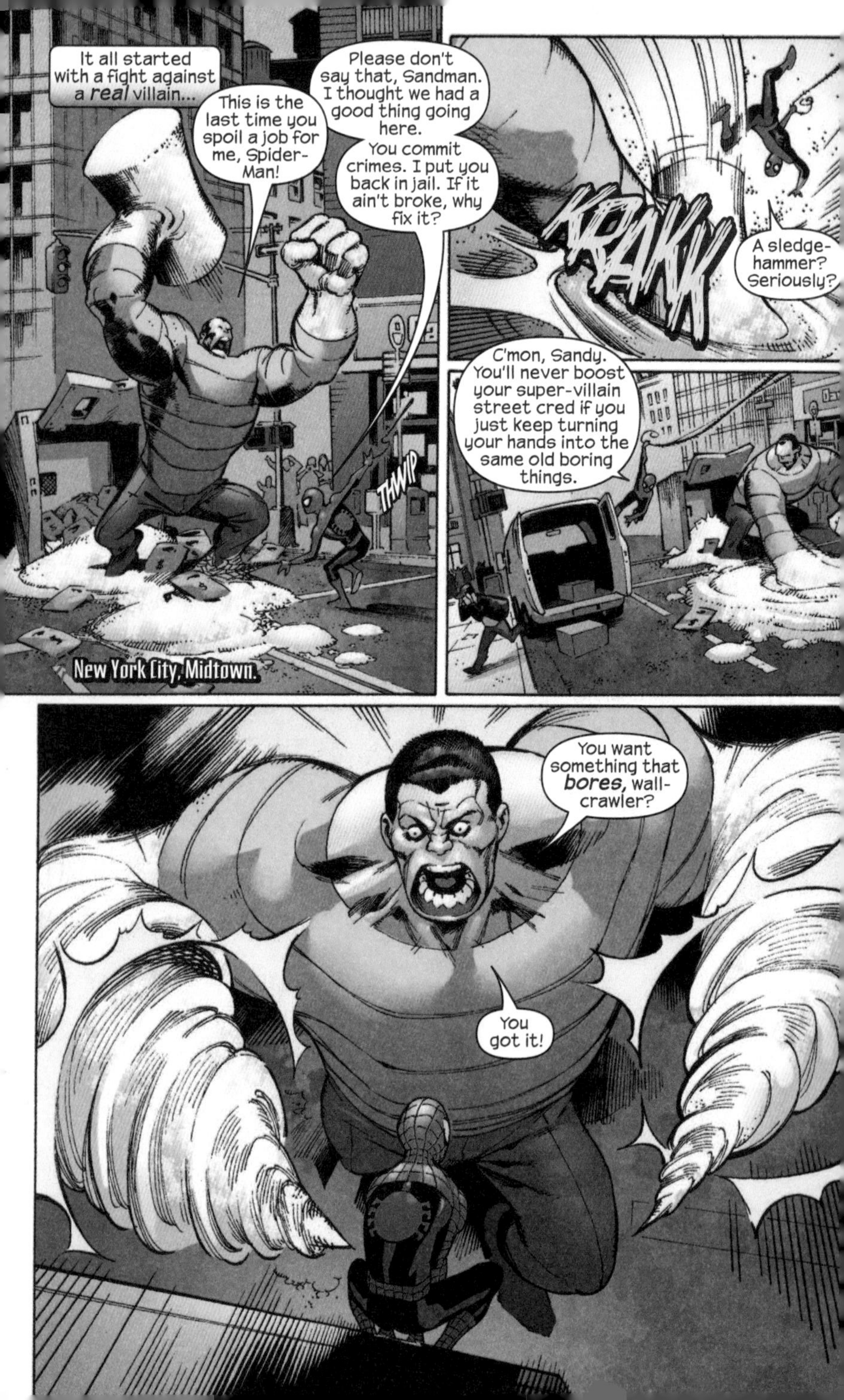

It all started with a fight against a *real* villain...
This is the last time you spoil a job for me, Spider-Man!
Please don't say that, Sandman. I thought we had a good thing going here.
You commit crimes. I put you back in jail. If it ain't broke, why fix it?
THWIP
New York City, Midtown.
KRAKK
A sledge-hammer? Seriously?
C'mon, Sandy. You'll never boost your super-villain street cred if you just keep turning your hands into the same old boring things.
You want something that *bores,* wall-crawler?
You got it!

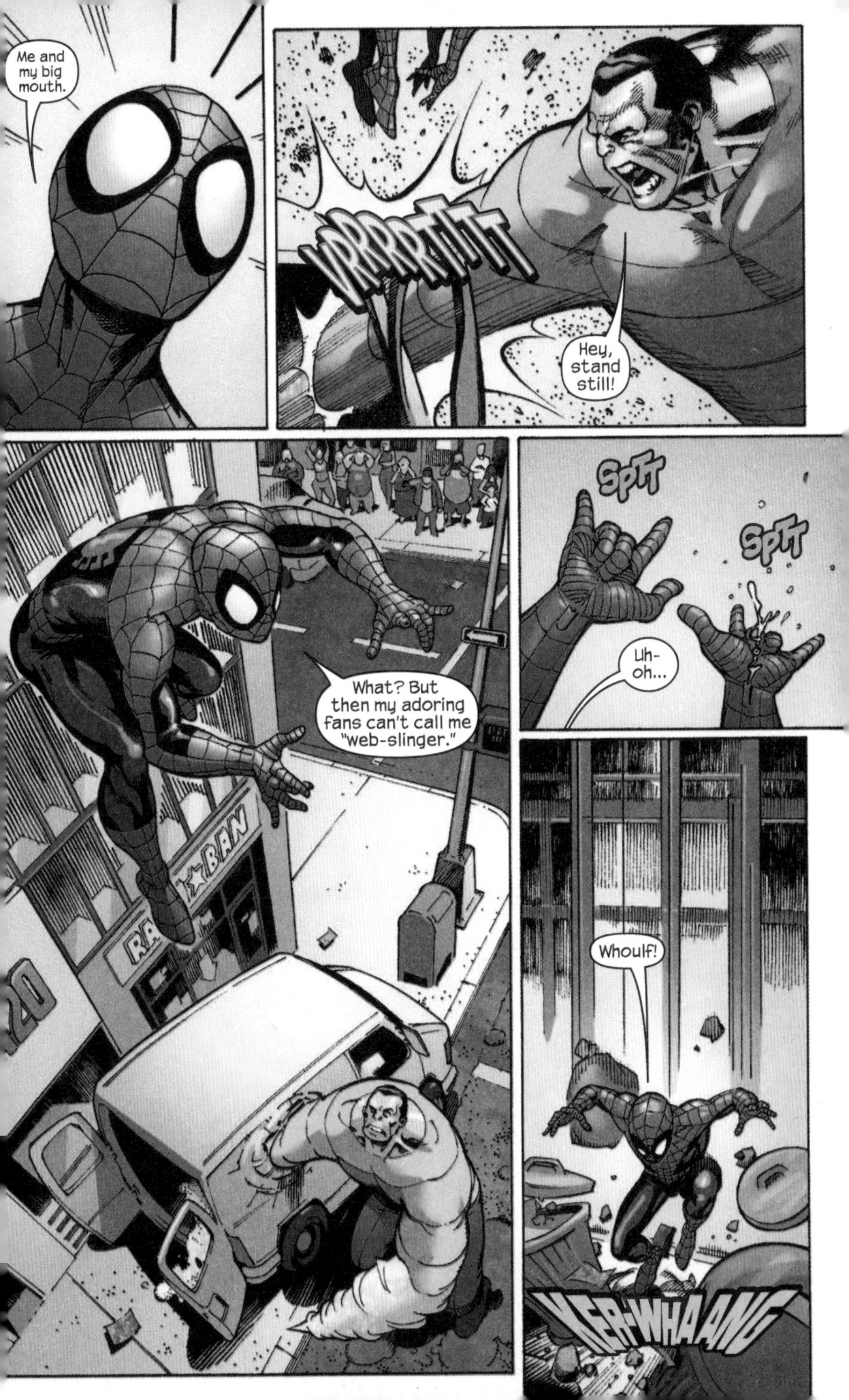
Me and my big mouth.
VRRRRTTTT
Hey, stand still!
What? But then my adoring fans can't call me "web-slinger."
SPTT
SPTT
Uh-oh...
Whoulf!
KER-WHAANG

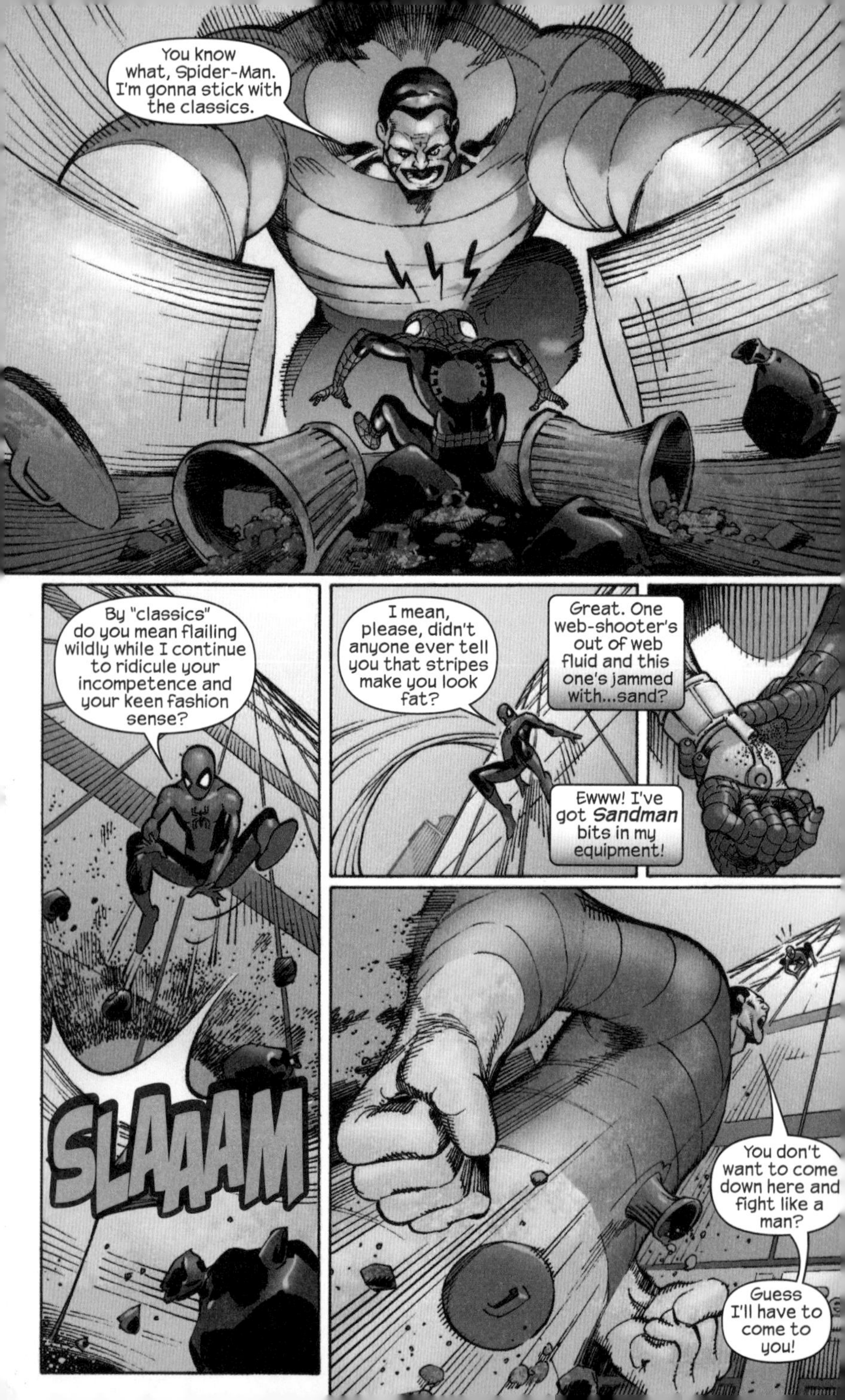
You know what, Spider-Man. I'm gonna stick with the classics.
By "classics" do you mean flailing wildly while I continue to ridicule your incompetence and your keen fashion sense?
I mean, please, didn't anyone ever tell you that stripes make you look fat?
Great. One web-shooter's out of web fluid and this one's jammed with...sand?
Ewww! I've got Sandman bits in my equipment!
SLAAAM
You don't want to come down here and fight like a man?
Guess I'll have to come to you!

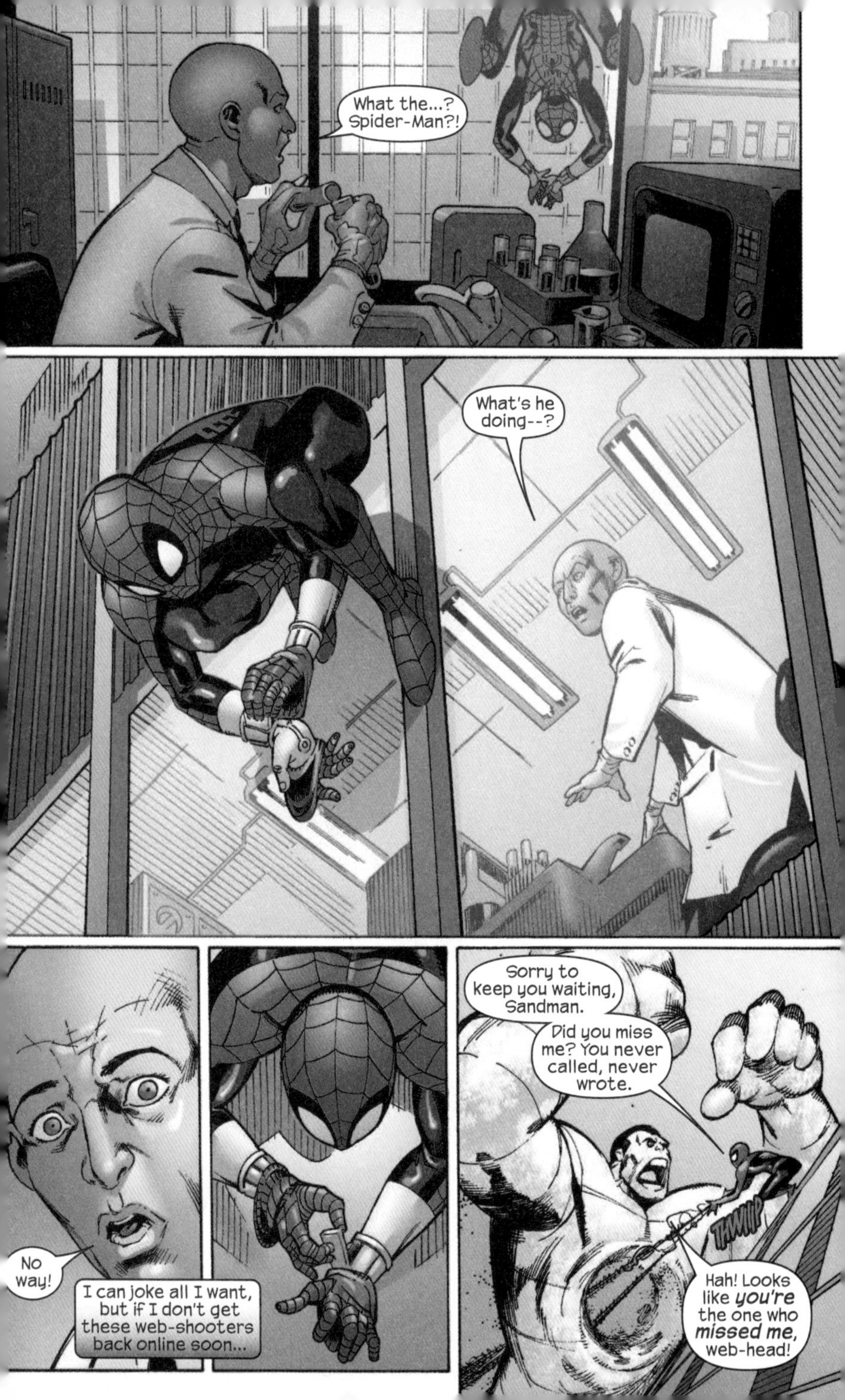
What the...? Spider-Man?!
What's he doing--?
No way!
I can joke all I want, but if I don't get these web-shooters back online soon...
Sorry to keep you waiting, Sandman.
Did you miss me? You never called, never wrote.
THWIP
Hah! Looks like *you're* the one who *missed me,* web-head!

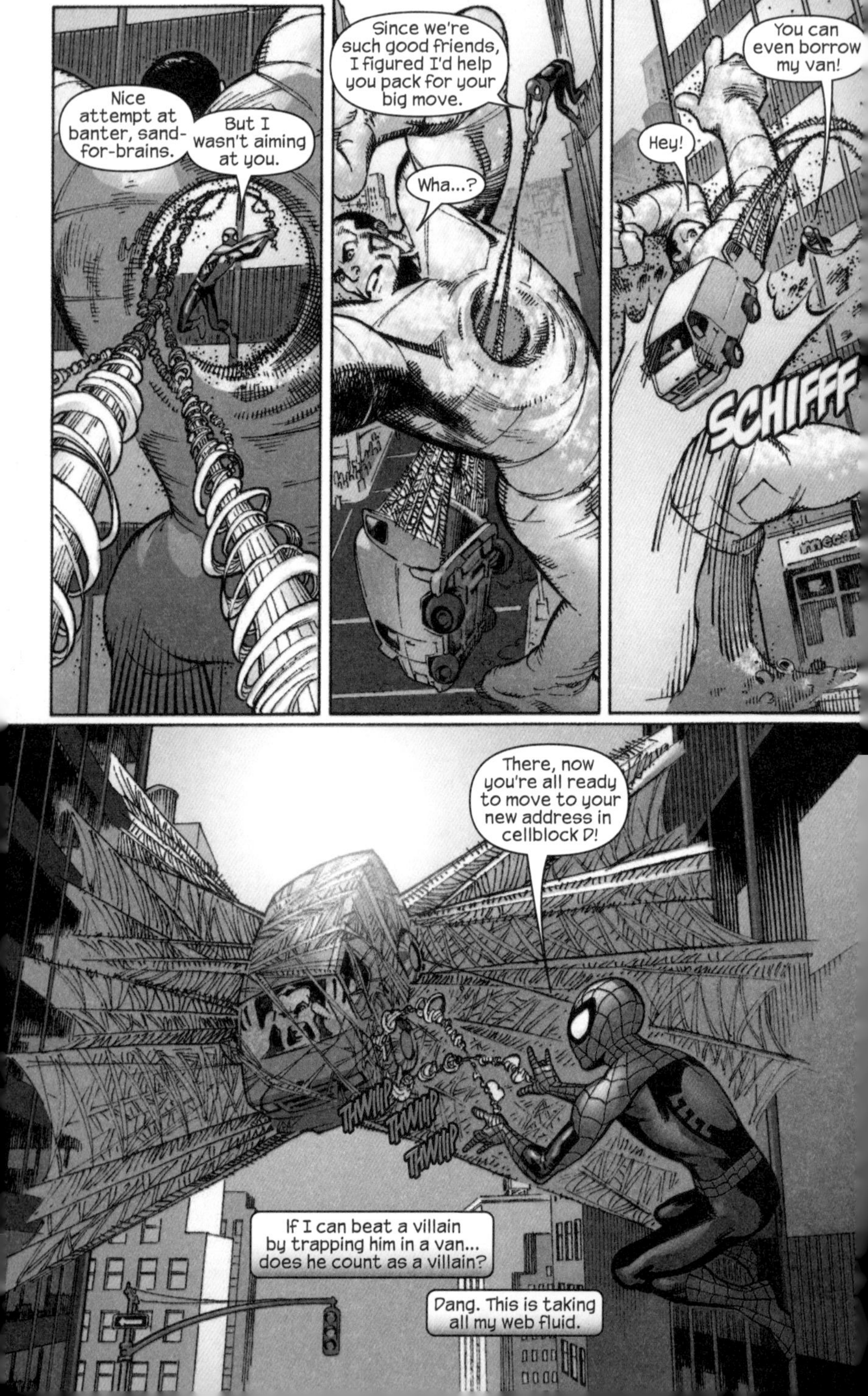
Nice attempt at banter, sand-for-brains.
But I wasn't aiming at you.
Since we're such good friends, I figured I'd help you pack for your big move.
Wha...?
You can even borrow my van!
Hey!
SCHIFFF
There, now you're all ready to move to your new address in cellblock D!
THWIIP
THWIIP
THWIIP
If I can beat a villain by trapping him in a van... does he count as a villain?
Dang. This is taking all my web fluid.

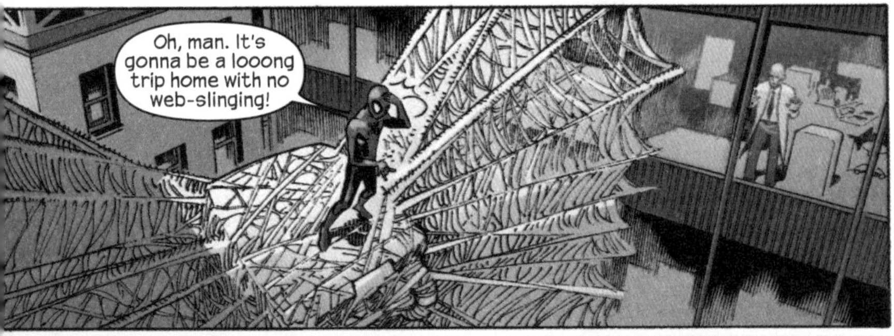
Oh, man. It's gonna be a looong trip home with no web-slinging!

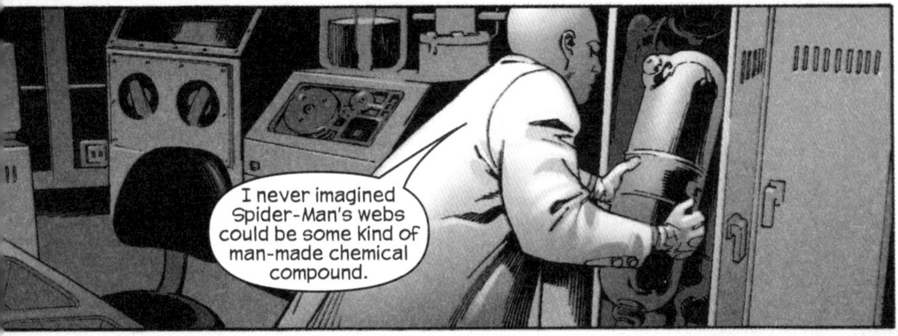
I never imagined Spider-Man's webs could be some kind of man-made chemical compound.

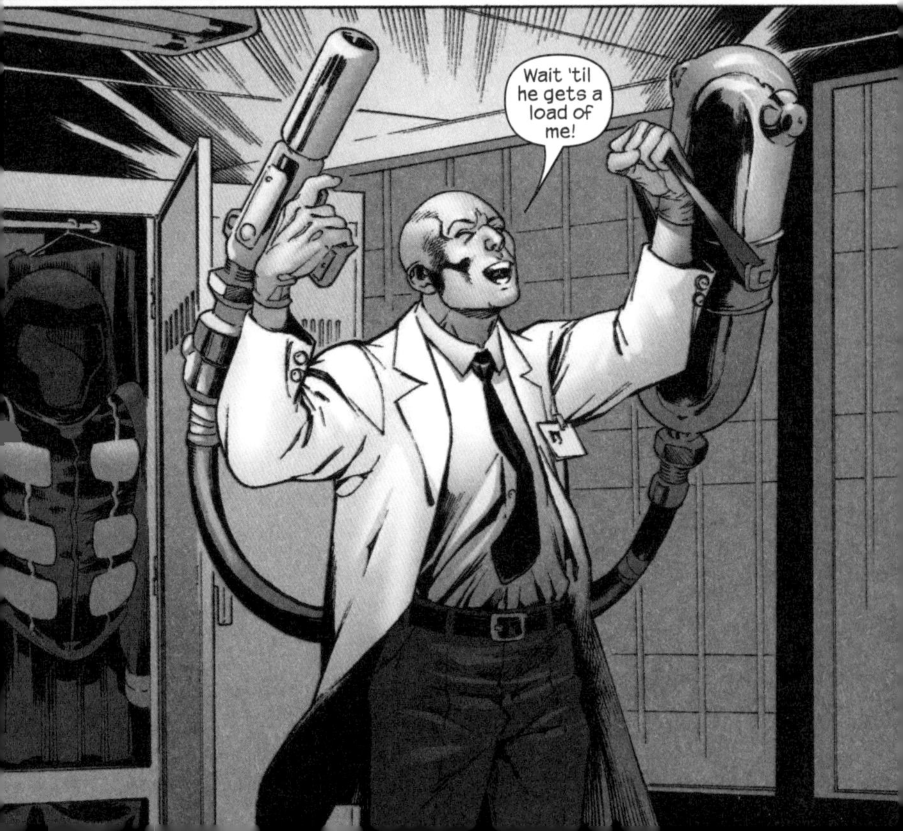
Wait 'til he gets a load of me!

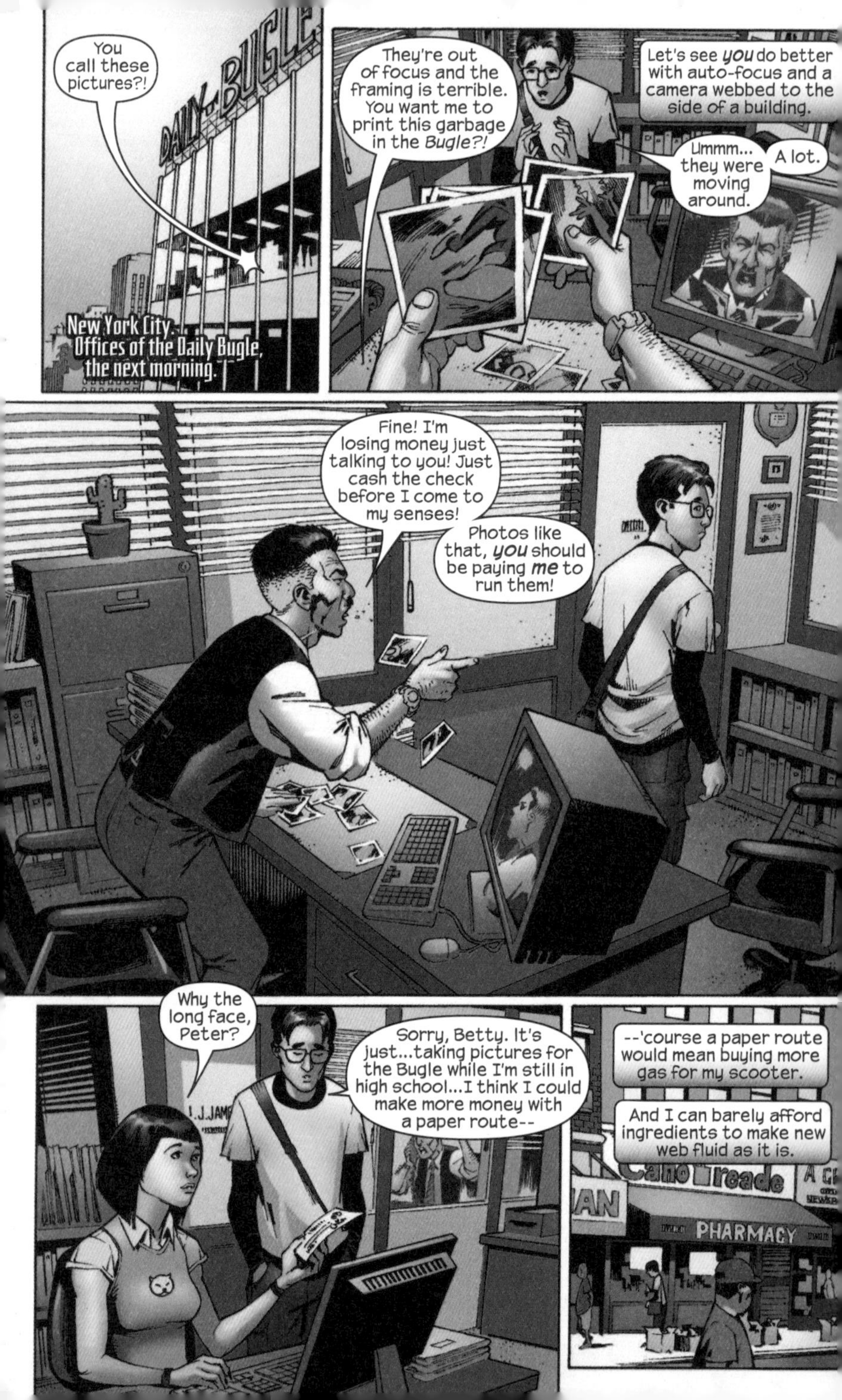

You call these pictures?!
DAILY BUGLE
New York City. Offices of the Daily Bugle, the next morning.
They're out of focus and the framing is terrible. You want me to print this garbage in the *Bugle*?!
Let's see ***you*** do better with auto-focus and a camera webbed to the side of a building.
Ummm... they were moving around.
A lot.
Fine! I'm losing money just talking to you! Just cash the check before I come to my senses!
Photos like that, ***you*** should be paying ***me*** to run them!
Why the long face, Peter?
Sorry, Betty. It's just...taking pictures for the Bugle while I'm still in high school...I think I could make more money with a paper route--
--'course a paper route would mean buying more gas for my scooter.
And I can barely afford ingredients to make new web fluid as it is.
PHARMACY

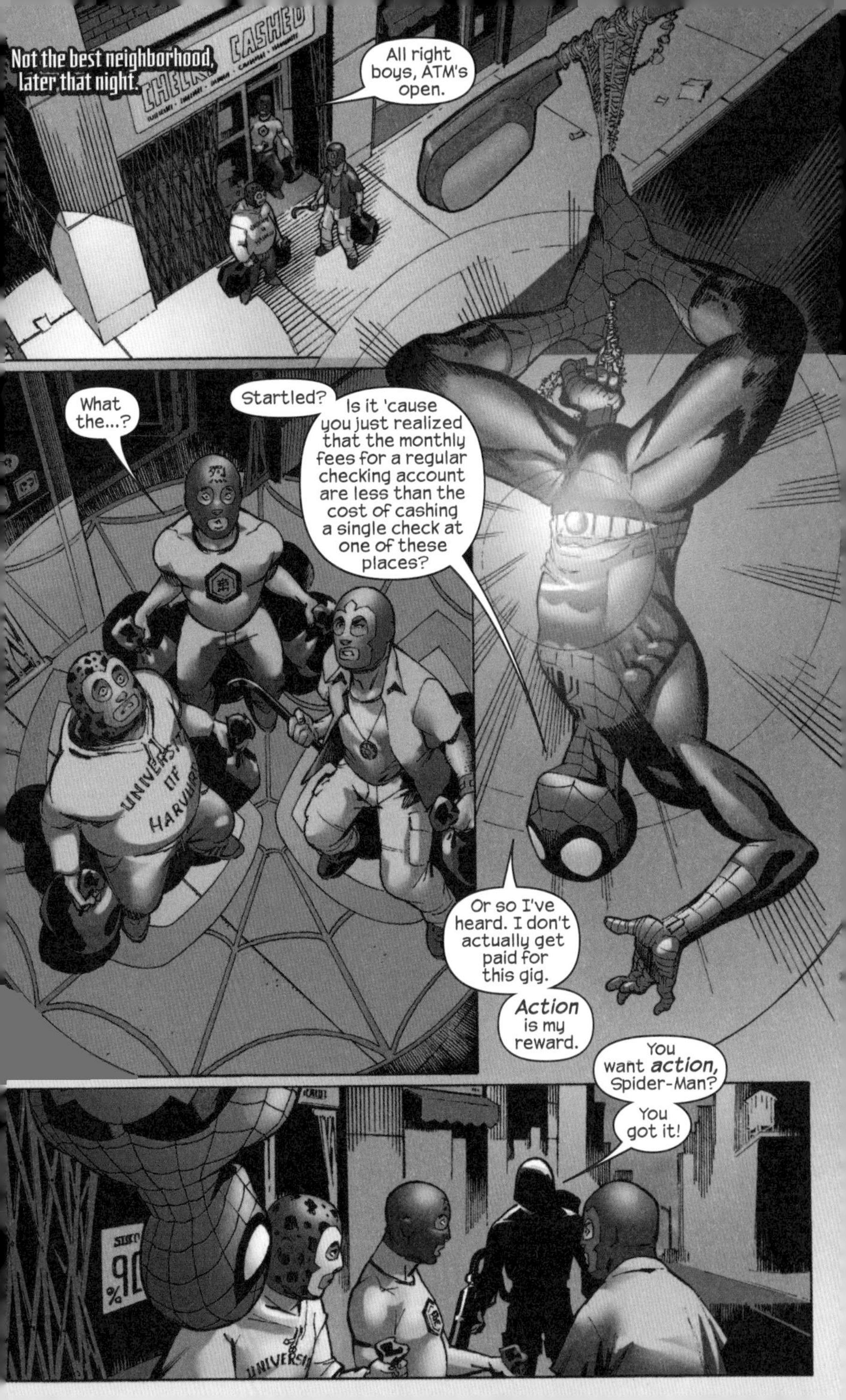
Not the best neighborhood, later that night.
All right boys, ATM's open.
What the...?
Startled?
Is it 'cause you just realized that the monthly fees for a regular checking account are less than the cost of cashing a single check at one of these places?
Or so I've heard. I don't actually get paid for this gig.
Action is my reward.
You want *action*, Spider-Man?
You got it!

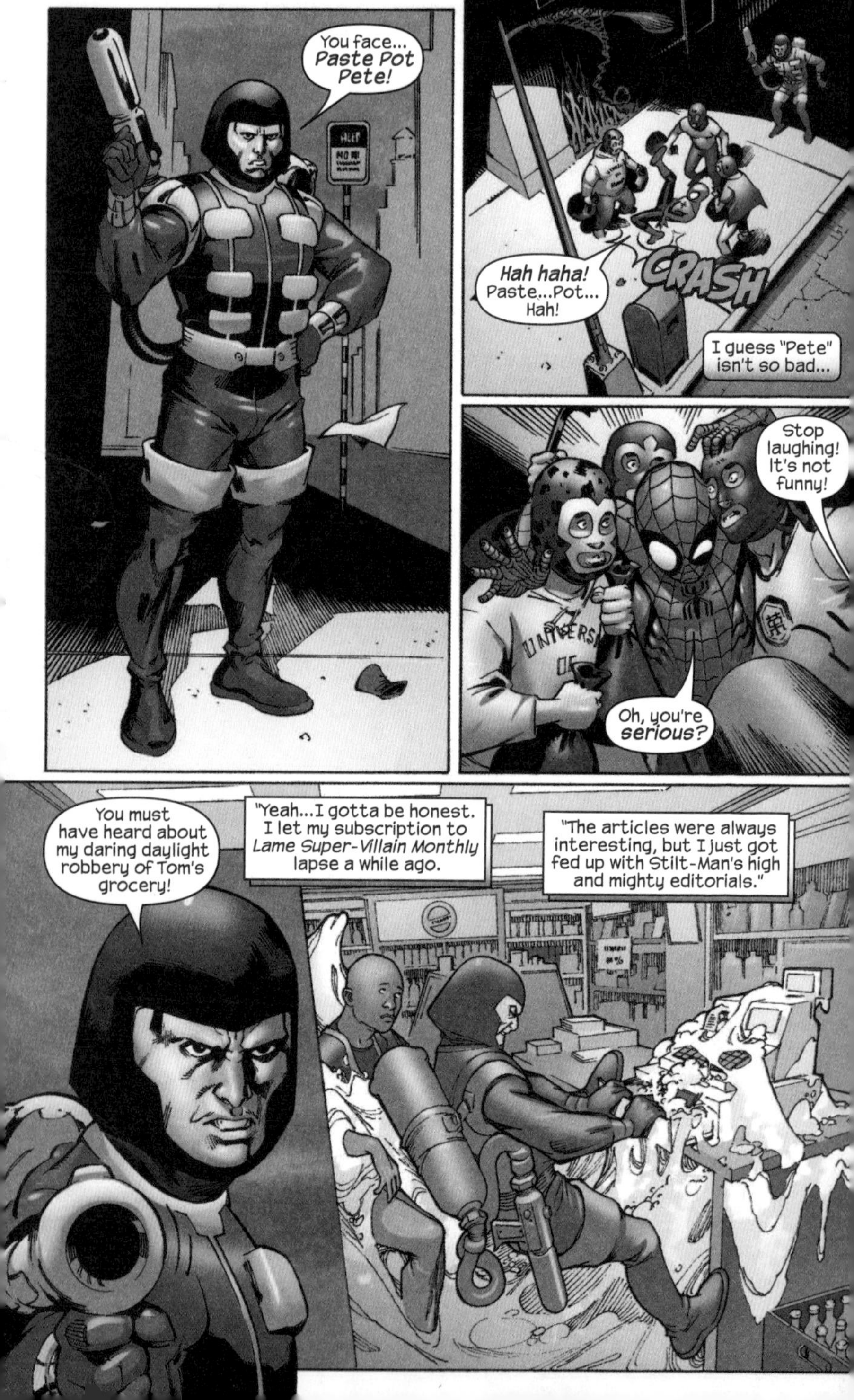
You face... Paste Pot Pete!
Hah haha! Paste...Pot... Hah!
CRASH
I guess "Pete" isn't so bad...
Stop laughing! It's not funny!
Oh, you're serious?
You must have heard about my daring daylight robbery of Tom's grocery!
"Yeah...I gotta be honest. I let my subscription to Lame Super-Villain Monthly lapse a while ago.
"The articles were always interesting, but I just got fed up with Stilt-Man's high and mighty editorials."

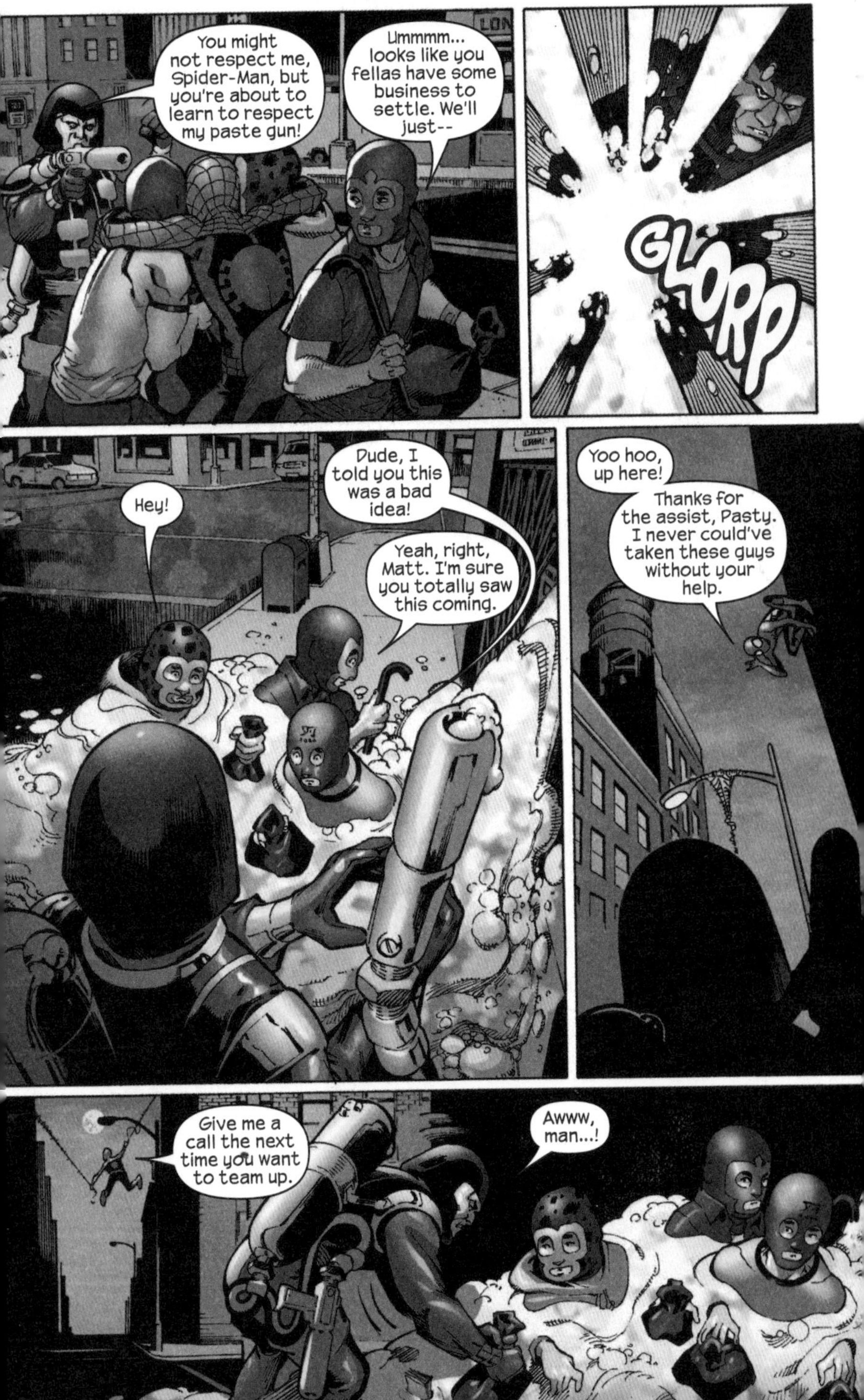
You might not respect me, Spider-Man, but you're about to learn to respect my paste gun!
Ummmm... looks like you fellas have some business to settle. We'll just--
GLORP
Hey!
Dude, I told you this was a bad idea!
Yeah, right, Matt. I'm sure you totally saw this coming.
Yoo hoo, up here!
Thanks for the assist, Pasty. I never could've taken these guys without your help.
Give me a call the next time you want to team up.
Awww, man...!

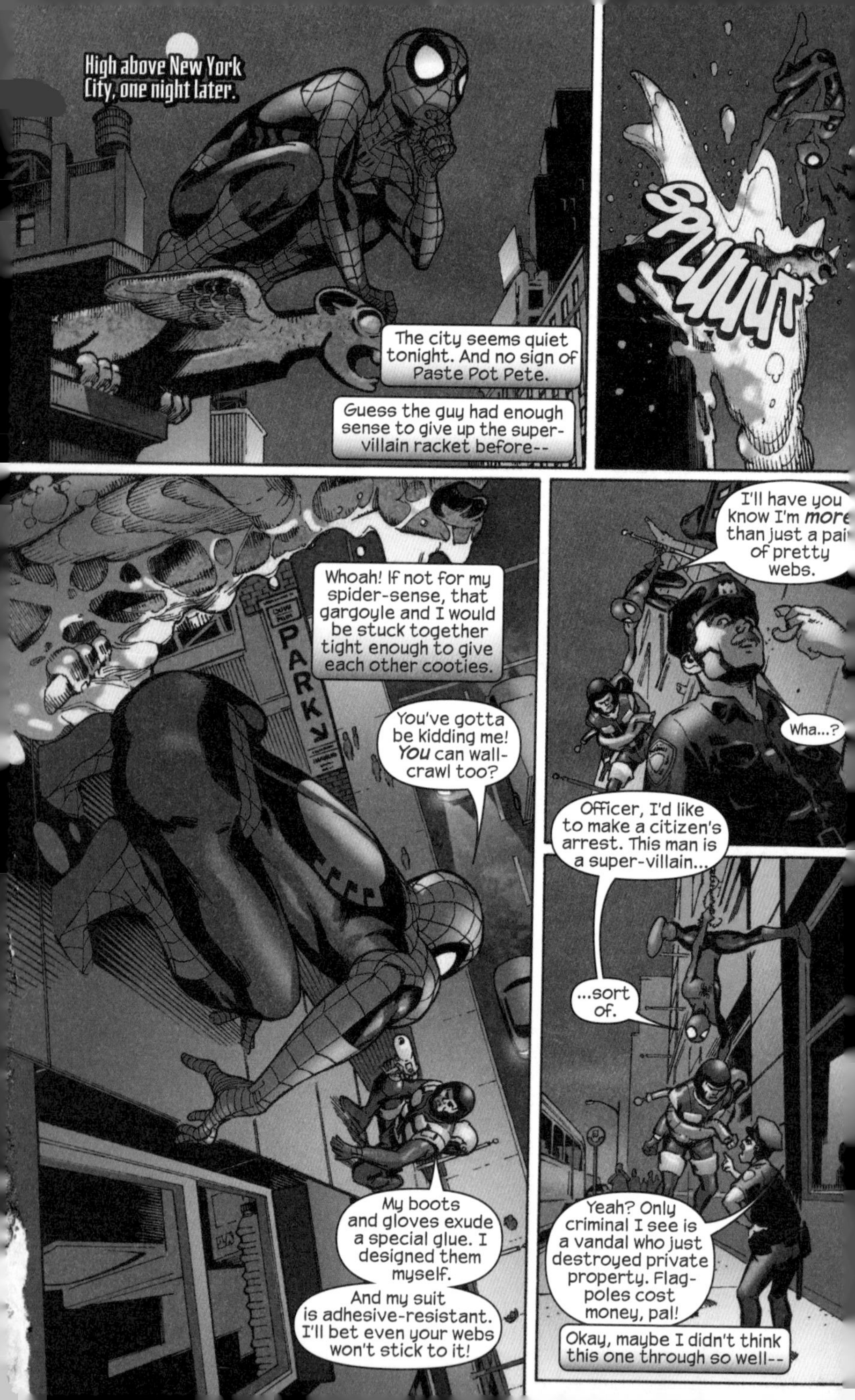

High above New York City, one night later.
The city seems quiet tonight. And no sign of Paste Pot Pete.
Guess the guy had enough sense to give up the super-villain racket before--
SPLUUUT
Whoah! If not for my spider-sense, that gargoyle and I would be stuck together tight enough to give each other cooties.
PARK
You've gotta be kidding me! *You* can wall-crawl too?
My boots and gloves exude a special glue. I designed them myself.
And my suit is adhesive-resistant. I'll bet even your webs won't stick to it!
I'll have you know I'm *more* than just a pai of pretty webs.
Wha...?
Officer, I'd like to make a citizen's arrest. This man is a super-villain...
...sort of.
Yeah? Only criminal I see is a vandal who just destroyed private property. Flag-poles cost money, pal!
Okay, maybe I didn't think this one through so well--

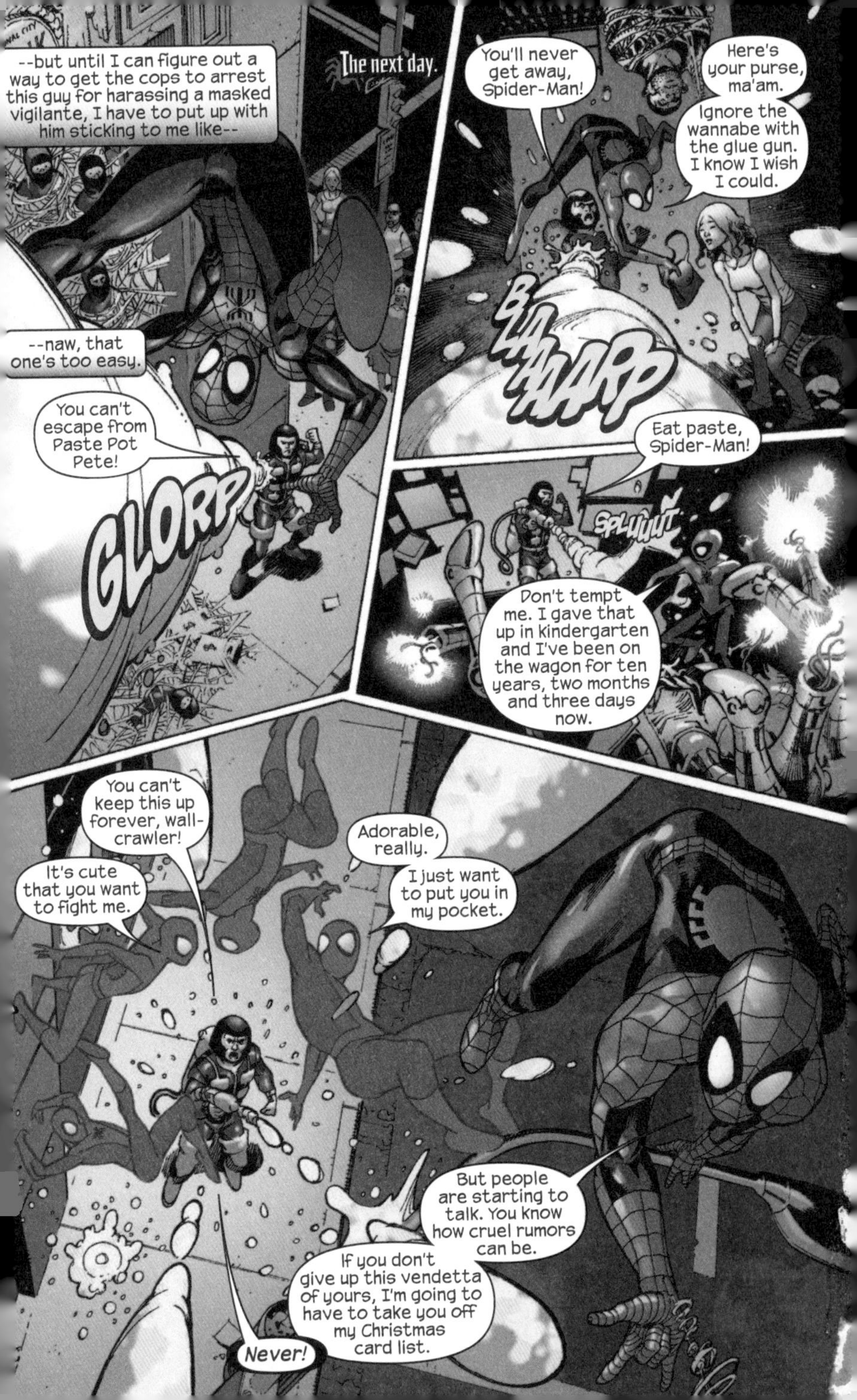

--but until I can figure out a way to get the cops to arrest this guy for harassing a masked vigilante, I have to put up with him sticking to me like--
The next day.
You'll never get away, Spider-Man!
Here's your purse, ma'am.
Ignore the wannabe with the glue gun. I know I wish I could.
BLAAAARP
--naw, that one's too easy.
You can't escape from Paste Pot Pete!
GLORP
Eat paste, Spider-Man!
SPLUUUT
Don't tempt me. I gave that up in kindergarten and I've been on the wagon for ten years, two months and three days now.
You can't keep this up forever, wall-crawler!
It's cute that you want to fight me.
Adorable, really.
I just want to put you in my pocket.
But people are starting to talk. You know how cruel rumors can be.
If you don't give up this vendetta of yours, I'm going to have to take you off my Christmas card list.
Never!

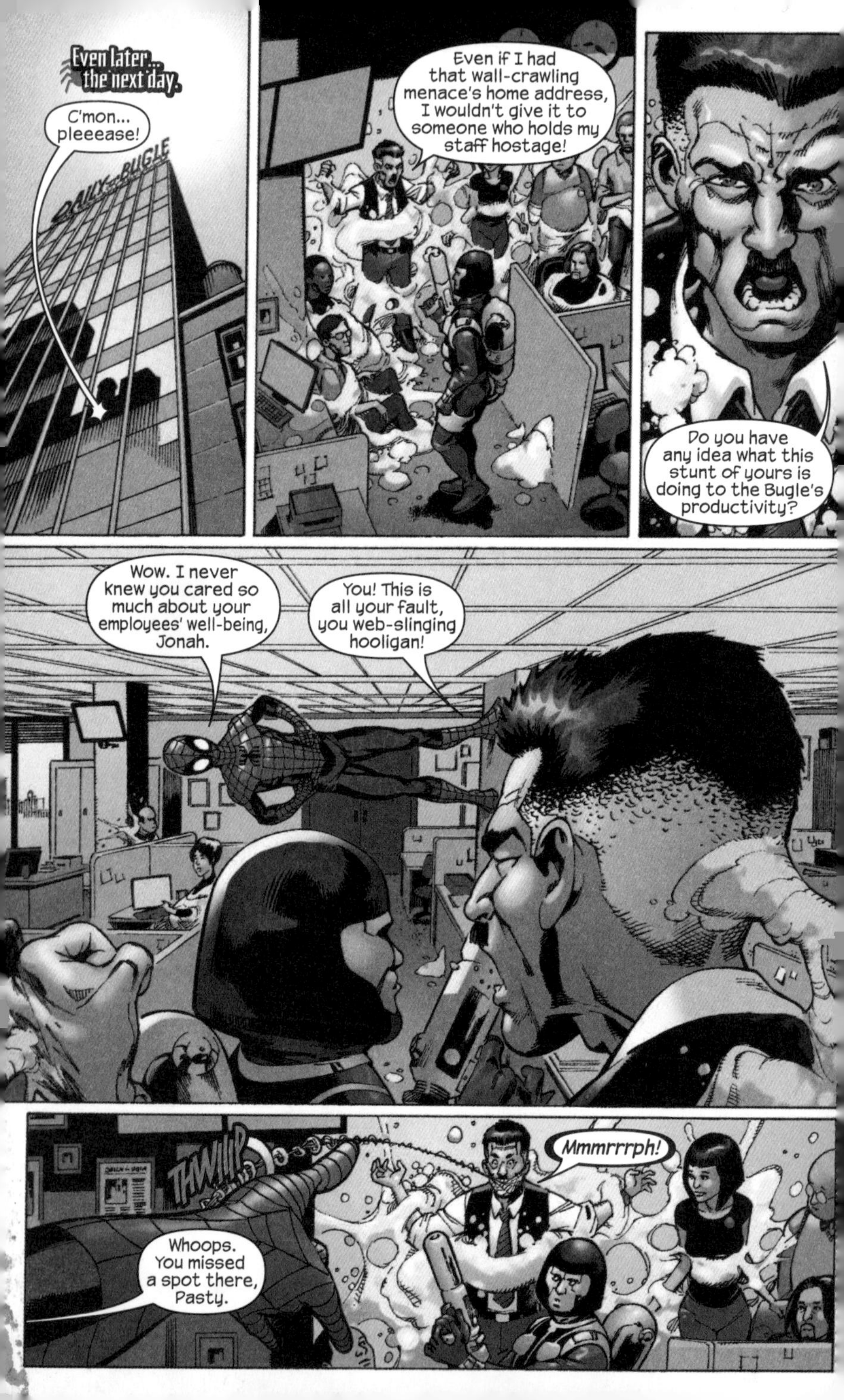
Even later... the next day.
C'mon... pleeease!
DAILY BUGLE
Even if I had that wall-crawling menace's home address, I wouldn't give it to someone who holds my staff hostage!
Do you have any idea what this stunt of yours is doing to the Bugle's productivity?
Wow. I never knew you cared so much about your employees' well-being, Jonah.
You! This is all your fault, you web-slinging hooligan!
THWIP
Mmmrrrph!
Whoops. You missed a spot there, Pasty.

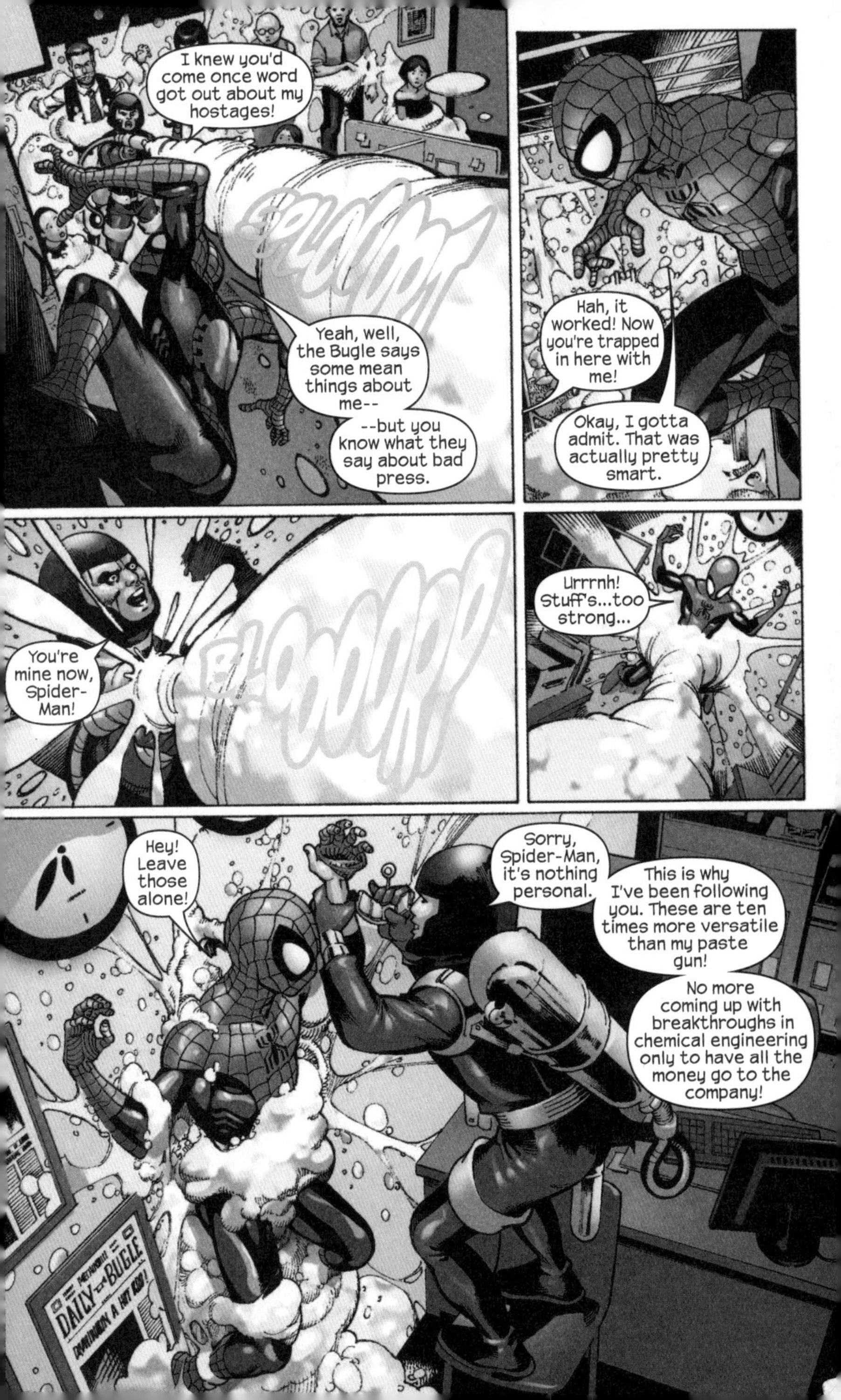
I knew you'd come once word got out about my hostages!
SPLOOSH!
Yeah, well, the Bugle says some mean things about me--
--but you know what they say about bad press.
Hah, it worked! Now you're trapped in here with me!
Okay, I gotta admit. That was actually pretty smart.
You're mine now, Spider-Man!
Urrrnh! Stuff's...too strong...
Hey! Leave those alone!
Sorry, Spider-Man, it's nothing personal.
This is why I've been following you. These are ten times more versatile than my paste gun!
No more coming up with breakthroughs in chemical engineering only to have all the money go to the company!
DAILY BUGLE

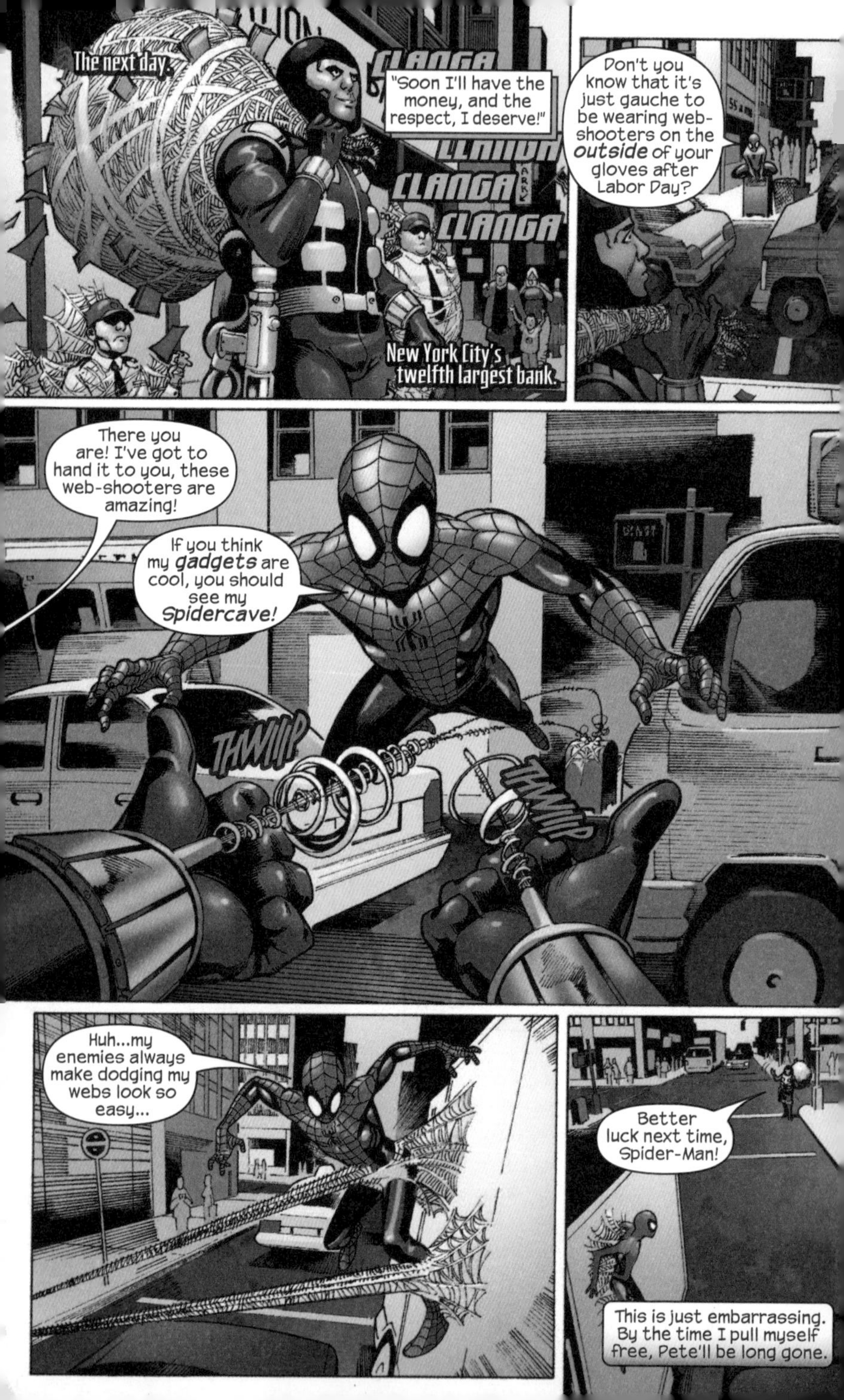
The next day.
CLANGA
"Soon I'll have the money, and the respect, I deserve!"
CLANGA
CLANGA
CLANGA
New York City's twelfth largest bank.
Don't you know that it's just gauche to be wearing web-shooters on the outside of your gloves after Labor Day?
There you are! I've got to hand it to you, these web-shooters are amazing!
If you think my gadgets are cool, you should see my Spidercave!
THWIIP
THWIIP
Huh...my enemies always make dodging my webs look so easy...
Better luck next time, Spider-Man!
This is just embarrassing. By the time I pull myself free, Pete'll be long gone.

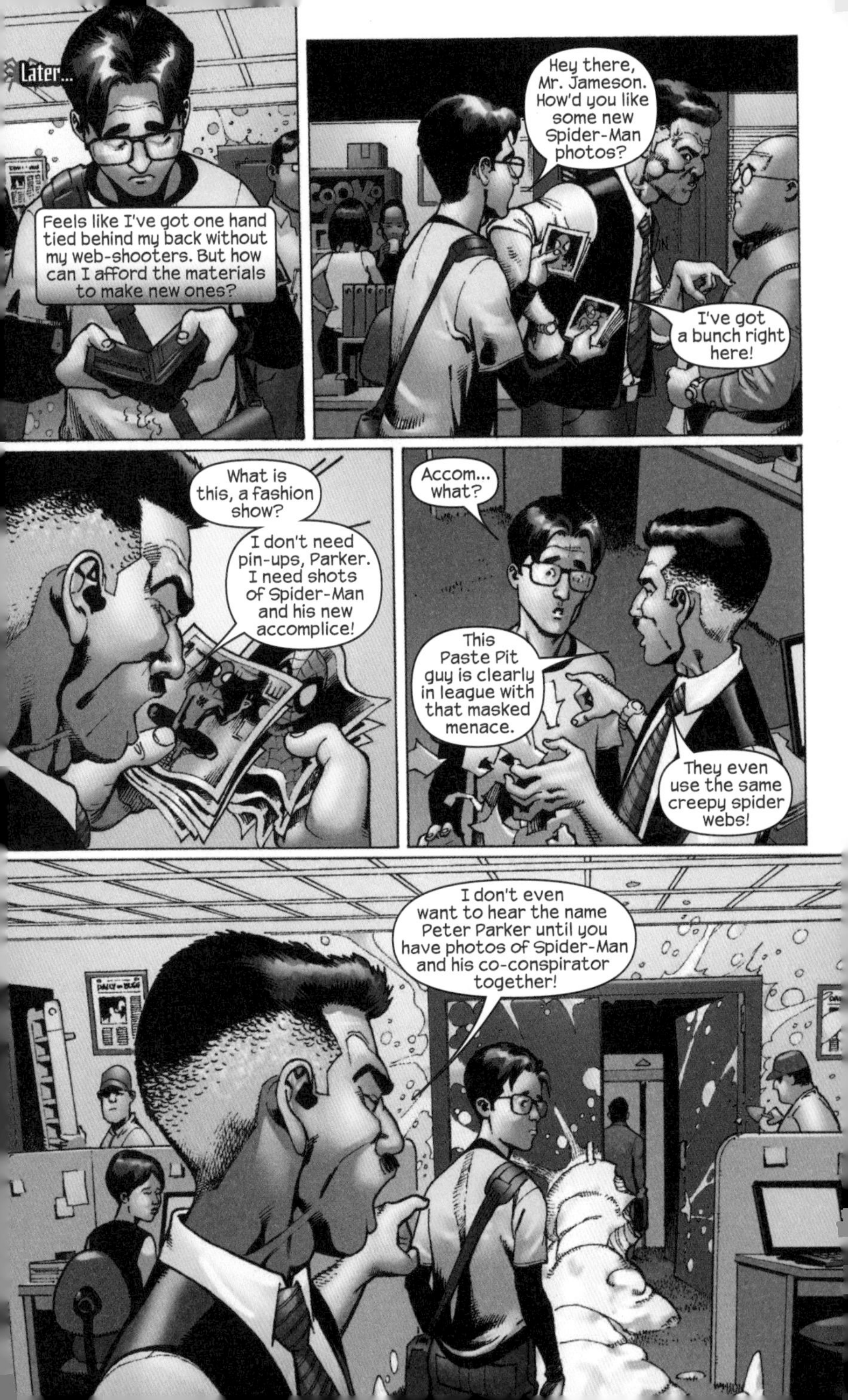
Later...
Feels like I've got one hand tied behind my back without my web-shooters. But how can I afford the materials to make new ones?
Hey there, Mr. Jameson. How'd you like some new Spider-Man photos?
I've got a bunch right here!
What is this, a fashion show?
I don't need pin-ups, Parker. I need shots of Spider-Man and his new accomplice!
Accom... what?
This Paste Pit guy is clearly in league with that masked menace.
They even use the same creepy spider webs!
I don't even want to hear the name Peter Parker until you have photos of Spider-Man and his co-conspirator together!

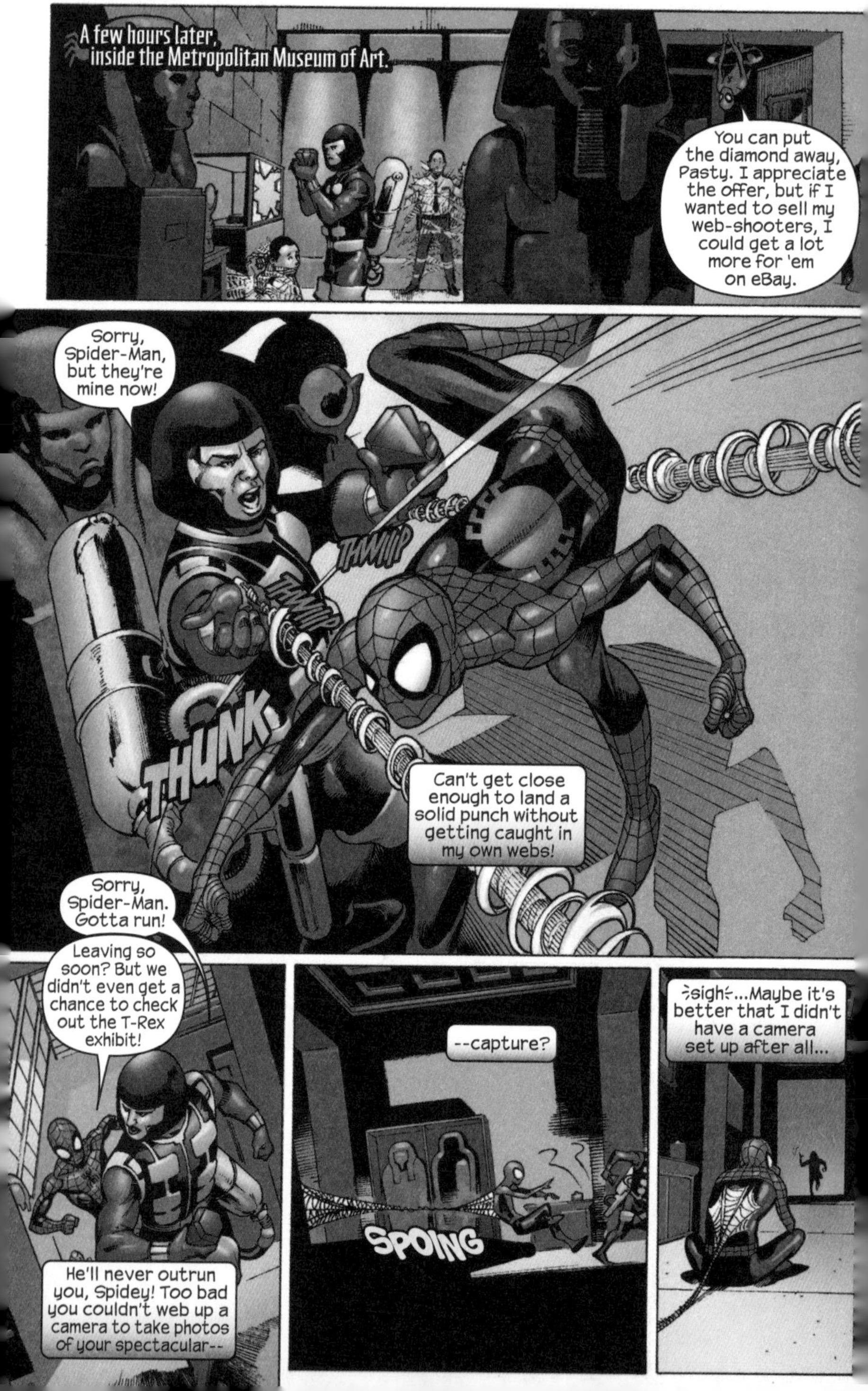

A few hours later, inside the Metropolitan Museum of Art.
You can put the diamond away, Pasty. I appreciate the offer, but if I wanted to sell my web-shooters, I could get a lot more for 'em on eBay.
Sorry, Spider-Man, but they're mine now!
THWIIP
THWIIP
THUNK
Can't get close enough to land a solid punch without getting caught in my own webs!
Sorry, Spider-Man. Gotta run!
Leaving so soon? But we didn't even get a chance to check out the T-Rex exhibit!
He'll never outrun you, Spidey! Too bad you couldn't web up a camera to take photos of your spectacular--
--capture?
SPOING
sigh...Maybe it's better that I didn't have a camera set up after all...

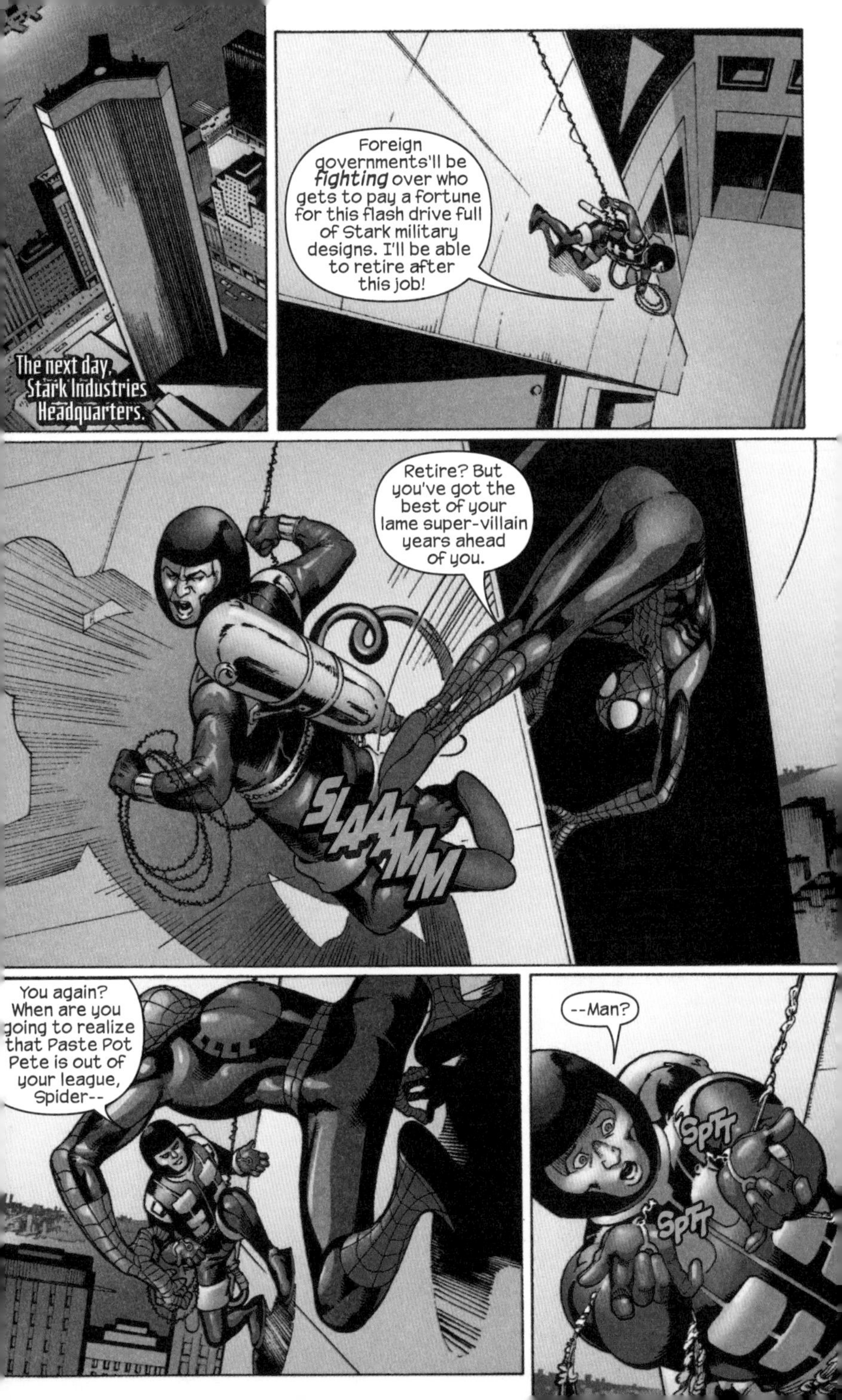
The next day, Stark Industries Headquarters.
Foreign governments'll be fighting over who gets to pay a fortune for this flash drive full of Stark military designs. I'll be able to retire after this job!
Retire? But you've got the best of your lame super-villain years ahead of you.
SLAAAMM
You again? When are you going to realize that Paste Pot Pete is out of your league, Spider--
--Man?
SPTT
SPTT

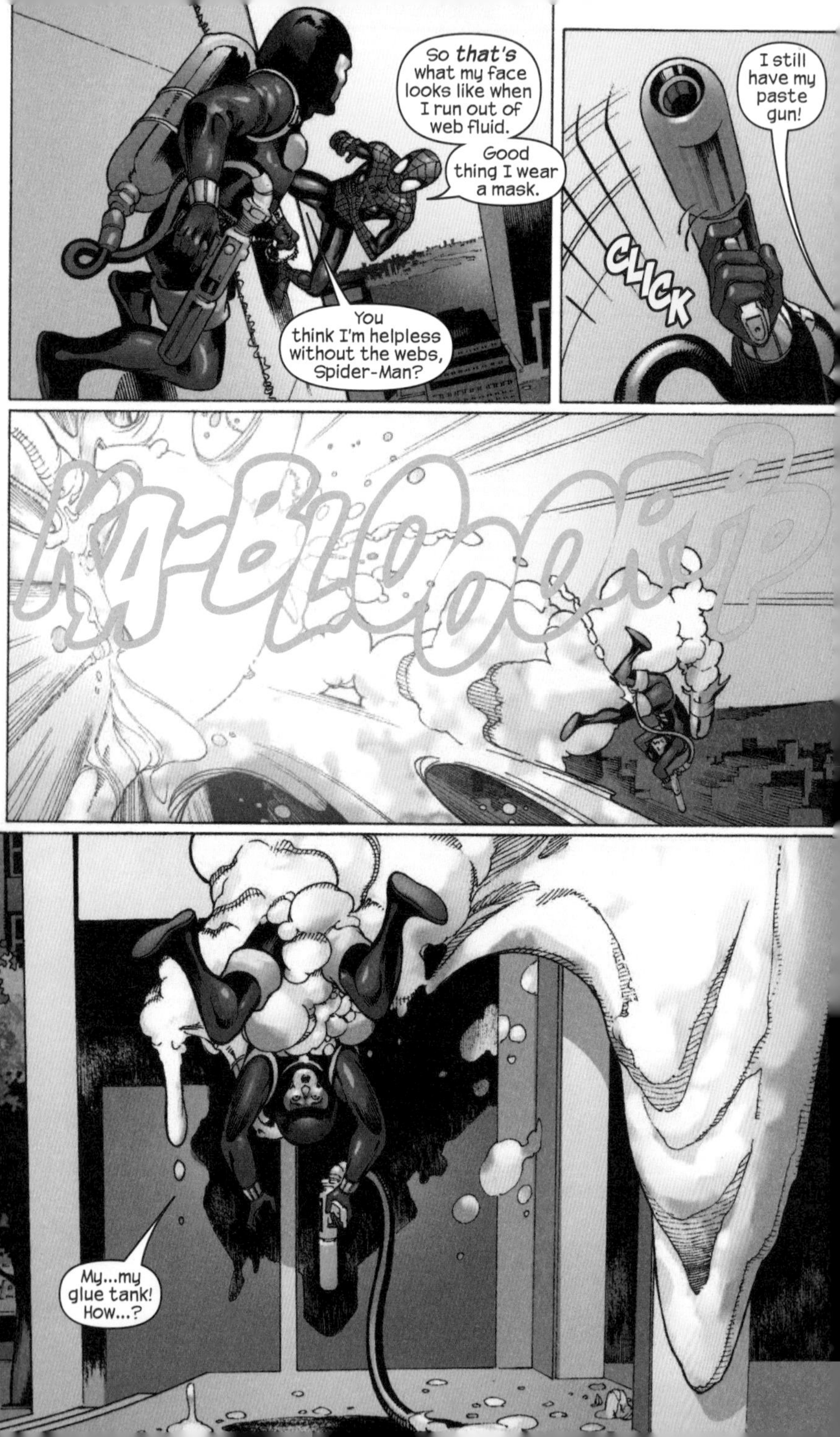
So that's what my face looks like when I run out of web fluid.
Good thing I wear a mask.
You think I'm helpless without the webs, Spider-Man?
I still have my paste gun!
CLICK
KA-BLOOOOSH
My...my glue tank! How...?

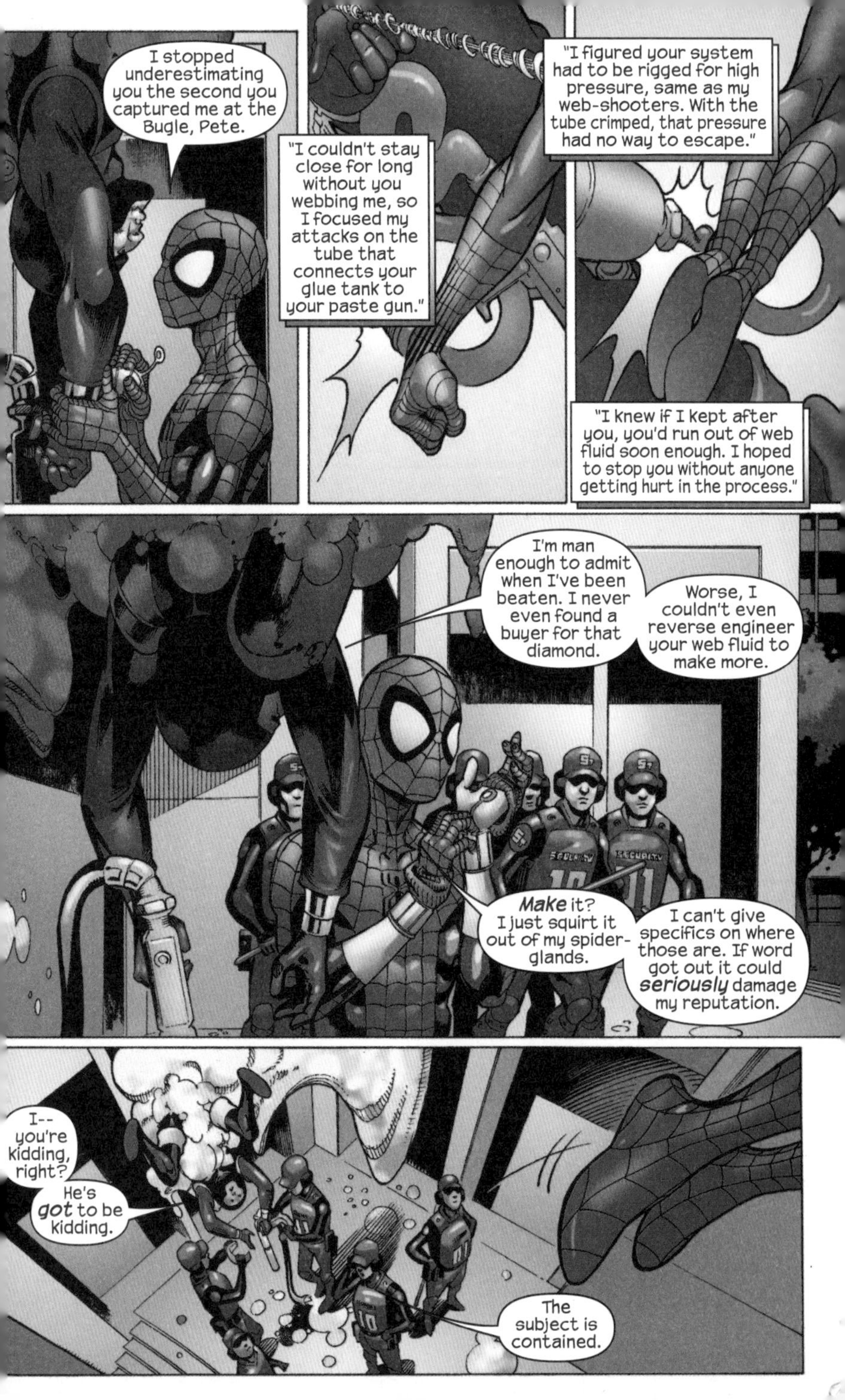
I stopped underestimating you the second you captured me at the Bugle, Pete.
"I couldn't stay close for long without you webbing me, so I focused my attacks on the tube that connects your glue tank to your paste gun."
"I figured your system had to be rigged for high pressure, same as my web-shooters. With the tube crimped, that pressure had no way to escape."
"I knew if I kept after you, you'd run out of web fluid soon enough. I hoped to stop you without anyone getting hurt in the process."
I'm man enough to admit when I've been beaten. I never even found a buyer for that diamond.
Worse, I couldn't even reverse engineer your web fluid to make more.
Make it? I just squirt it out of my spider-glands.
I can't give specifics on where those are. If word got out it could *seriously* damage my reputation.
I-- you're kidding, right?
He's *got* to be kidding.
The subject is contained.

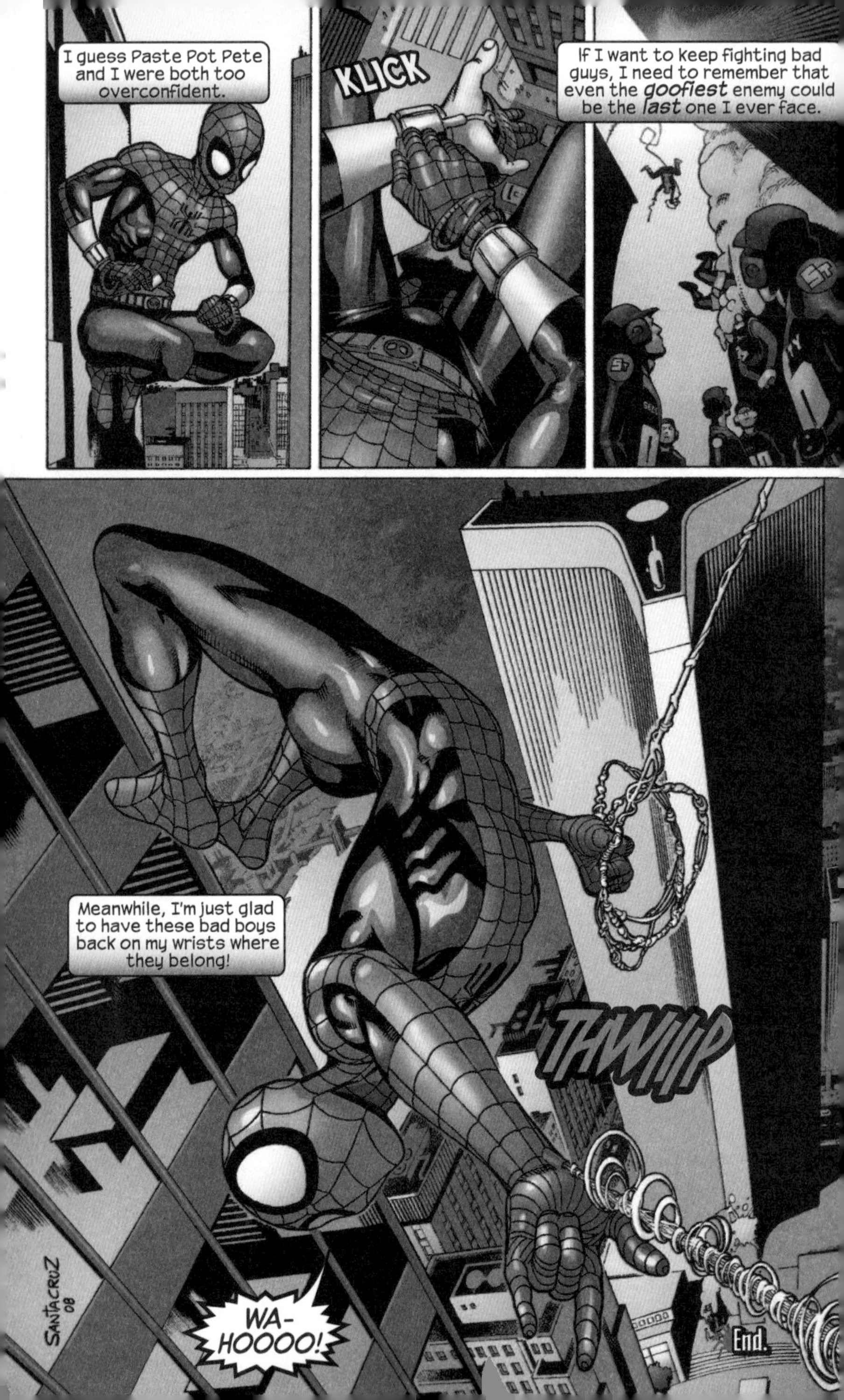
I guess Paste Pot Pete and I were both too overconfident.
KLICK
If I want to keep fighting bad guys, I need to remember that even the goofiest enemy could be the last one I ever face.
Meanwhile, I'm just glad to have these bad boys back on my wrists where they belong!
THWIIP
WA-HOOOO!
SANTACRUZ 08
End.

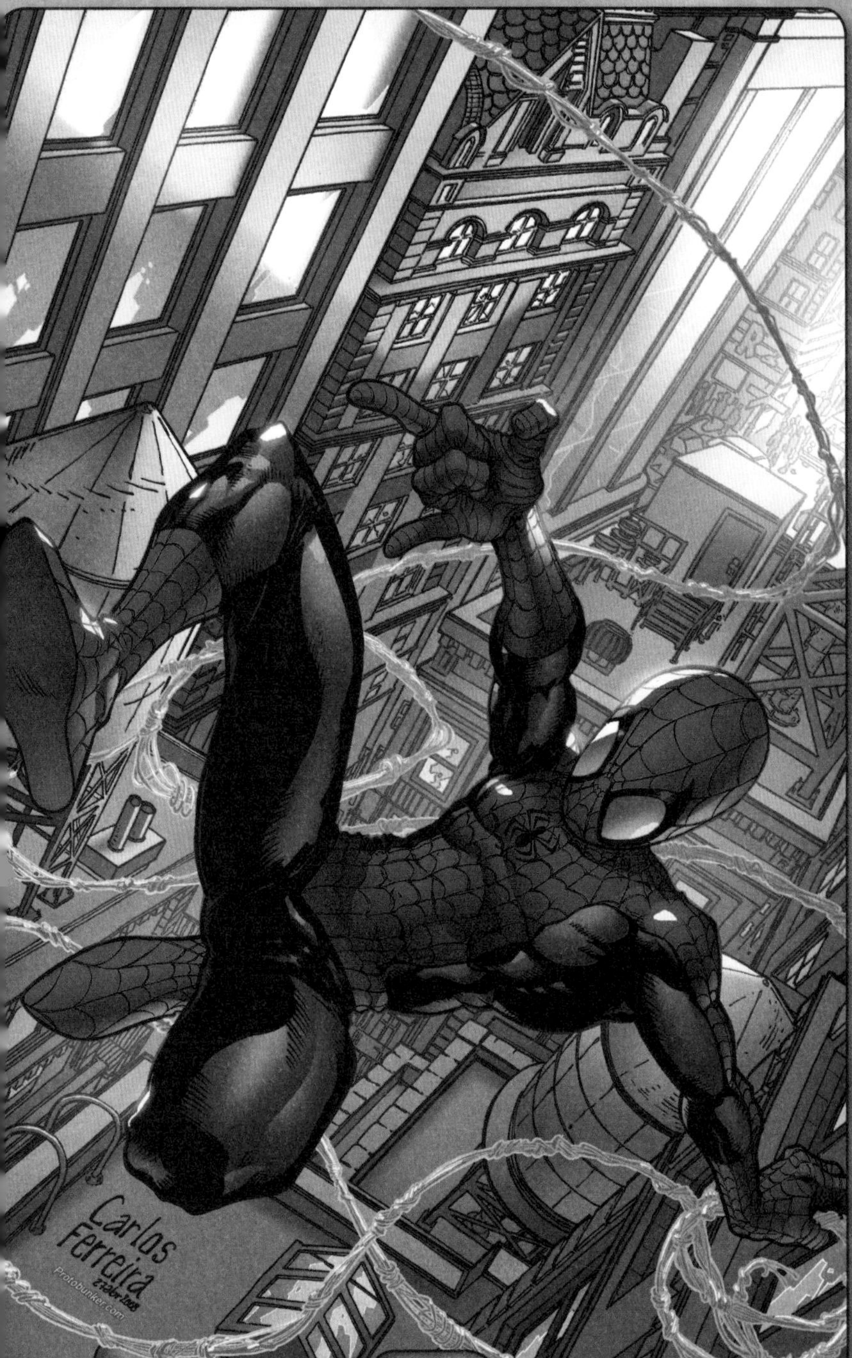
Carlos Ferreira
Protobunker.com
#52

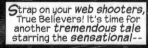

Strap on your *web shooters*, True Believers! It's time for another *tremendous tale* starting the *sensational*--

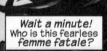

Wait a minute! Who is this fearless *femme fatale*?

Is she *friend* or *foe*?

And, *most importantly*, isn't there some kind of *rule* in the *super hero handbook* about picking *similar codenames*?

Remember, webheads, there's *only one* Amazing Spider-Man. Accept--

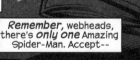

MARC SUMERAK WRITER · SANFORD GREENE PENCILER · NATHAN MASSENGILL INKER · SOTOCOLOR'S A. STREET COLORIST · DAVE SHARPE LETTERER · JOE SABINO PRODUCTION · CARLOS FERREIRA COVER ARTIST · RALPH MACCHIO CONSULTING · NATHAN COSBY EDITOR · JOE QUESADA EDITOR IN CHIEF · DAN BUCKLEY PUBLISHER · ALAN FIN EXECUTIVE PRODUCE

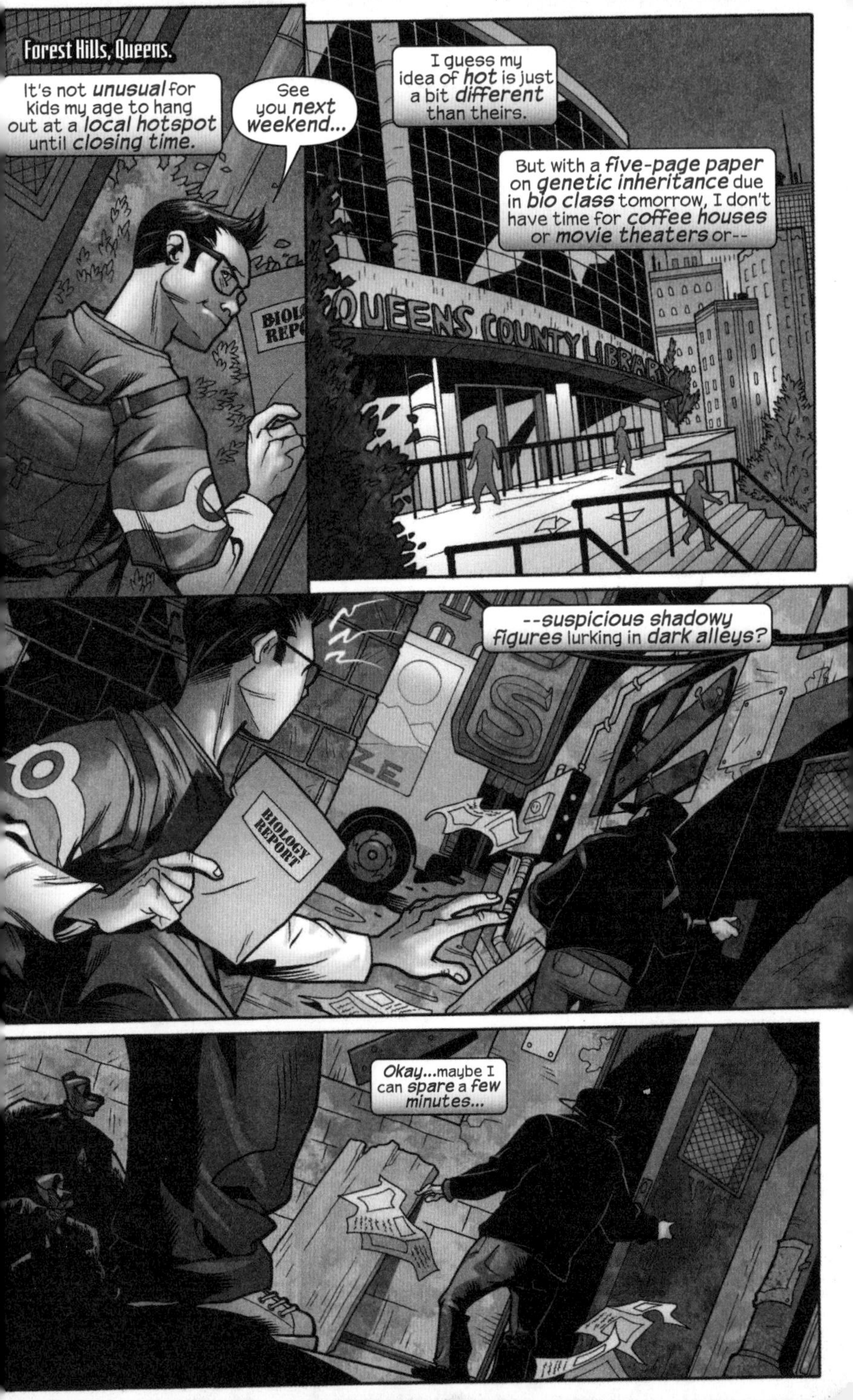
Forest Hills, Queens.
It's not unusual for kids my age to hang out at a local hotspot until closing time.
See you next weekend...
BIOLO REPO
I guess my idea of hot is just a bit different than theirs.
But with a five-page paper on genetic inheritance due in bio class tomorrow, I don't have time for coffee houses or movie theaters or--
QUEENS COUNTY LIBRARY
--suspicious shadowy figures lurking in dark alleys?
BIOLOGY REPORT
Okay...maybe I can spare a few minutes...

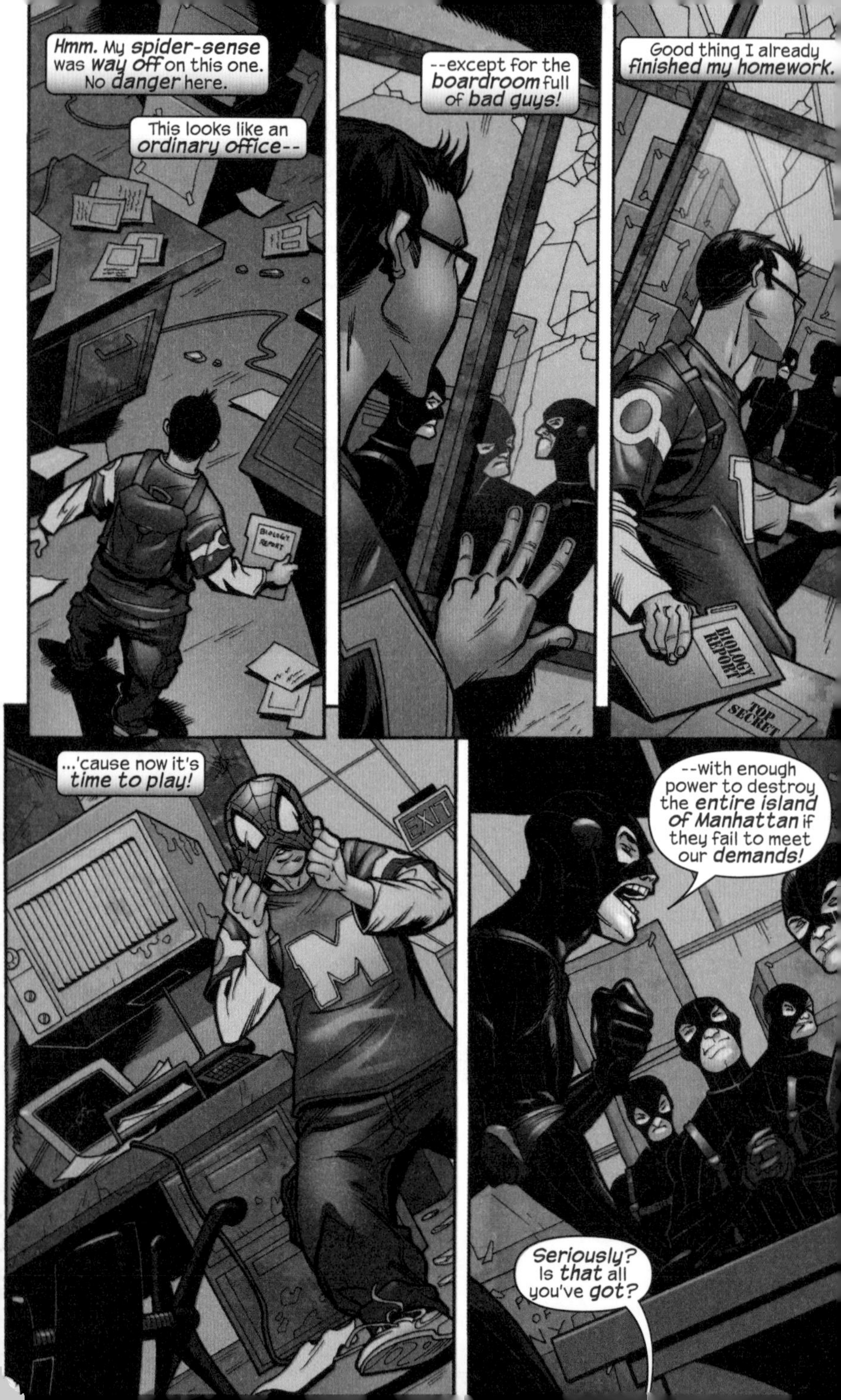
Hmm. My spider-sense was way off on this one. No danger here.
This looks like an ordinary office--
--except for the boardroom full of bad guys!
Good thing I already finished my homework.
BIOLOGY REPORT
TOP SECRET
...'cause now it's time to play!
EXIT
--with enough power to destroy the entire island of Manhattan if they fail to meet our demands!
Seriously? Is that all you've got?

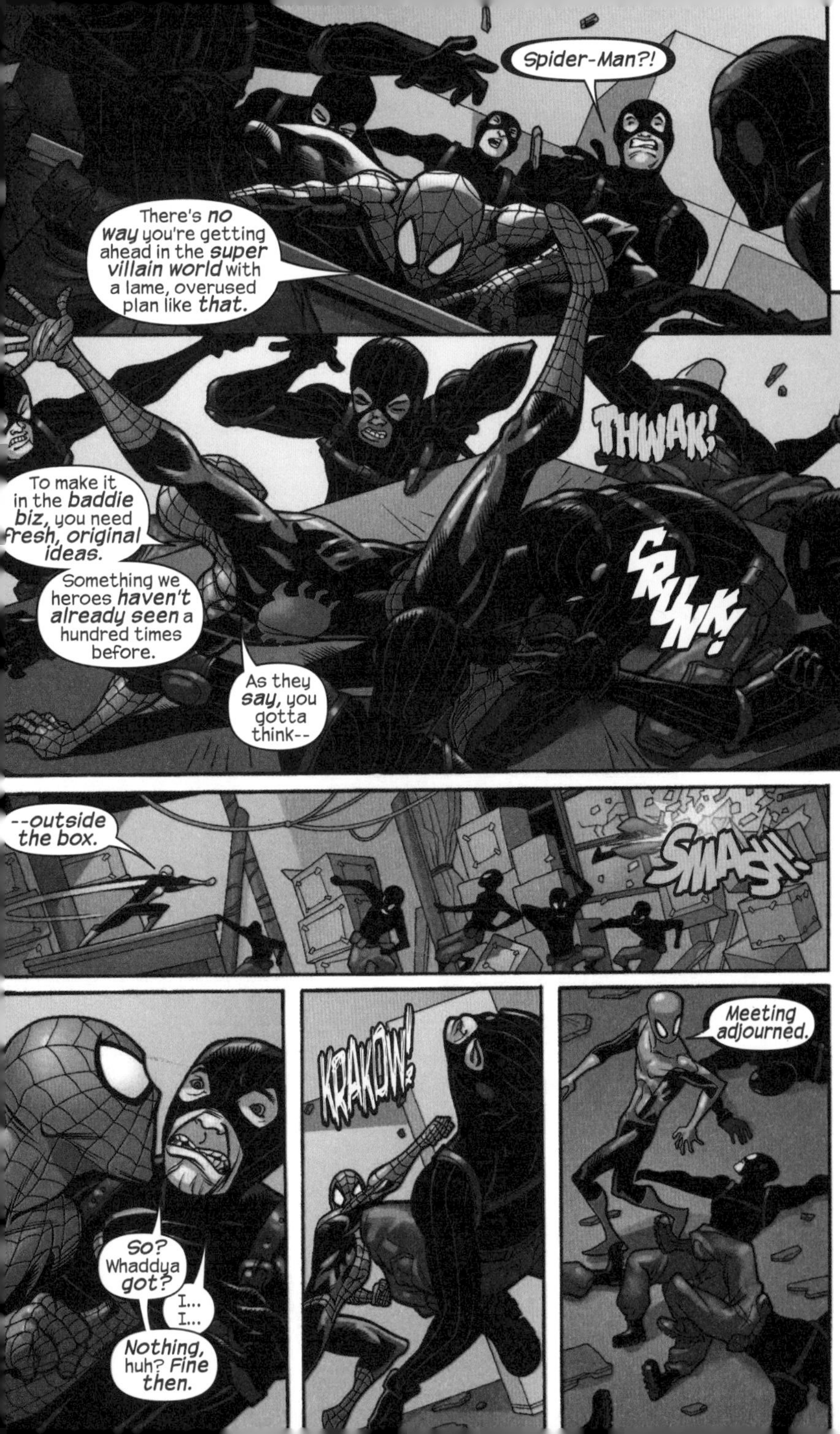

Spider-Man?!
There's no way you're getting ahead in the super villain world with a lame, overused plan like that.
THWAK!
To make it in the baddie biz, you need fresh, original ideas.
Something we heroes haven't already seen a hundred times before.
CRUNK!
As they say, you gotta think--
--outside the box.
SMASH!
So? Whaddya got?
I... I...
Nothing, huh? Fine then.
KRAKOW!
Meeting adjourned.

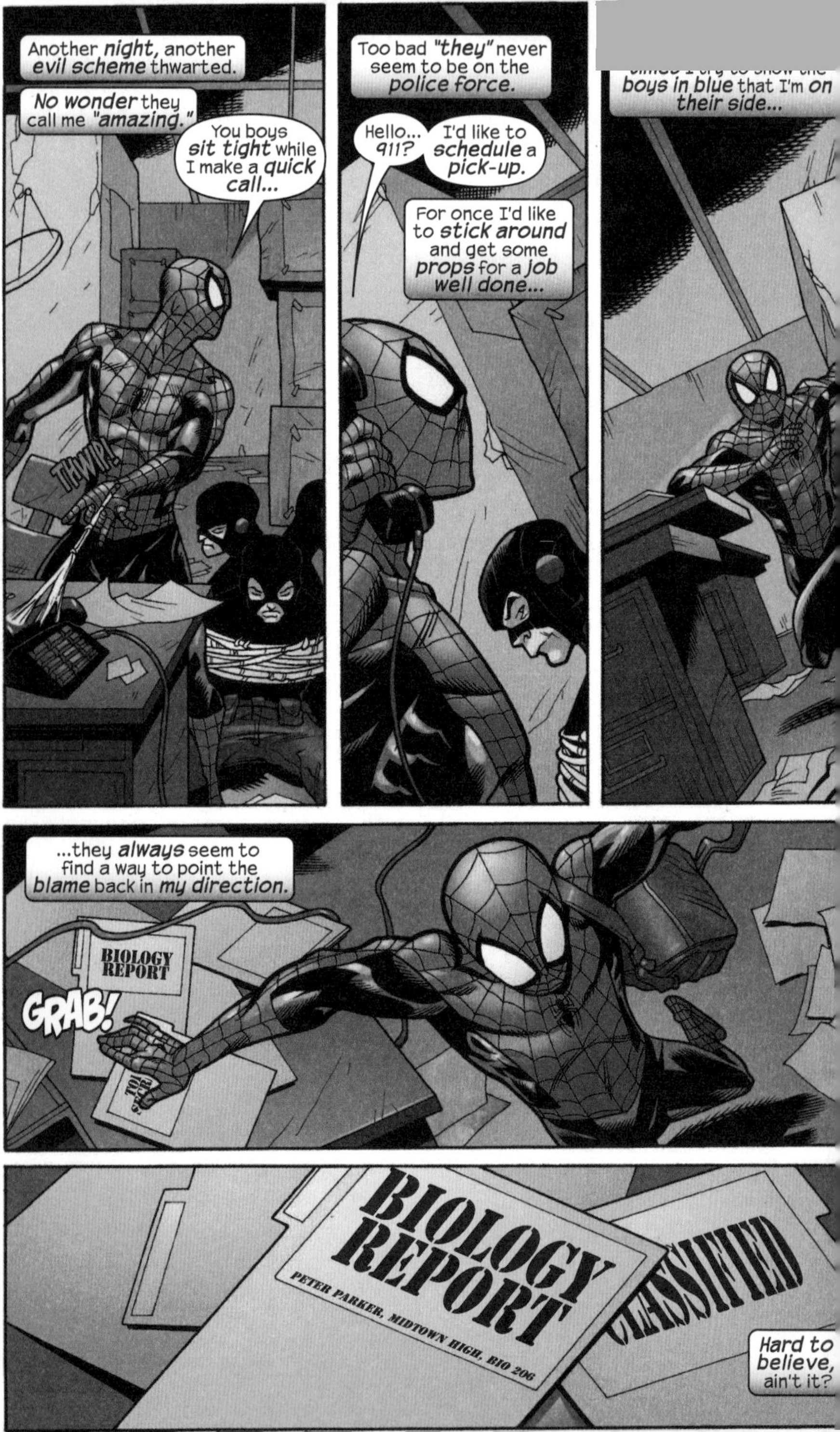

Another night, another evil scheme thwarted.
No wonder they call me "amazing."
You boys sit tight while I make a quick call...
THWIP!
Too bad "they" never seem to be on the police force.
Hello... 911?
I'd like to schedule a pick-up.
For once I'd like to stick around and get some props for a job well done...
boys in blue that I'm on their side...
...they always seem to find a way to point the blame back in my direction.
BIOLOGY REPORT
GRAB!
BIOLOGY REPORT
PETER PARKER, MIDTOWN HIGH, BIO 206
CLASSIFIED
Hard to believe, ain't it?

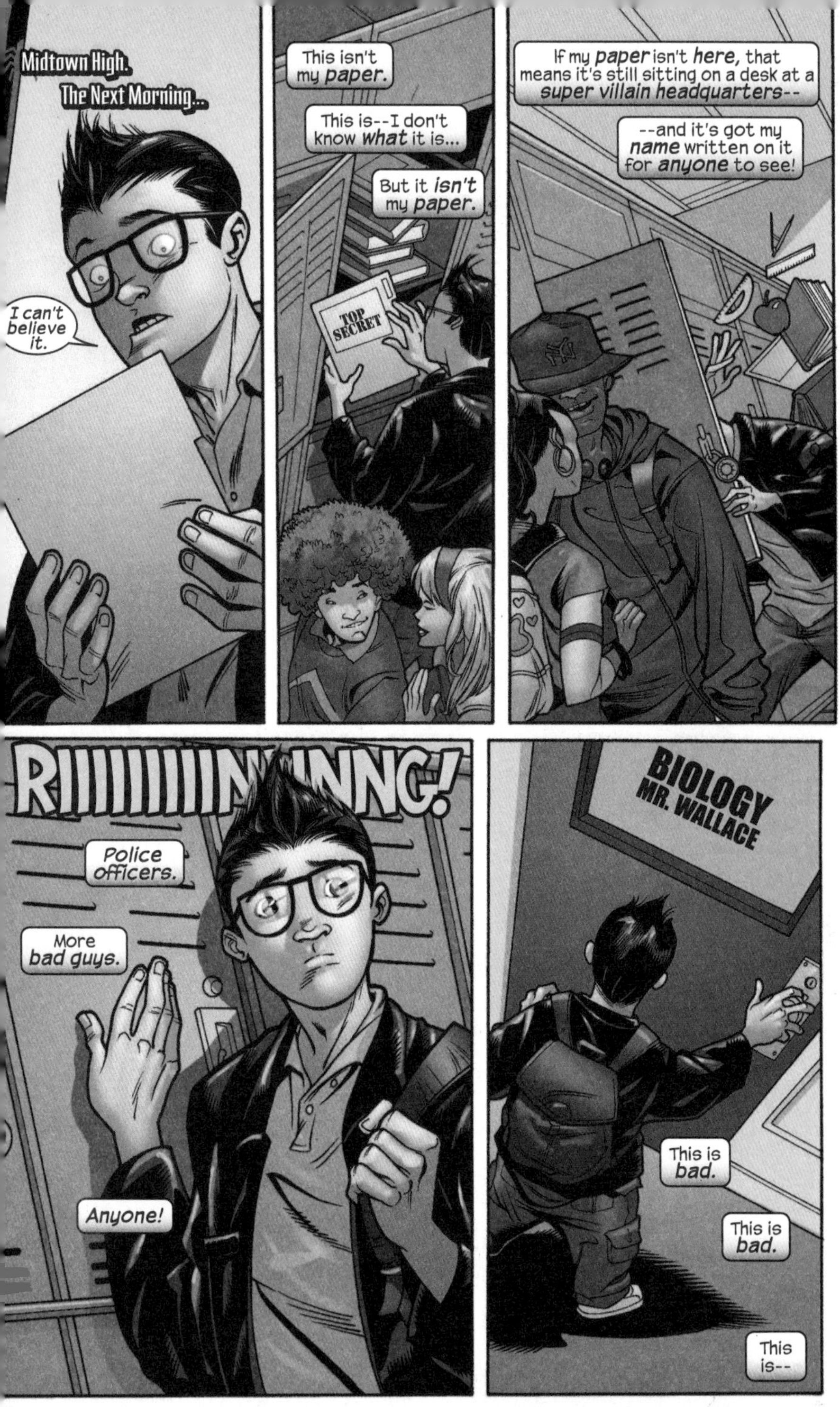
Midtown High.
The Next Morning...
I can't believe it.
This isn't my paper.
This is--I don't know what it is...
But it isn't my paper.
TOP SECRET
If my paper isn't here, that means it's still sitting on a desk at a super villain headquarters--
--and it's got my name written on it for anyone to see!
RIIIIIIIIINNNNG!
Police officers.
More bad guys.
Anyone!
BIOLOGY
MR. WALLACE
This is bad.
This is bad.
This is--

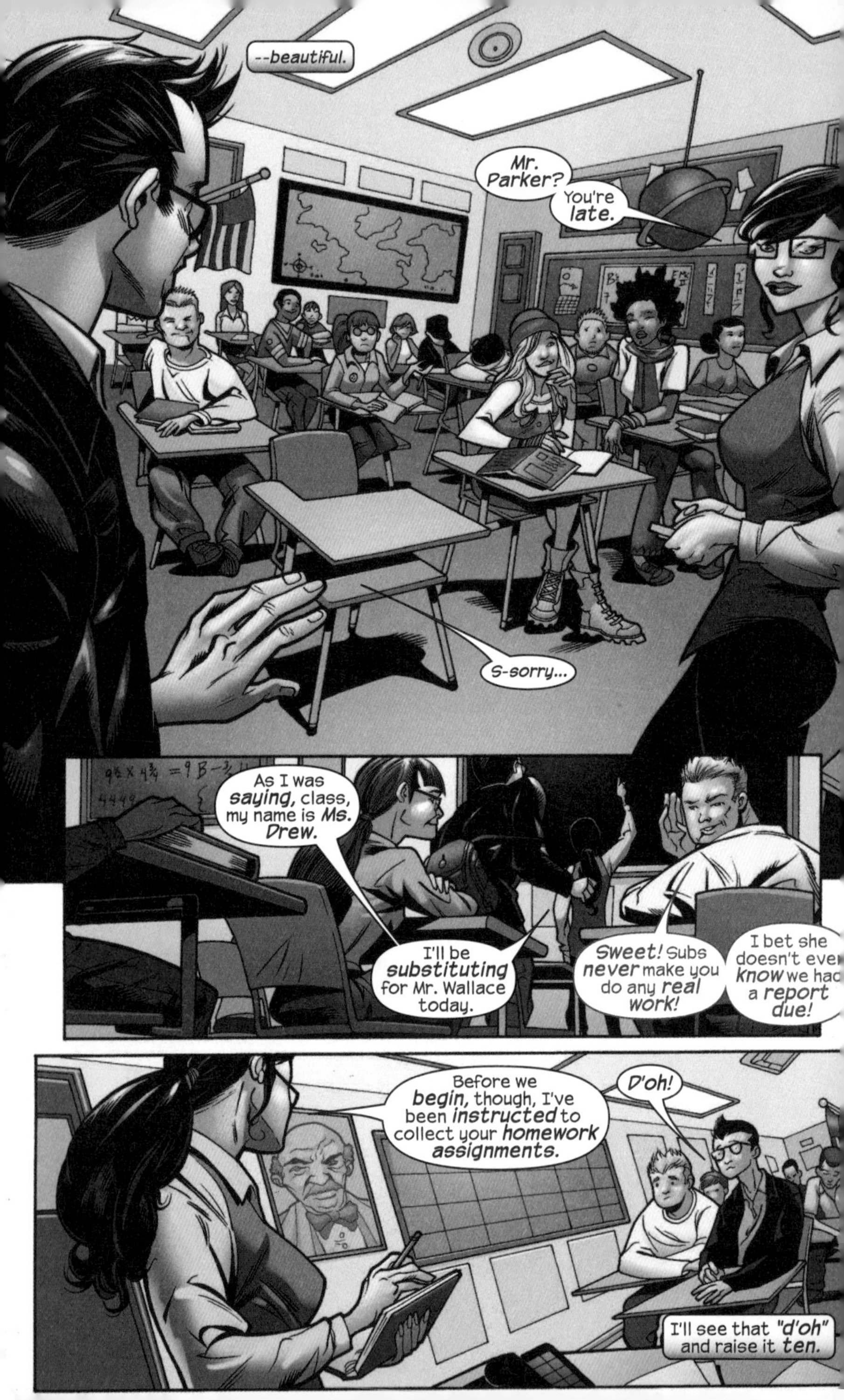
--beautiful.
Mr. Parker?
You're late.
S-sorry...
As I was saying, class, my name is Ms. Drew.
I'll be substituting for Mr. Wallace today.
Sweet! Subs never make you do any real work!
I bet she doesn't even know we had a report due!
Before we begin, though, I've been instructed to collect your homework assignments.
D'oh!
I'll see that "d'oh" and raise it ten.

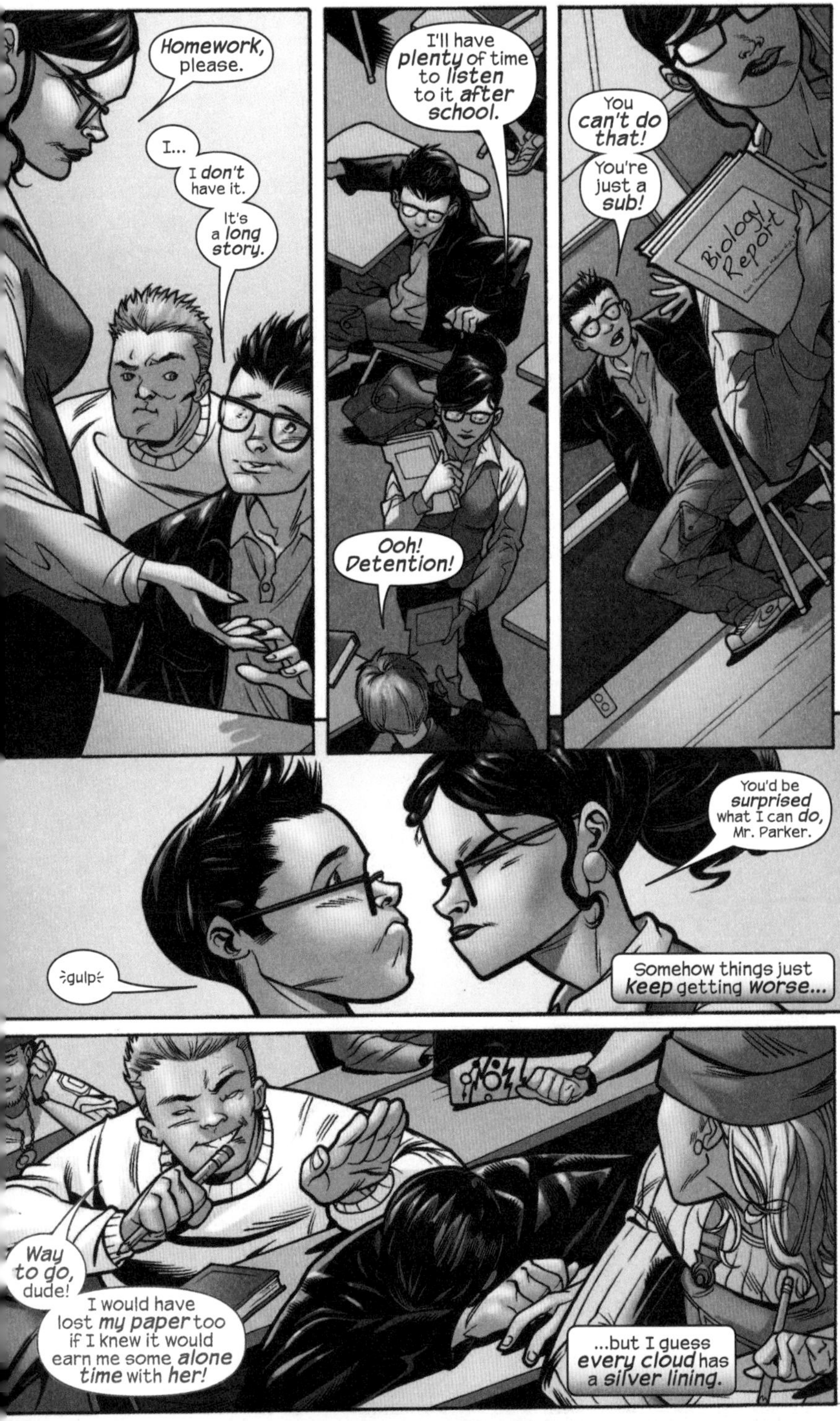
Homework, please.
I...
I don't have it.
It's a long story.
I'll have plenty of time to listen to it after school.
Ooh! Detention!
You can't do that!
You're just a sub!
Biology Report
You'd be surprised what I can do, Mr. Parker.
gulp
Somehow things just keep getting worse...
Way to go, dude!
I would have lost my paper too if I knew it would earn me some alone time with her!
...but I guess every cloud has a silver lining.

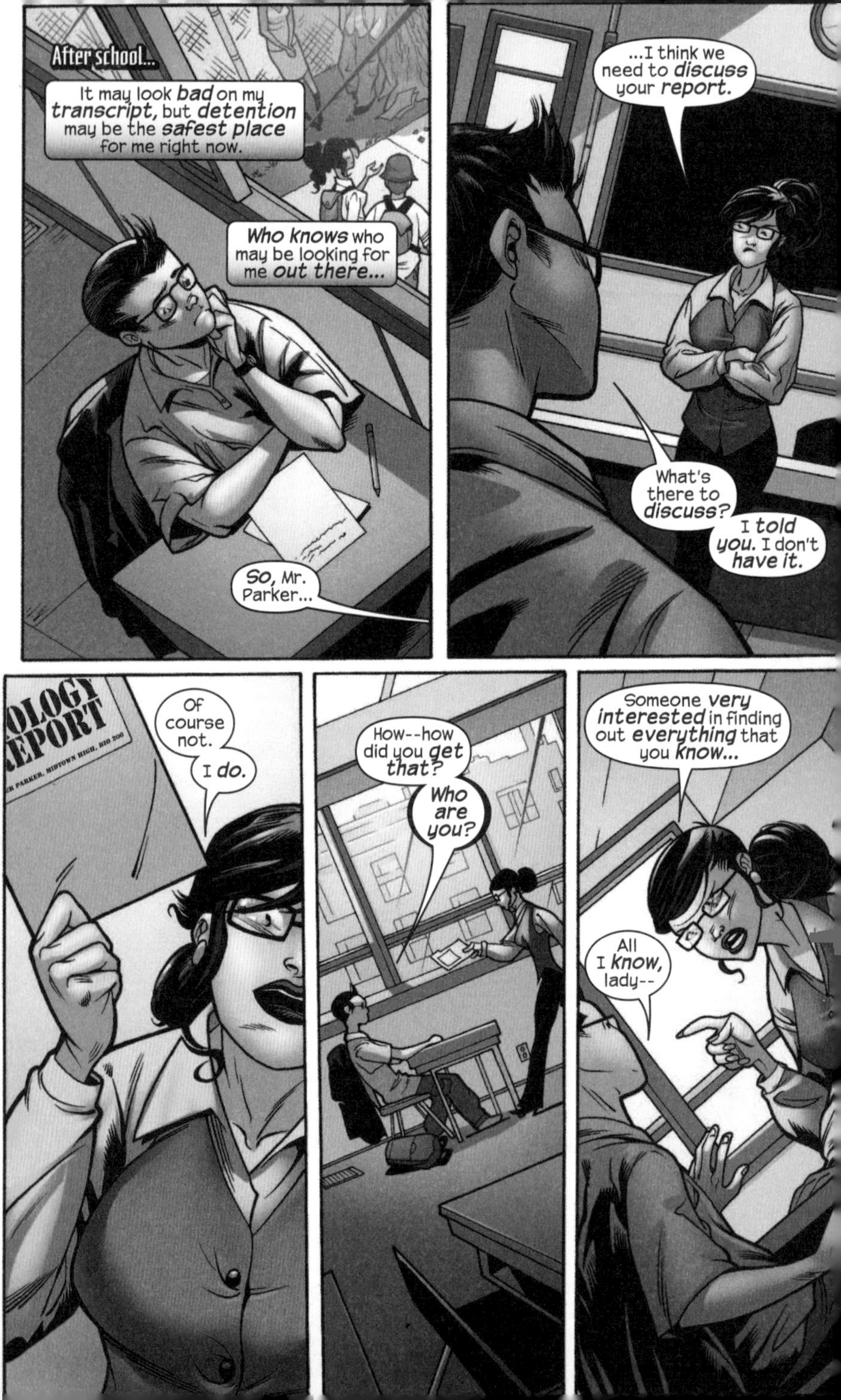
After school...
It may look bad on my transcript, but detention may be the safest place for me right now.
Who knows who may be looking for me out there...
So, Mr. Parker...
...I think we need to discuss your report.
What's there to discuss?
I told you. I don't have it.
Of course not.
I do.
How--how did you get that?
Who are you?
Someone very interested in finding out everything that you know...
All I know, lady--

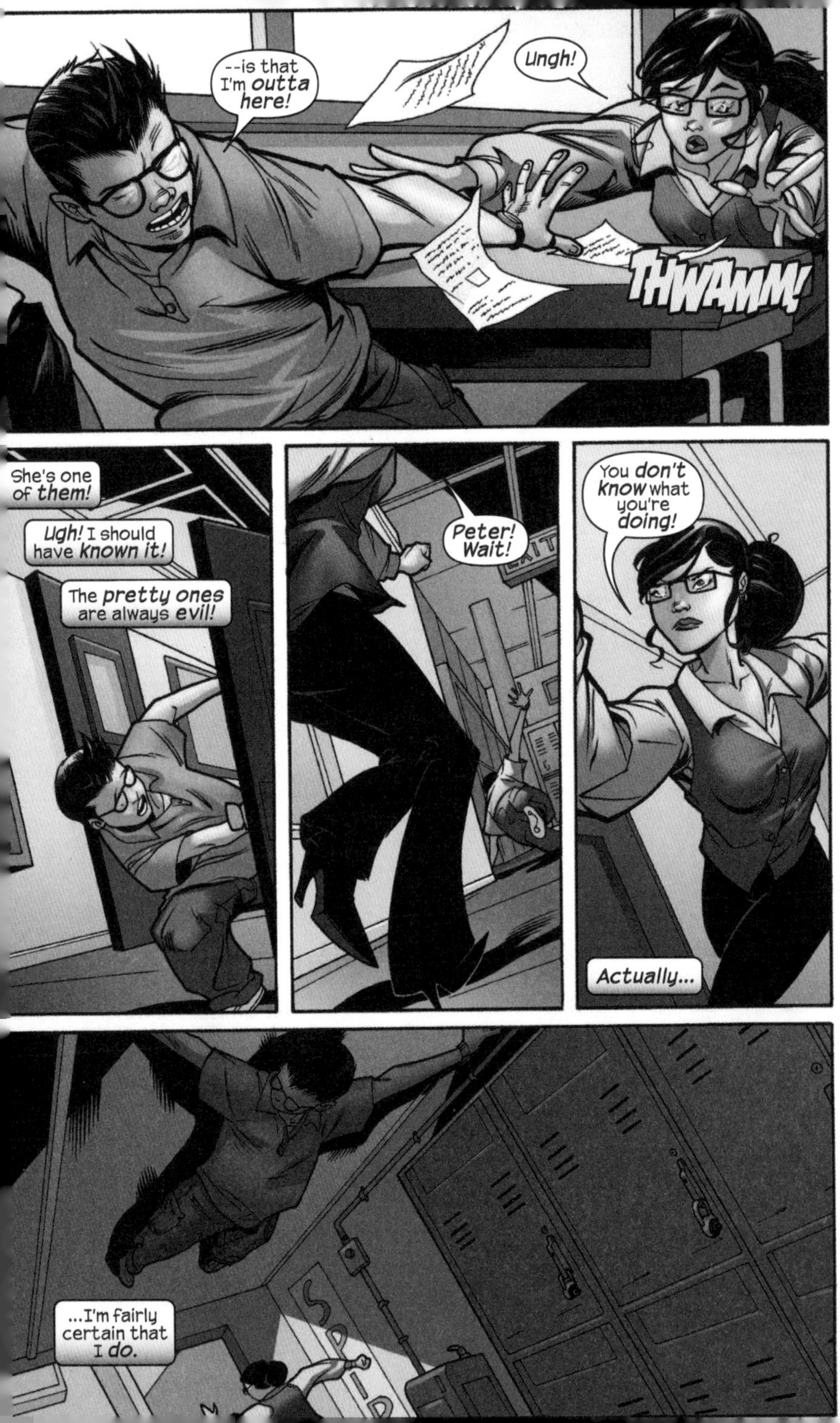
--is that I'm outta here!
Ungh!
THWAMM!
She's one of them!
Ugh! I should have known it!
The pretty ones are always evil!
Peter! Wait!
You don't know what you're doing!
Actually...
...I'm fairly certain that I do.

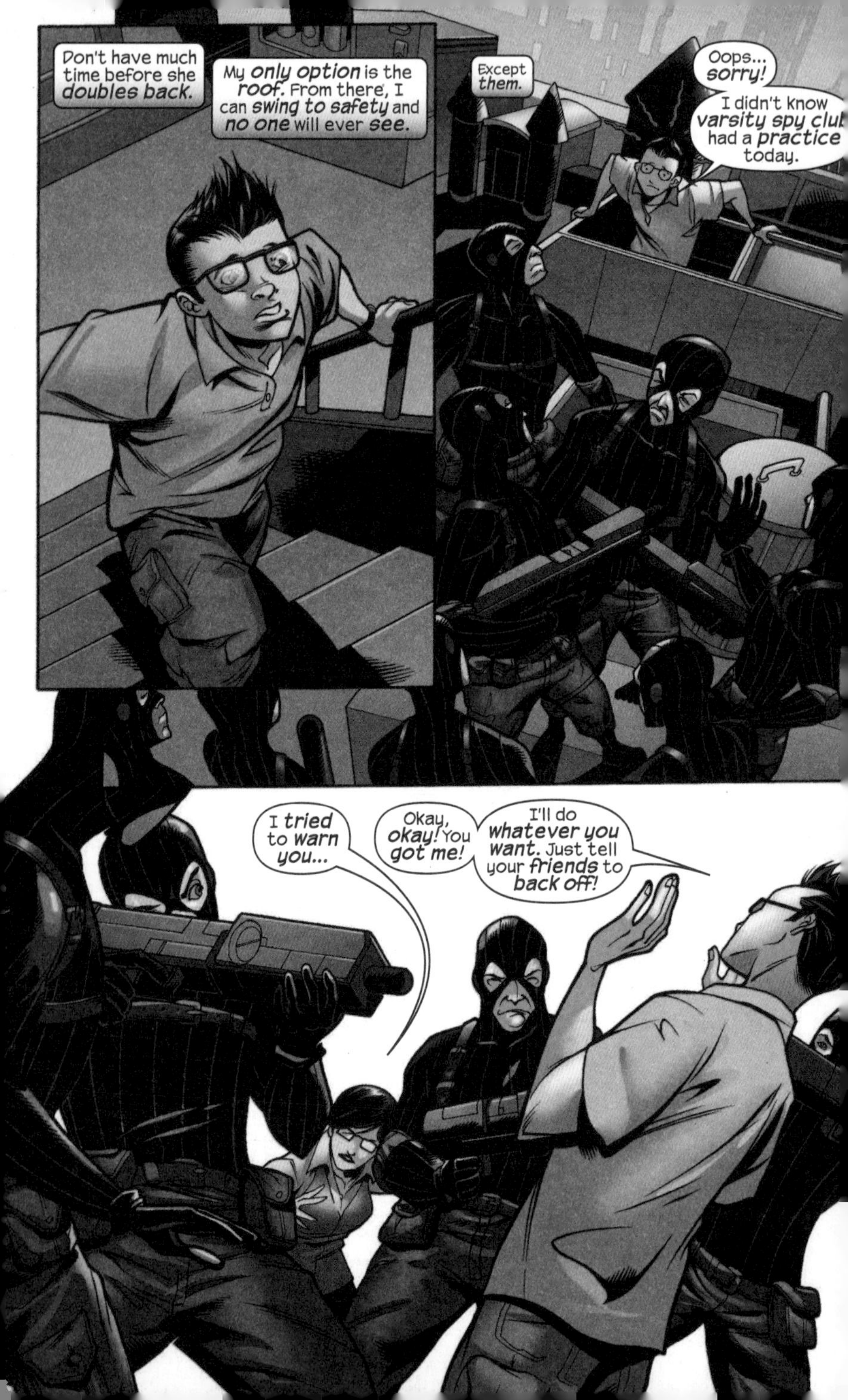
Don't have much time before she doubles back.
My only option is the roof. From there, I can swing to safety and no one will ever see.
Except them.
Oops... sorry!
I didn't know varsity spy club had a practice today.
I tried to warn you...
Okay, okay! You got me!
I'll do whatever you want. Just tell your friends to back off!

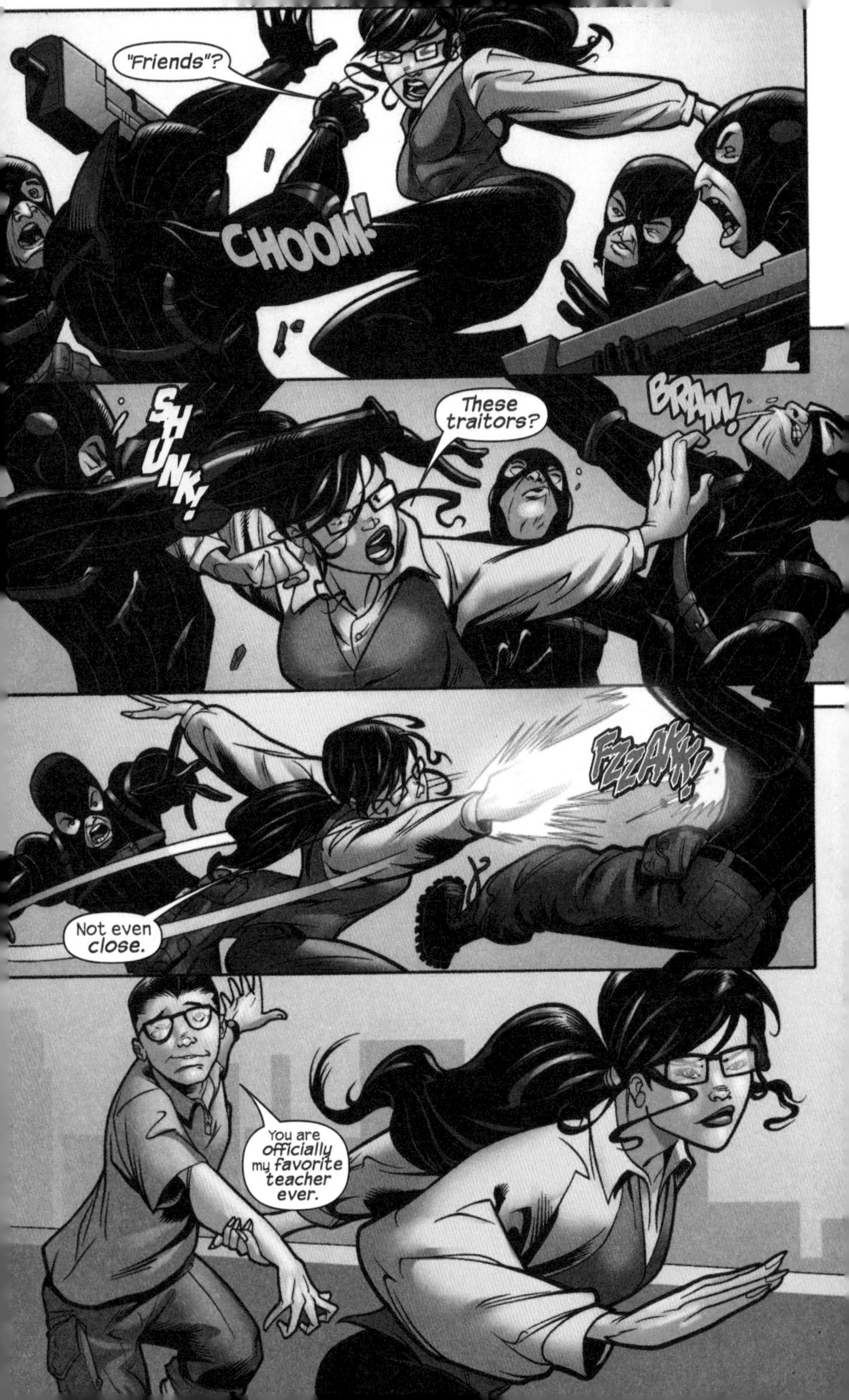
"Friends"?
CHOOM!
SHUNK!
These traitors?
BRAM!
FZZAKK!
Not even close.
You are officially my favorite teacher ever.

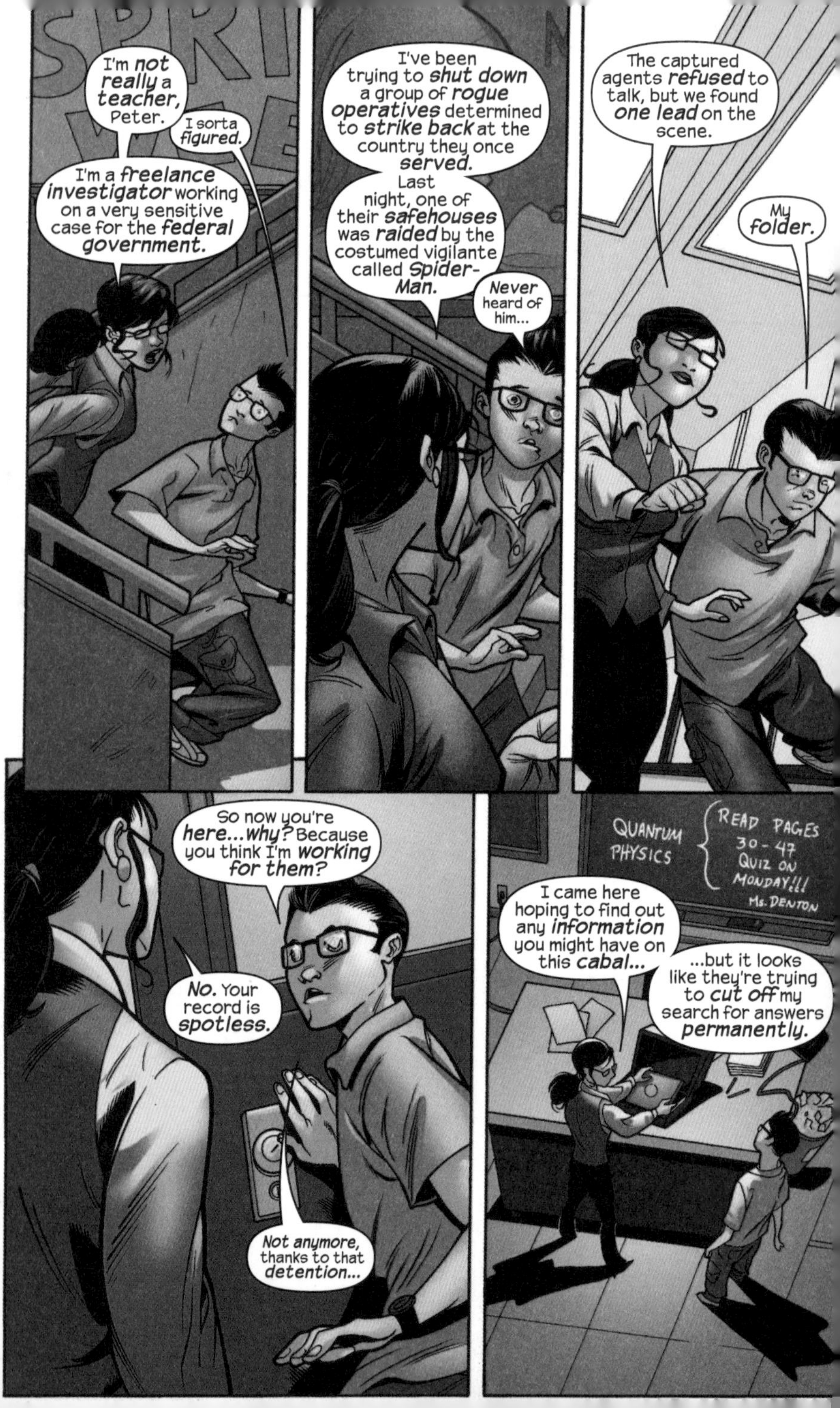
I'm not really a teacher, Peter.
I sorta figured.
I'm a freelance investigator working on a very sensitive case for the federal government.
I've been trying to shut down a group of rogue operatives determined to strike back at the country they once served.
Last night, one of their safehouses was raided by the costumed vigilante called Spider-Man.
Never heard of him...
The captured agents refused to talk, but we found one lead on the scene.
My folder.
So now you're here...why? Because you think I'm working for them?
No. Your record is spotless.
Not anymore, thanks to that detention...
QUANTUM PHYSICS
READ PAGES 30 - 47
QUIZ ON MONDAY!!!
Ms. DENTON
I came here hoping to find out any information you might have on this cabal...
...but it looks like they're trying to cut off my search for answers permanently.

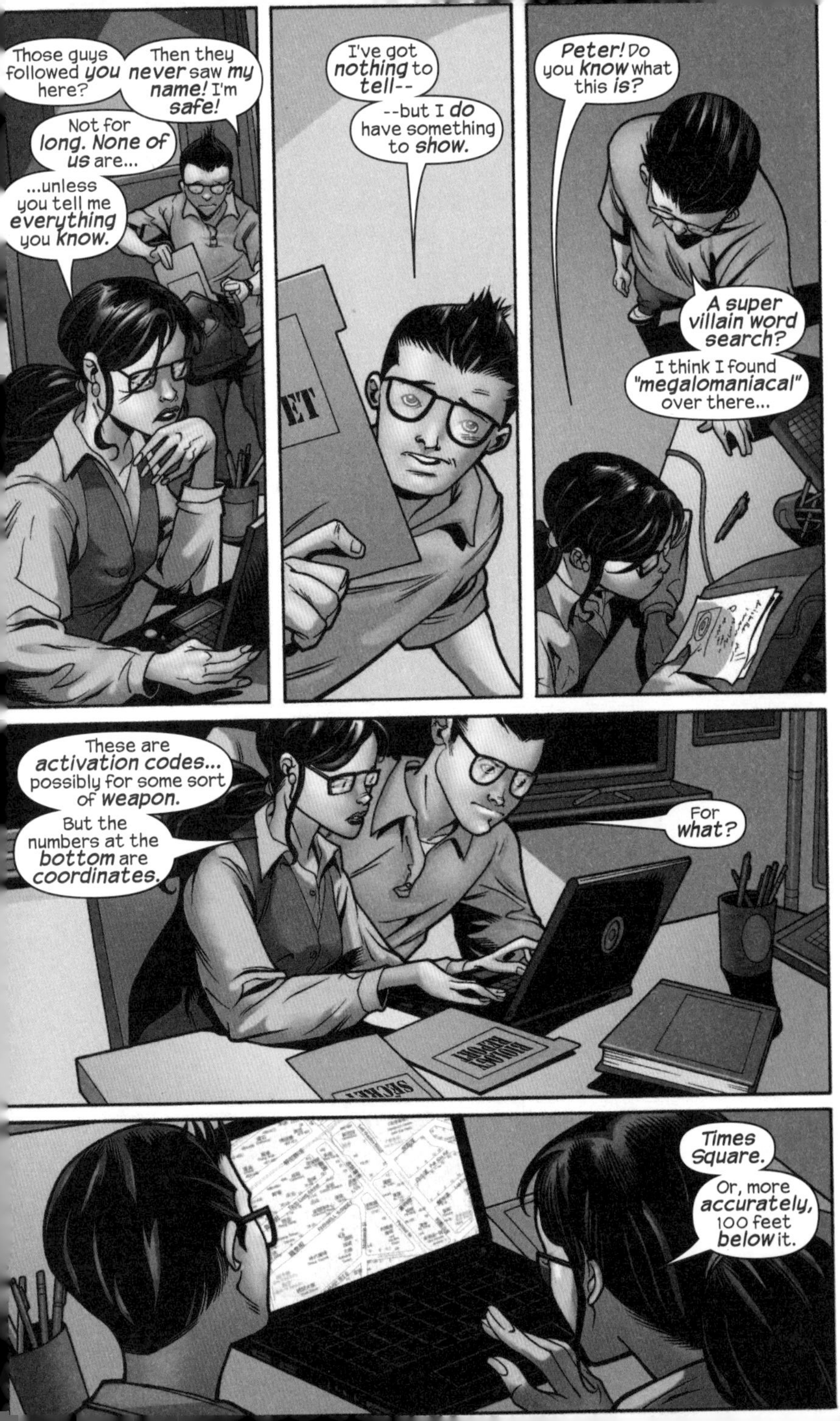
Those guys followed you here?
Then they never saw my name! I'm safe!
Not for long. None of us are...
...unless you tell me everything you know.
I've got nothing to tell--
--but I do have something to show.
Peter! Do you know what this is?
A super villain word search?
I think I found "megalomaniacal" over there...
These are activation codes... possibly for some sort of weapon.
But the numbers at the bottom are coordinates.
For what?
Times Square.
Or, more accurately, 100 feet below it.

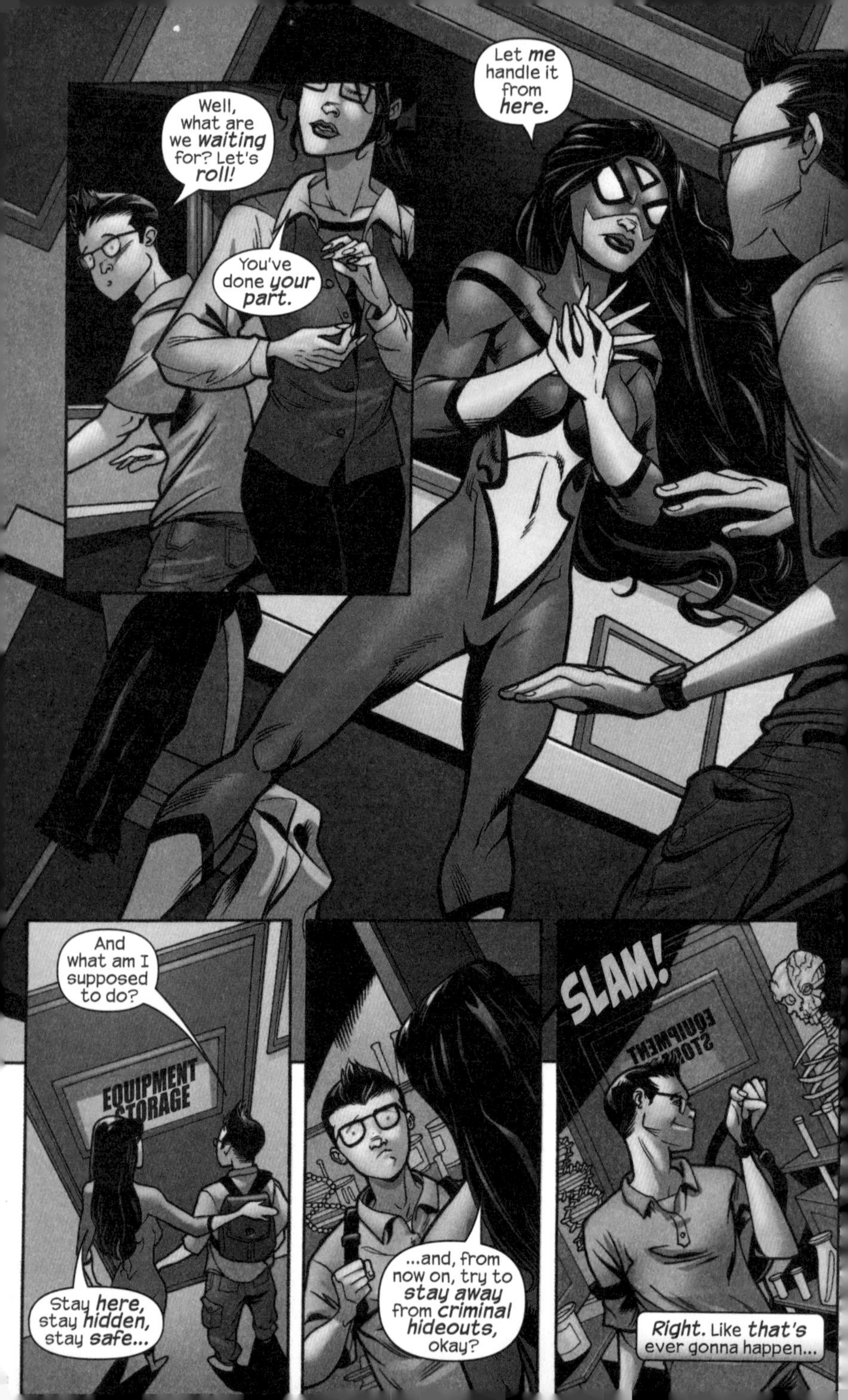
Well, what are we waiting for? Let's roll!
You've done your part.
Let me handle it from here.
And what am I supposed to do?
EQUIPMENT STORAGE
Stay here, stay hidden, stay safe...
...and, from now on, try to stay away from criminal hideouts, okay?
SLAM!
Right. Like that's ever gonna happen...

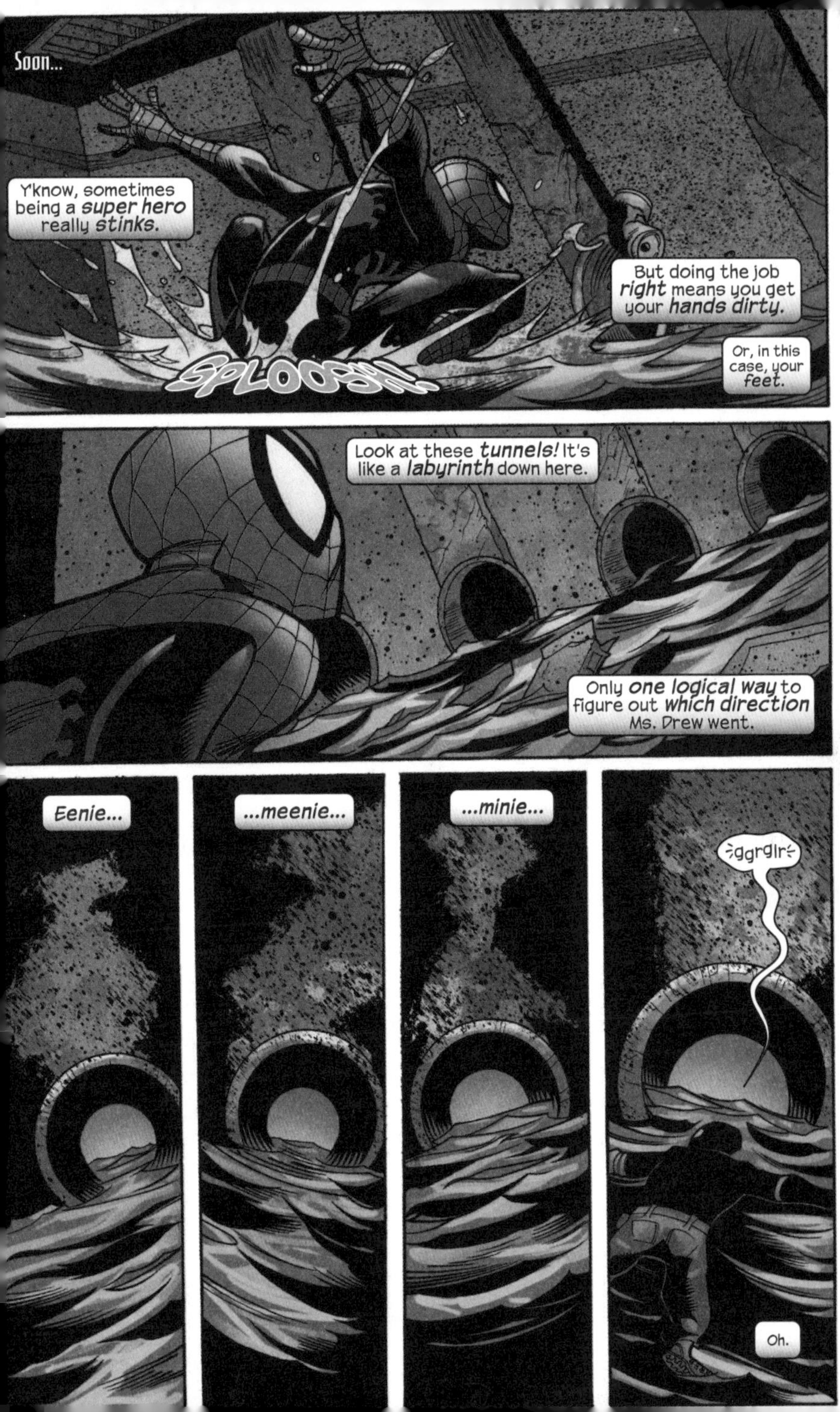
Soon...
Y'know, sometimes being a super hero really stinks.
SPLOOSH!
But doing the job right means you get your hands dirty.
Or, in this case, your feet.
Look at these tunnels! It's like a labyrinth down here.
Only one logical way to figure out which direction Ms. Drew went.
Eenie...
...meenie...
...minie...
ggrglr
Oh.

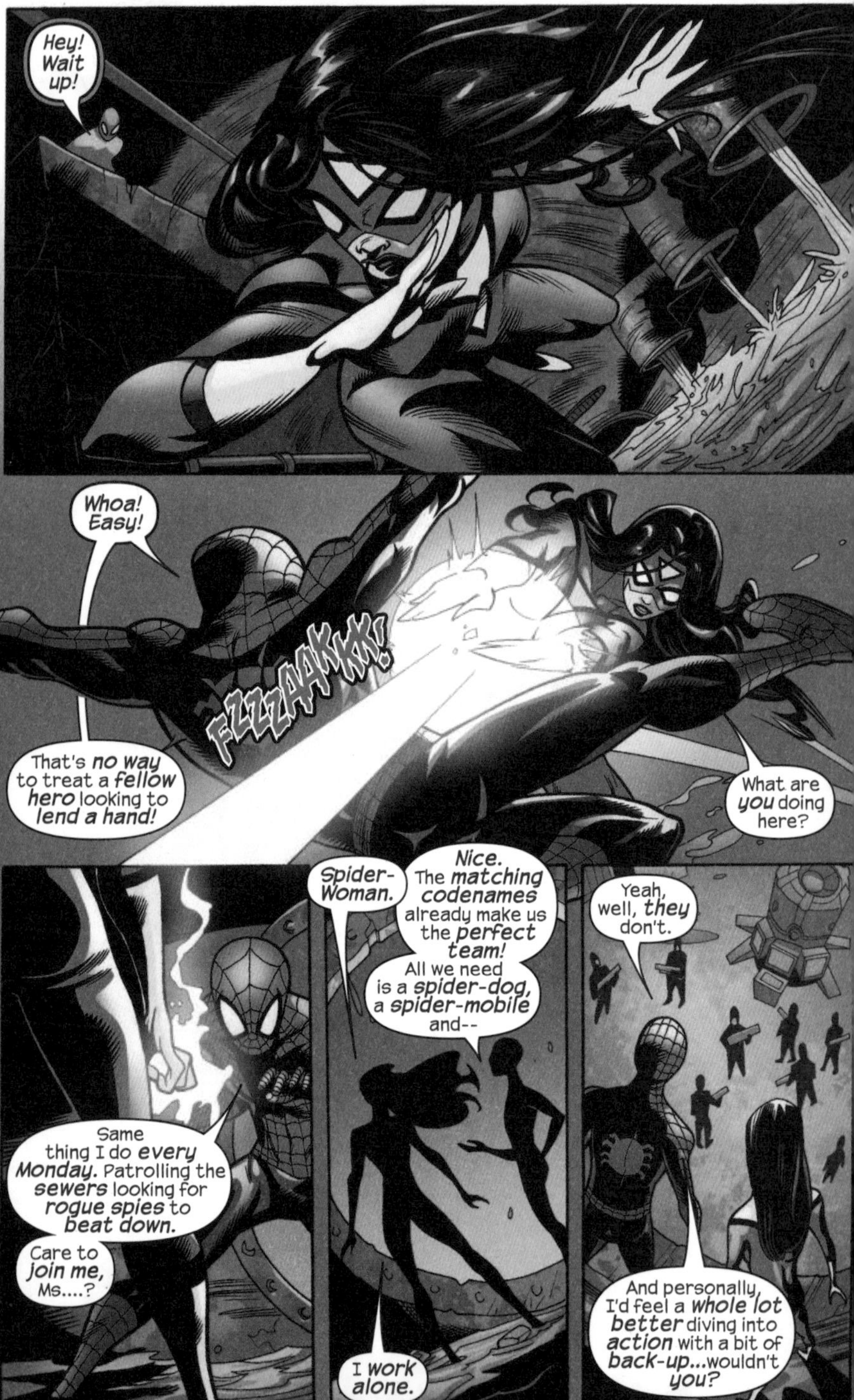

Hey! Wait up!
Whoa! Easy!
FZZZAAKKK!
That's no way to treat a fellow hero looking to lend a hand!
What are you doing here?
Same thing I do every Monday. Patrolling the sewers looking for rogue spies to beat down.
Care to join me, Ms....?
Spider-Woman.
Nice. The matching codenames already make us the perfect team!
All we need is a spider-dog, a spider-mobile and--
I work alone.
Yeah, well, they don't.
And personally, I'd feel a whole lot better diving into action with a bit of back-up...wouldn't you?

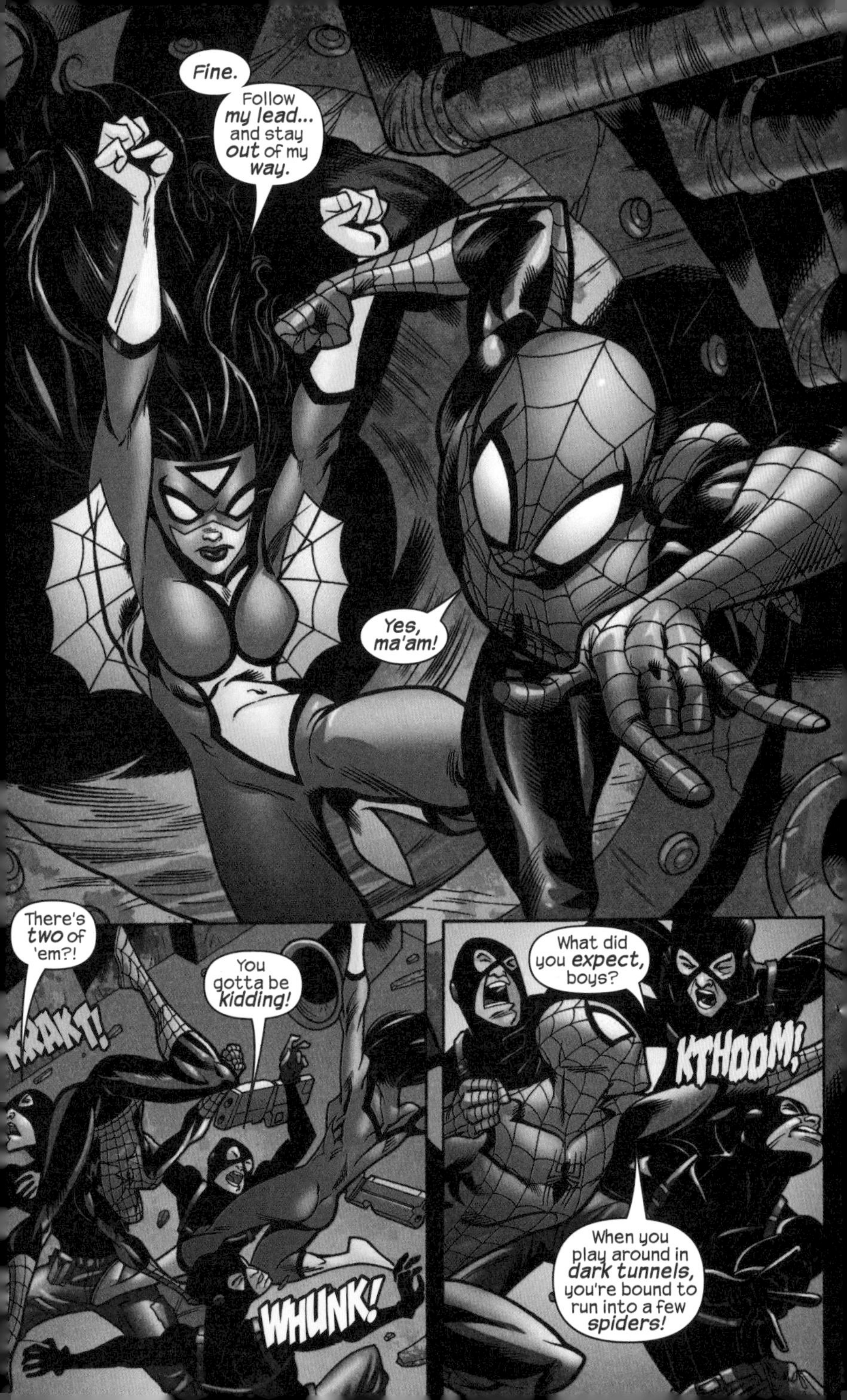
Fine.
Follow my lead... and stay out of my way.
Yes, ma'am!
There's two of 'em?!
KRAKT!
You gotta be kidding!
WHUNK!
What did you expect, boys?
KTHOOM!
When you play around in dark tunnels, you're bound to run into a few spiders!

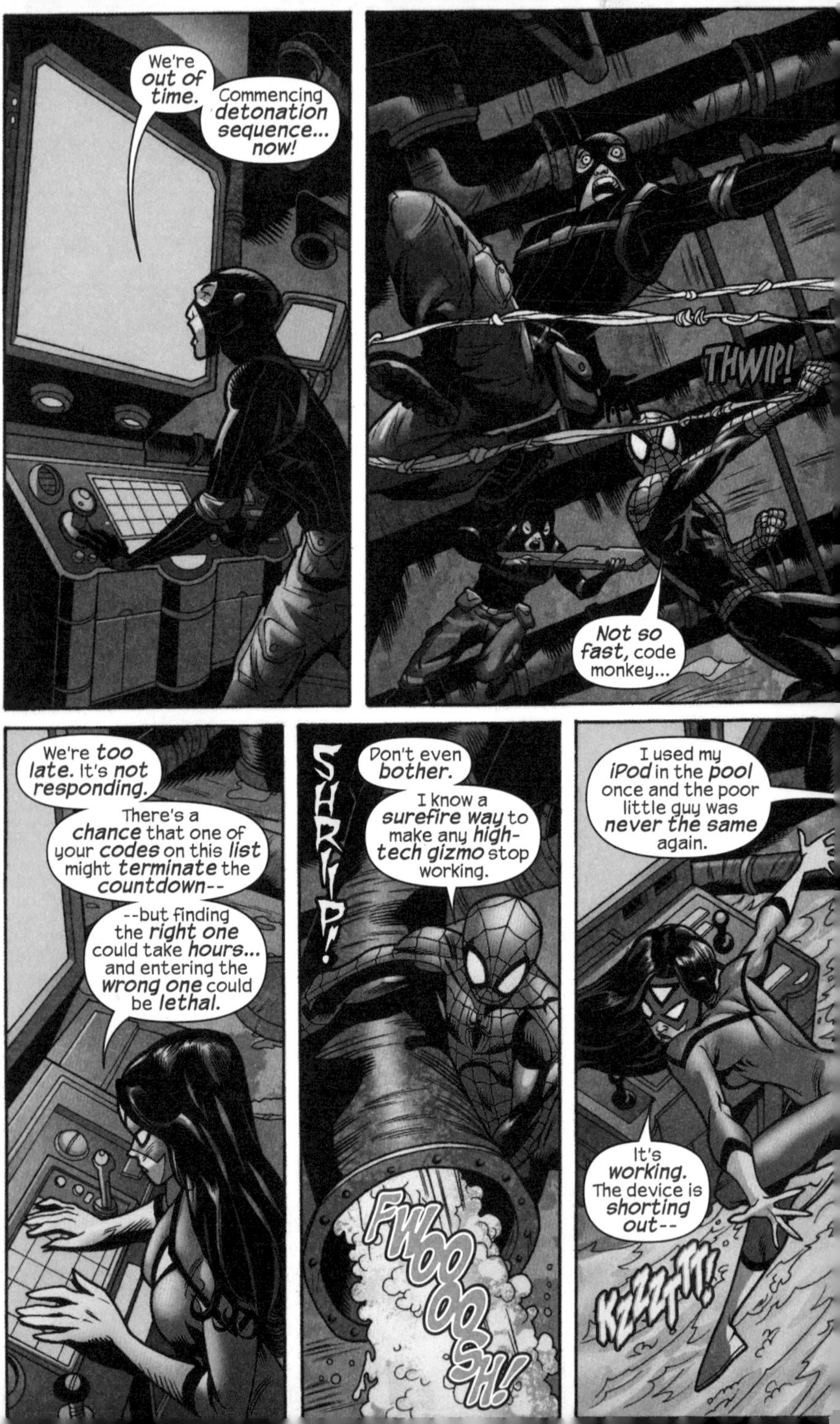
We're out of time.
Commencing detonation sequence... now!
THWIP!
Not so fast, code monkey...
We're too late. It's not responding.
There's a chance that one of your codes on this list might terminate the countdown--
--but finding the right one could take hours... and entering the wrong one could be lethal.
SHRIIP!
Don't even bother.
I know a surefire way to make any high-tech gizmo stop working.
FWOOOOSH!
I used my iPod in the pool once and the poor little guy was never the same again.
It's working. The device is shorting out--
KZZZTTT!

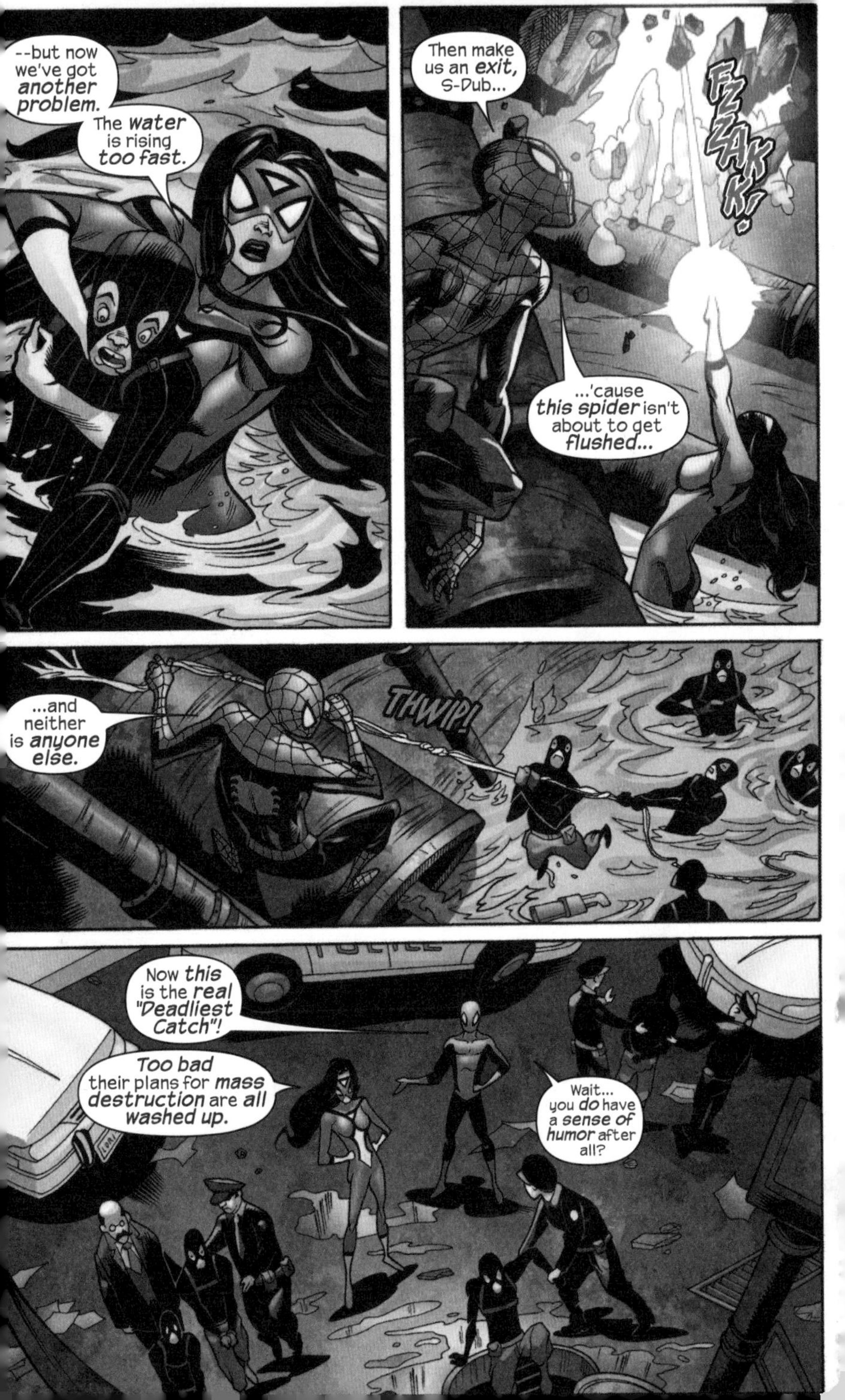
--but now we've got another problem.
The water is rising too fast.
Then make us an exit, S-Dub...
FZZAKK!
...'cause this spider isn't about to get flushed...
...and neither is anyone else.
THWIP!
Now this is the real "Deadliest Catch"!
Too bad their plans for mass destruction are all washed up.
Wait... you do have a sense of humor after all?

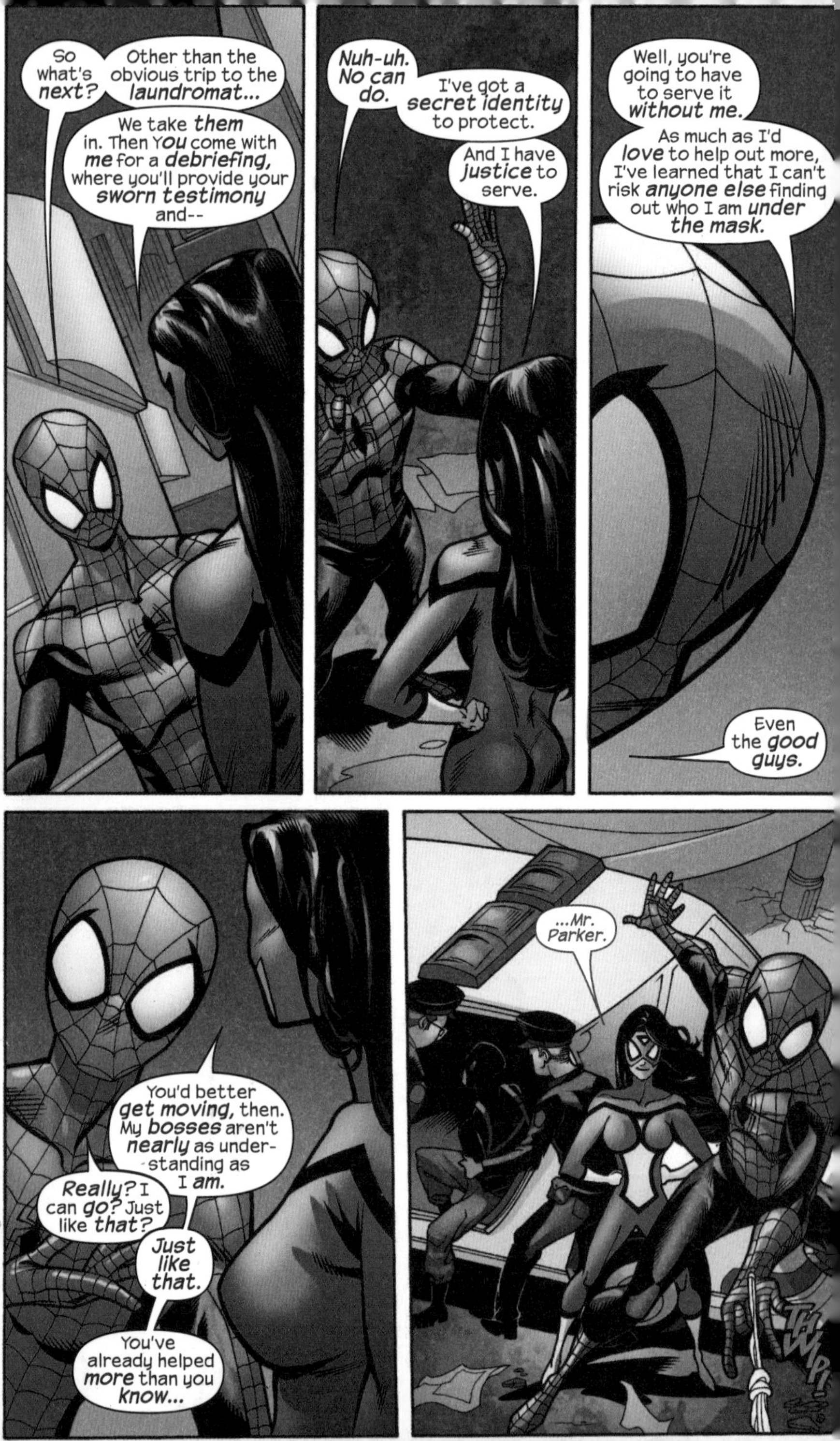

So what's next?
Other than the obvious trip to the laundromat...
We take them in. Then you come with me for a debriefing, where you'll provide your sworn testimony and--
Nuh-uh. No can do.
I've got a secret identity to protect.
And I have justice to serve.
Well, you're going to have to serve it without me.
As much as I'd love to help out more, I've learned that I can't risk anyone else finding out who I am under the mask.
Even the good guys.
You'd better get moving, then. My bosses aren't nearly as under-standing as I am.
Really? I can go? Just like that?
Just like that.
You've already helped more than you know...
...Mr. Parker.
THWIP!

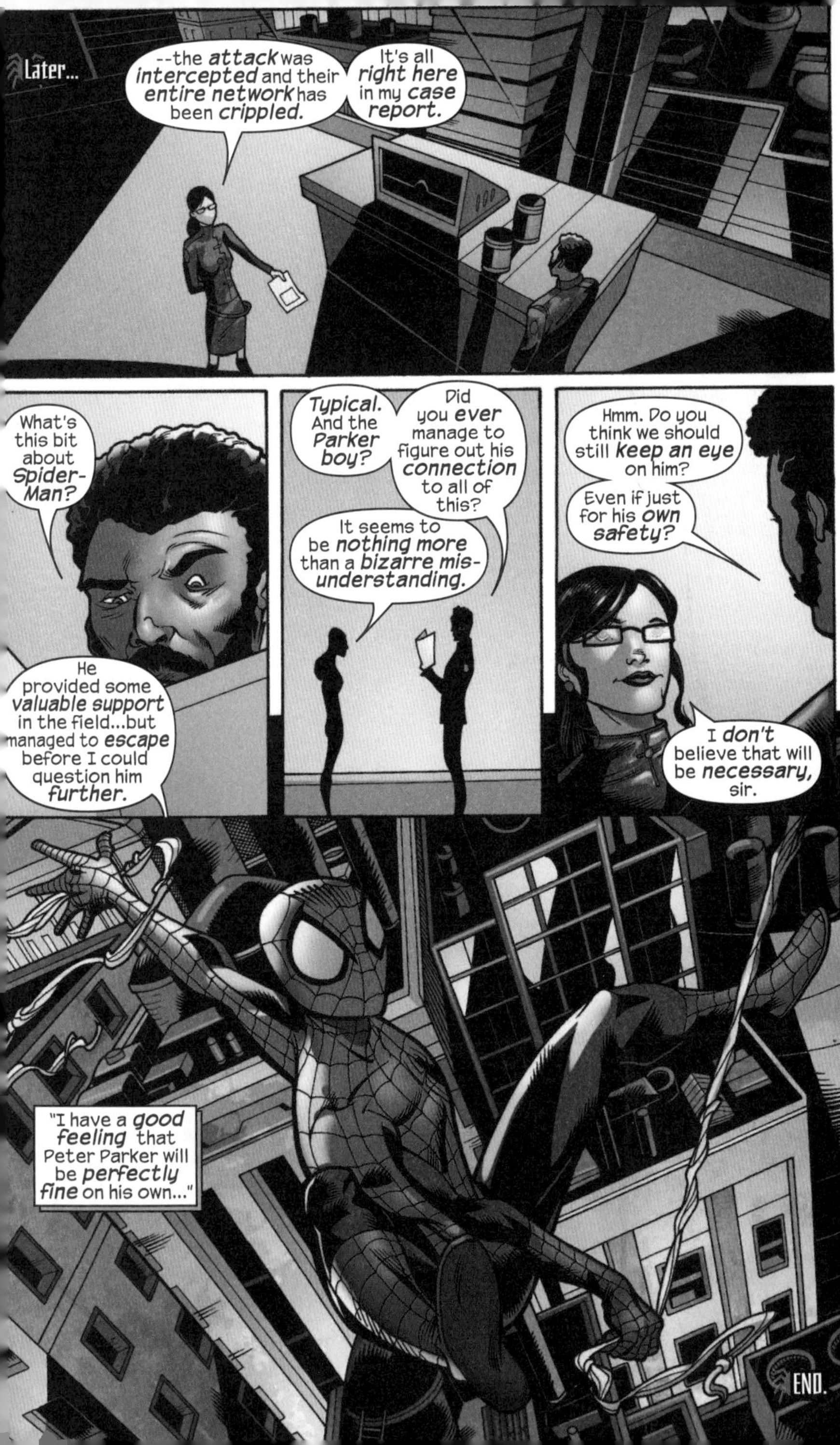
Later...
--the attack was intercepted and their entire network has been crippled.
It's all right here in my case report.
What's this bit about Spider-Man?
He provided some valuable support in the field...but managed to escape before I could question him further.
Typical. And the Parker boy?
Did you ever manage to figure out his connection to all of this?
It seems to be nothing more than a bizarre mis-understanding.
Hmm. Do you think we should still keep an eye on him?
Even if just for his own safety?
I don't believe that will be necessary, sir.
"I have a good feeling that Peter Parker will be perfectly fine on his own..."
END.

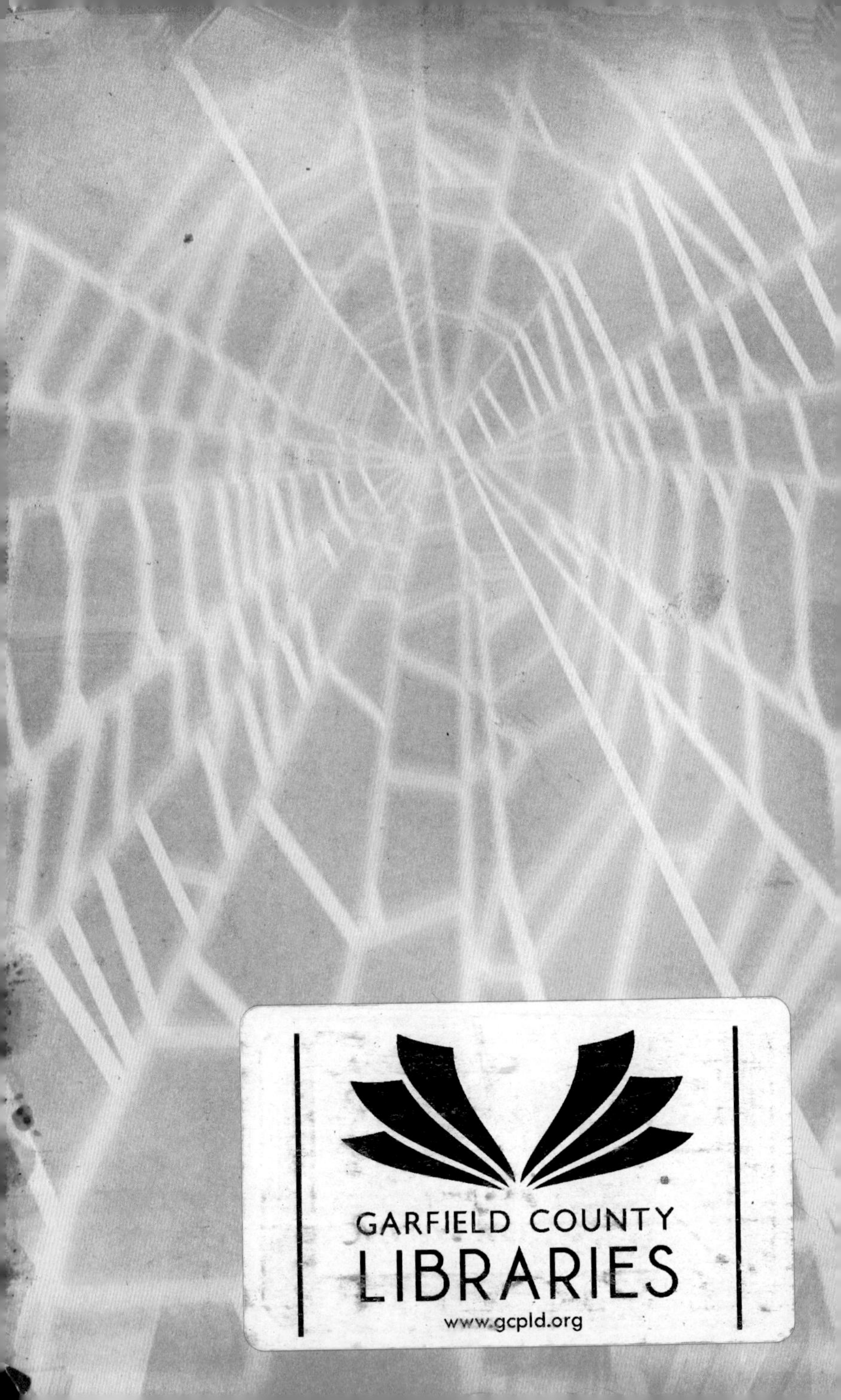